SHELBY DOLL

HOPETON HORROR

Hopeton Horror

A story of The Poor Mortal Wanderer

Standalone Novel

Shelby Doll

Road sign outside Alva, Oklahoma
Photo credit: Shelby Doll

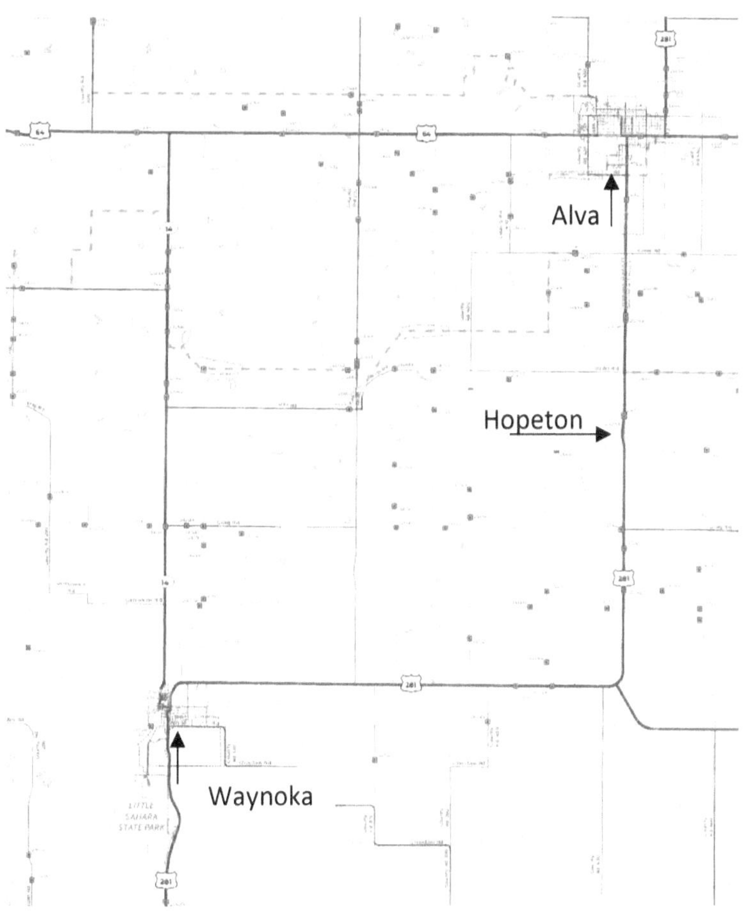

Partial map of Woods County, Oklahoma

https://oklahoma.gov/content/dam/ok/en/odot/maps/county-maps/woods.pdf

DEDICATION

For my family, who introduced and included me to so many days spent at the dunes.

For Waynoka, and every sandy excursion of craziness and fun that led to inspiring these words.

And of course, for Kraig.

1: Lizzy

I don't want to go to school. A foggy puff of breath coincides with the thought.

My head is centimeters away from banging against the steering wheel. An exaggerated groan releases the right amount of pressure. Taut shoulders slump instead of drawing closer, removing my forehead from the line of fire for now.

Empty fields blur together as they whiz by my window. Traces of snow, dotting the tufts of dormant grass and crops left amid the winter dirt, draw my peripheral to the otherwise flat stretches of farmland. It isn't quite cause to distract me like I want it to. The white-knuckled grip I have on the steering wheel doesn't lessen.

Only upsettingly recently did my nightmares, teleporting back to the locker-filled halls of hell, cease. *At least in the nightmares, it was high school.* Fortunate or not, landing an entry-level instructor position at the university in Alva was the best decent job I could find on such short notice. Thankfully, lacking a use for lockers.

Better than many of the other options, it's also significantly more relieving than continuing on the job hunt, is what I keep telling myself in hopes I don't spiral about where my life is going. All these big changes at once are sending me on a crash course toward a massive existential crisis. One more serious than I am prepared to handle, teetering on the edge of sanity.

It's Saturday now. This gives me tomorrow to collect myself and regain a firm grasp on my mental stability. That should be plenty of time before I need to be on campus with the reality of change crashing in around me.

The acceptance letter, approving me to become a professor, flashes in my mind. "Ms. Eliza Dern, newest member of the Arts Department," it said in generic, typewriter font. Accompanying the letter had been a certificate, printed on textured parchment paper, announcing my instructor status. A faded school mascot made up most of the background.

Overall, the document appeared far too professional for how amateur I am, stepping into such a role.

Another exhale escapes at the thought of what I left behind to return to my childhood hometown. I don't mean to look down on a good opportunity. Writing my short stories and columns in Oklahoma City didn't exactly pay the bills and provide me money to spare. It did get me to the point of making just enough to skate by while doing something I enjoyed. Hopefully, I can find something similar here at home.

Home. The grain elevator grows in size the closer I get to town.

Hopeton is barely a bump on the map, and only so because it makes the highway circumvent the cluster of houses, post office, bank, and church that make it up. There's the one road running north and south through town, parallel to the highway so they both cross the railroad tracks.

Even though there isn't much here, I admit it's cozy.

I know I didn't make it very far from the place I grew up. Moving to the biggest city in the state, a couple of hours away, isn't what I would call "making it." But it's further than a lot of people get away from their birthplace. For a time, I can say I lived outside my hometown zip code.

A few years isn't a lot for already having to move back. The unhelpful statement arises from dark recesses.

Coming around the last curve, my eyes stay glued to the road as long as they can. In the driveway of my mom's house, they have nowhere left to turn. This journey has merely begun, and I've quite had my fill.

The last meal I ate gurgles unsettlingly in the pit of my stomach. It was a quick drive here after burying her at one of the backroad cemeteries out in the country. There wasn't time to properly prepare myself for this next step.

Thinking about her, alone, out in the middle of nowhere, is almost enough to send tears down my cheeks. Technically, she was already living alone. That's the difference though. Living alone, she was still alive. Not six feet deep.

I don't know where she wanted to be buried. Maybe that's why this hurt is so intense.

Mom never mentioned a will. She was the picture of health, minus an understandable Dr. Pepper habit. At fifty-seven years old, she experienced no major issues I knew of. Yet, here I am, summoned to take care of her house, her things, and settle any debts.

The to-do list I have to make, if I were to try to list and sell the house, threatens to overwhelm me. Since I don't want to make this choice too lightly, I won't jump into it right now. I stop my train of thought in case continuing sends me into a panic attack.

My breath lets out, minus the condensation this time. A sigh that doesn't reduce any of the weight in my chest, though it does ease some tension.

Tears, beginning to form, recede to bring the details of the structure itself into shape. Her garden, lining the front porch, is flourishing. Evergreen plants and winter florals are well tended, blooming or simply standing nicely in the bed of rock and soil mixture. Without a weed or stray stem in sight, I would bet money she was taking care of them up to her collapse.

The siding on the house is looking to be in pretty good shape, almost fresh. Touched up, it's a lingering version of the pale yellow straight out of my childhood. *That's a good selling point if I have to go there. Just don't circle around to something that might set me off.*

Maintaining a critical eye does not last long on the walk up the porch steps. Memories of laughter and sunburnt summers penetrate the cold concentration of the present. Fuzziness shoves clear, constructive thoughts to the side as spots dot my vision.

I find myself resisting the urge to knock, forgetting for a moment there would be no answer. The front door still creaks at every centimeter of movement it endures. Protestation announcing upon entrance or exit in hopes that whosoever intrudes might learn a lesson. To stay in or out, not go back and forth between the two.

Inside the old farmhouse, everything is exactly how it was prior to me moving out. The perfect mix of old lady house and fairytale cottage astounds me. I didn't appreciate it as a kid when it felt more like a museum than my home. As an adult, I can admit, *Excellent taste, Mom.*

Books, old and new, line the walls. Floor to ceiling in some rooms, while others leave space for different décor. Plants, real and fake, take up residence along the curtained window sills and hang in various corners to break up the array of paintings. Wallpaper decorates a couple rooms, whereas dark paint peeks out from the scarce, bare spots of others. It's cozy, almost timeless.

Unsure where to begin, a fingernail ends up in my mouth. Incoherent thoughts race until the sharp pain, gnawing too far beyond the sensitive skin, returns me to myself. An unwelcome realization dawns on me, that I need to start in her room.

Boxes constitute the majority of the kitchen. Easily, a couple end up in my arms to escort me up the stairs. Creaks squeal and groan under each step as I ascend. Silence greets me at the landing to overlook the living room.

I don't mean to pause at her door. Homeostasis was within my grasp by the time I'd made it up the stairs; I didn't expect to require another deep breath in preparation.

A shaky hand rises in front of me to push open the door. Spotless. Her room is spotless. As if she picked up in case anyone would care to look.

Slow, mechanical movements strip the bed, folding everything together to place into one of the bigger boxes. *I already have my own bedspread. There's no sentiment in keeping these.*

The dresser drawers are packed to the brim. A sense of normality manifests in an eye roll. These old houses aren't known for having closets; everything ends up shoved into a drawer.

Each item is removed with caution. An inspection conducted in case I want to keep anything. Most of the clothes go in another box or directly into the trash. Mom and I don't share much in common when it comes to fashion. *Didn't,* I correct myself. Mom and I *didn't* share much in common. A sniffle thinly holds in the sudden barrage of tears. Alongside furious blinks as I attempt to continue, bearing some modicum of composure.

Too few boxes fill up quickly.

Straightening to stand upright has sharp barbs of pain emanating underneath my shoulder blades, my hunched position to clear out drawers showing my age.

Another creaky trip down the stairs. I'm distracted stretching out my aches when a flash outside the front window captures my attention. Stopping in my tracks all but sends me sliding the rest of the way down.

Regaining balance allows me to stare more intently at a tree waving in the breeze outside. Infuriatingly easing my frazzled nerves, the huffy exhale that follows hardly resembles a laugh. *It's the wind blowing the tree, making shadows. Get a grip.*

After a couple more rounds of cleanup, involving less jaw-dropping action, full boxes overrun the empty ones in a corner of the kitchen.

An engine revving echoes throughout the hollow house. Mom's place, being the last one before the intersection to hop on the highway at the south side of town, has nothing to block traffic sounds. The houses across the street don't reach as far.

One final trip on the stairs, without incident, has the master bedroom and upstairs bathroom cleared out. Some things I'll be able to donate; most will likely end up at the dump, and that's okay. The tiniest sliver of crushing weight removes itself from the mass attached to my soul. My reward for accomplishing a dreaded task.

Any celebration halts as eye contact is made with my old room. On the ground floor, it was mostly emptied at the time I moved out. All that should be left in there is a bed and vacant dresser. *I hope.* An impulse drives me to open the door and search the drawers to make sure there isn't anything stashed in there or under the bed. Nothing. Good.

Now, down here in general should be easier. Especially if I end up leaving most of what Mom already had.

In my quest to have the life and career I wanted for myself, my social and home life took up the role of sacrificial lamb. My own apartment minimally furnished, let alone decorated. Furniture existed out of necessity, not comfort or company. Who knew owning nothing would be advantageous when everything I possess fits in my car? *That's a sad notion. I'm not chancing a spiral. Moving on.*

Loads of books. I love books. Those stay.

The plants, I might see if I can keep the real ones alive, and if they don't make it, well, at least I tried. Fake plants always look nice to me, so we'll see how sparse it looks when the real ones die. Yes, I said *when* and not *if.* I know me.

Really, that's it. Except for the furniture, and that's all well taken care of.

Enough daylight to outline the trees and field beyond the window gives me the kick I need to load up the boxes in my car. Better to get it all done today if I can, rather than putting it off.

Plans formulate of what my route will be through Alva. Not that it's a large town, housing a whopping population of around five thousand people, whereas Hopeton has about forty. I haven't roamed these roads in a hot minute. Time clouds the street names and landmarks I'd used to guide me in my teenage years.

I can rid myself of these boxes and knock out some grocery shopping while I'm at it. One more glance at what's left in the house reveals the fridge is close to empty, and so are the cupboards. Mom had to be ready to go shopping. Her half-started list stares at me from its home on the kitchen counter. She was one of those people who didn't forget the list at home or make it up on the spot in the middle of the store. *I wonder what that's like*, I joke to myself in an effort to stall the tears.

My car, weighed down carrying Mom's things instead of mine, inches along the stretch of road that comprises

Hopeton. A bright red flyer in the window of the post office catches my eye. "Winter Block Party" is the caption above a date set for next Saturday evening. *That should be nice.* It'll get me some face time among the current residents without them being compelled to knock on my door to express condolences.

On the highway, my car chugs and wheezes up to speed, as exhausted as I am. The eventual rhythmic humming of the road lulls me into a zoned-out trance. No music has played out of the radio since leaving Oklahoma City to head for the funeral. I can't bring myself to turn it on now.

Staring out the window over fields that've rolled by during many drives from my childhood, I can't hold in the tears a moment longer. I don't bother to wipe at them until they blur my vision and block the road. Then the sleeve of my hoodie reaches up as more form. *I've become a hazard to those besides myself.*

I can't wait for this to get easier. Obviously, grief never really goes away. It hits in the little moments here and there and means you knew great love, so the hole in your heart is the love with nowhere to go. Blah, blah. It still sucks. Plus, knowing our relationship, I didn't expect to be feeling much of anything.

The flatlands and outskirts of Alva melt into a full-fledged town around me. Only then do the tears let up, and I can focus through puffy, red eyes.

Just my luck, is my initial reaction once it registers who the owner of the thrift store is. Though I'm unsure if it is in relief or anticipation. This woman knew my mom and was at her funeral. *I knew I recognized that face.*

Sniffles act as my buffer during our conversation. She offers me condolences again, in addition to, "Of course I can take these donation boxes. Don't worry, I'll toss the trash ones myself."

Well, that takes care of that. While I am happy I didn't start bawling at the mention of my mom, it might have worked as a nice exit strategy if the talking went on too long.

Another task done chips away at the monster making itself at home inside me.

A numbness takes over my extremities as I crawl into the car to head for the grocery store. My hands and feet might as well be made of stone at how they drag my movements.

The tiny parking lot outside the grocer is less than half full. A hopeful sign I won't have to deal with any more people recognizing me. My hood comes up for good measure and to brace against the chill whipping up out of nowhere.

Warmth inside the door combats the cold stinging my cheeks and nose. Shaking myself off provides a second of peace, prior to my day getting worse.

Less than three steps inside the door is a sea of sympathetic faces staring into my soul. Large windows span the front half of the store to provide an unobstructed view of anyone entering. Of course, I recognize a handful of people who probably remember me too. Those I don't, most likely already heard all about who I am and why I'm here, if I had to guess. *Gossip travels fast.*

As my eyes dart between theirs, the pounding inside my chest ceases before catapulting into overdrive as the impulse to hurl right here and now takes immediate priority. A couple of people my mom's age appear on the verge of tears, as though they want to give me a hug to share sorrows. One person even starts toward me.

Shakily, my hands rise. "I appreciate the sympathies, but I really just want to get some shopping done and go home."

Oh, look at that, my voice is as shaky as my hands.

Several people furrow their brows or scoff. Others nod, their mouths pulled in taut smiles and walk away. Part of me regrets shutting down good intentions; another part is very glad I don't have to suffer any stories or awkward attempts to make me feel better.

Good people mean well, but they're still people. I'm not normally a people person and today is not the day to change that.

Similarly to the drive to Alva, my trip through the store happens in a trance state where nothing is readily in focus. Items end up in my hands, then in the cart or returned to the shelf. Any chance at conversation with the cashier shuts down when he takes in the blank expression plastered on my face. Knowing it's there doesn't make it easier to remove.

A pinstripe of light on the horizon betrays the last bit of sun clinging to the sky. Darkness covers almost everything beyond the artificial perimeter created by two streetlamps. Night ascending sends my brain into bedtime mode, regardless of the actual time. This is not conducive to an already stale mood from the day I've had. *I am so ready to not be perceived.*

Mom's house, coming into view around the bend in the highway, reminds me of the sinking weight in my chest I had done my best to stop thinking about. It's as bad pulling up to the shadowed dwelling as it was in the daylight. Deafening emptiness oozes from the black windows. One of which is open.

Huh, weird. I swore all the windows were closed.

Grocery bag straps dig into my fingers the short walk to the porch. The screen door, wide open, waves at me in the light breeze like a welcome party. *Man, I am losing it.*

Flicking the heavy switch in the kitchen temporarily blinds me in a burst of brightness. Many blinks span the time it takes to unpack everything and preheat the oven for my gourmet dinner of frozen pizza.

Heat blasts my face in the few seconds the door gapes open. An agonizing, stomach-churning wait for the molten meal to cool is the hardest part. Cheese bubbles and sizzles as saliva begins to drip out the side of my mouth.

This turns into as good a time as any to move my things into the master bedroom. Though once confronted with the bareness, alone in my thoughts, it quickly evolves into the type of distraction I don't want.

My mind hyper-focuses on the fact that I'm taking up the same space she should be and refuses to move on to another topic. Depositing my folded clothes into the drawers where hers resided. Spreading my sheets onto the bed she would be getting ready to occupy. These simple tasks rip the breath out of my chest.

The smell of melted cheese and marinara sauce wafts up the stairs, bringing me back from the edge I am close to tumbling over. Stomach growls reignite operation of my lungs, which were failing at their one job.

Bare feet slapping across the cool wood of the dining room grounds me. A buildup of pressure behind my eyes relaxes, allowing them to be drawn to the boombox sitting against the wall. Without intention, I switch it on to keep the silence from crushing me.

It's set to some classical station that's quite off-putting at first, but there isn't the energy expendable to find another station, let alone know what I want to listen to. As I dredge out a pizza cutter from somewhere, the wordless melody starts to grow on me. Humming along, nothing to steer my brain besides the music itself, I find the last of the pressure gone.

Some normality returned gives me confidence to sit down and eat in front of the old television. An audible click accompanies switching off the boombox, rippling the suddenly heavy silence.

Taking up residence in front of the ancient television set, I sink into the newest-looking piece of furniture. Mom's favorite recliner. "Oversize and fluffy," she would call it, saying it reminded her of Dad.

A local newscast is in the middle of weather predictions. "Looking to get colder this week since we're working through the beginning of the year," rattles off the smiling weatherman.

My mind veers off on a tangent about how I love getting to bury myself in hoodies and sweatshirts. It's a great excuse to not give the impression of having a figure.

During the last few bites of my pizza, the topic turns to obituaries. Face paling as they regain my attention, a lightheadedness dries out my mouth. I almost change the channel or turn the thing off completely. Somehow I suck it up to hear them call out, "Debbie Dern, 1967 to 2024, survived by her daughter, Eliza Dern—newest faculty member of the university campus in Alva."

A groan coincides with the next announcement before any thought finishes in my head. *Oh, great, now everyone at campus is going to know and give their condolences.* Groaning again to myself and the room, I slide down in the chair a little thinking that's as much news as I can handle.

As I prepare to shove myself up, a banner flashes across the screen stating "Inmate Escaped." A photo of the sign outside Alva, warning passersby that hitchhikers may be escaping inmates, appears above the banner, halting any movement.

My heart and butt sink down further in the chair.

Well, that's great news for the first night home.

2: Casey

Damn it. Double damn it. I can't stand this school, this town, this state. Ugh, I need to get out. Enraged thoughts slam around, much like how I want to throw my head against a wall.

Taking a deep, crisp breath does nothing to calm me. My fists clench and unclench as I force them to take up the rhythm of my stride. *Just because I feel stuck right now doesn't mean I always will.* This is the mantra I have been trying to drill into myself. It isn't working very well.

If anything, at least I'm not stuck in the small town I came from, merely another one almost identical to it. My eyes rolling nearly pop a blood vessel, aggressively straining at the socket. *Alva is barely big enough to be a city, let alone whyever the hell it has a college campus.*

Trudging through the light dusting of snow to class on said campus, my mind races to complete some checklist it created as an attempt to regulate this mood. Where it loses me is how Debbie Dern has a daughter who could come, nearly at the drop of a hat, to bury her and tidy up her affairs. It makes me wonder how much she knows.

For a moment, this line of thinking does help me to forget how I got myself into coming to this stupid school to take these ridiculous classes so I could get a slip of fancy paper. My fingers relax, immediately soothing the ache starting to build in tense joints.

I finally caved and decided to follow up on the notion of college, thinking, *Maybe it will provide a greater purpose or calling through higher education.* The rationalization being that I'd know if this is the piece I'm missing, the thing I require in order for everything else to fall into place so it would all make sense. In reality, I've found more reasons to hate humanity.

And hate myself, for that matter.

At these words, a whisper of cold metal, exactly as it rested against my face a different day, causes me to shiver. The muscle memory of a gun, weighed down by a full clip, primed and ready, drags me out of the present. Heavy silence fills my ears, replacing light morning traffic as the echo of another time pushes itself onto me. Reliving the sensation, my arm tingles at the impulse to reenact how it felt bringing this weapon to rest at my temple. Finger on the trigger, ready to pull. For some reason, it didn't.

Forcing myself out of the lifelike memory, my mind seeks with renewed direction to change the subject. *There's no place for me among this inane familiarity.* Pushing on as if I experienced any other thought. If college isn't the answer, and the jobs I've held so far weren't the answer, what's next?

Hopefully, this problem is solving itself by utilizing my new outlet. Oof, I've got to stop talking to myself this way. *Get a grip, man.*

A stiff breeze snaking in my shirt collar wrenches me from the backslide. My steps slowed while I was lost in thought and allowed the bite in the air to penetrate my inadequate layers. Ninety percent of the students and faculty are wearing hoodies, coats, or sweaters. I, dumbass that I am, didn't take the weather into consideration and am wearing a winter vest over a long sleeve shirt. I'm freezing my ass off. *At least it gives me something else to focus on.*

My first class today is an elective I was practically forced into due to overflow and options left, apparently. Art. Or something to such effect. A groan rumbles in my throat at those hard-working tuition dollars.

Today, officially the first day of the new semester, maybe I can exhibit a better attitude. *Doubtful.*

The room is about half full when I arrive. A mix of kids fresh out of high school, baby-faced and naïve, mingle amid people a touch closer to my age. Those trying to change trajectories or whatever else might bring one to college close to their thirties. Then there's a couple of students sporting enough grey hair or wrinkles to pass for grandparents.

Scanning the positions and belongings of this odd array of persons more closely, I note how their occupancy is spread throughout the room. My goal is to find a seat surrounded by the fewest people. There, right smack in the middle, an empty table calls to me.

The obstacle course of chairs and students poke legs out every which way. Careful of my footing, I make my way to the targeted seat as I note the pretty thing sitting at the instructor's desk. Refraining from snapping my neck for a better view, I settle for a peek out of my periphery.

An unknown source of patience permits me to be seated before fully inspecting her. My mask of indifference slips as a corner of my mouth hangs open.

Luckily, she appears nervous herself, pausing to take a breath to address us. "Good morning, everyone. Welcome to Art. Please call me Ms. Lizzy. Let's try to all have a good semester, okay?"

Her tone sets the question up as a joke. Low chuckles sound around me in response. A half smile she tacks onto it would've fooled me too if it weren't for a glint of something in her eyes, darting face to face. The fact I only saw it because I was staring so intently at her dawns on me as a blush heats my cheeks.

I wonder how old she is and what her stance is on dating students? Never really knowing an inclination towards romance or romantic situations, the idea becomes intriguing coupled with her. Several tangents ensue prior to realizing I've completely zoned out while she continued. In spite of discussing a topic I care little about, when she speaks, I find myself actually wanting to pay attention.

Maybe this class won't be so bad after all.

***

I stand corrected. Over an hour of listening to color theory, perspective, and illusion makes my brain melt. Though she is wonderful to listen to, it's difficult retaining what she explains. I don't appreciate the premise of this class. I'm more of a writer. *I guess it's still a type of art.*

At dismissal, to be able to move on to the next hell— I mean class—an overwhelming desire to talk to Ms. Lizzy floods me. Existing as another face in a crowd of staring students isn't enough. I need her to know, specifically, that I exist.

My eyes remain locked on her as the others disperse. A wobble accompanies cautious steps to navigate people and wayward seats. I assume Lizzy is short for some first name such as Elizabeth or whatnot. Something I intend on finding out. This and other trivial matters divert attention, adding to the uproar my existence has turned into as I work towards the front of the room.

Before I can get clear of the chairs and tables, some other fiend beats me to her. Traitorous bodily reactions bring me to a standstill. Shoulders slump and tense, a stone heart falls into my empty stomach, a breath releases as a silent gasp, fists clench, and my forearms tighten as if preparing to take a swing at something. Or someone.

Well, I don't want to stand here awkwardly until they're done holding a conversation. A scowl replaces the mask. The rest of my body situates itself back to normal.

Lowering my head to keep walking by her desk, I hear the student ask, "So, are you new around here? Seeing anybody? I could show you a good time, gorgeous."

He didn't even let her answer the questions. How dare he be first at doing the same thing I was going to do, and then have the audacity to be worse at it? My scowl deepens. Eyes pointed at the floor, strain at maintaining this expression. This is the least of my concerns as my pace slows in anticipation of her response.

In the hall, I come to a halt beyond the door and listen.

"Uh, I'm actually from here, and I don't choose dates out of my student pool. Though I am flattered, you should focus on the lessons when in class," she says, radiating confidence that sparks a smirk beneath my furrowed brow.

His huffy emergence from the room intensifies my moment of petty amusement.

Scraping follows as her chair scoots away from the desk. Footsteps coming towards the door skyrockets my heartrate. *She's coming this way.*

No coherent thoughts form mid scramble, deciding what to do. Too much time passes to reach a decision. The click-clack of footsteps grow louder. Wide-eyed, I pivot right smack into her as she walks through the doorway.

She recovers quickly for bouncing off my chest. Breathless, she laughs. "Holy crap, I am so sorry. I thought everyone was gone already."

A smile tugs on the corners of her mouth. The light it emanates reaching her eyes.

Her eyes that are staring at me, noticing me, acknowledging my existence. I know she refused this other nuisance, but maybe she would give me a chance? We appear closer in age. I bet I could offer her more than that heathen of a boy.

Could I though? Wasn't I just arguing to myself because I don't know my purpose in life? Hmm, I still think I could offer her more in the way of... I've been talking to myself too long. Say something!

"Sorry, I left my penkil in your ass." A moment passes while my brain processes what I said. "I mean, lucky pencil in your class!"

Her cheeks glow red faster than she can hide the reaction under her hand. A cough hardly subdues the laugh she politely attempts, and fails, to choke down.

My own cheeks heat as I force out a laugh. Weighing an explanation against a retreat, I spin on my heel to put distance between us as quickly as possible.

Around the corner, her words chase after me. "I'll keep an eye out for your pencil."

If I could will myself out of existence, this would be the time.

Immense effort is expended to pull myself toward the next class. Suffering the rest of the day, nothing else sinks in. Between that fiasco of a first impression and recovering from this weekend, there is no learning to be done today.

This preoccupation continues during the walk home. Temperature doesn't register on my radar. Assignments designated during the day tickle the back of my mind. Yet nothing takes priority to my current conundrum: Ms. Lizzy.

How quickly the idea of her took over my mind should probably bother me.

Becoming a constant in her life might help present me as safe or stable. *What's an authentic way to get close to her?* There aren't tutors for art classes, are there? I might need to look into it.

The apartment lock clicks open. A sigh precludes my bag dropping beside me as I numbly plop down on the couch.

For now, the focus should be to keep cool, take it slow. Even with these thoughts, I'm getting ahead of myself. Especially needing to make up for my slip-up. *Maybe try not to fuck anything else up. Other plans are in the works that require attention.*

There's the train to derail my distracted daydreaming. Also reminding me to contact Geoffrey on our next move.

Overwhelmed by future planning and possibilities, I mentally shake myself.

Mustering the will to knock out some class work, my brain yearns for a mental reset. If I take in one more fraction or contraction, I think I'm going to shoot myself.

That joke is in poor taste. The automatic remark cuts through insensitive flippancy in regard to a serious, and clearly possible, scenario.

Sinking into the cool leather of the couch, the TV is on before I recognize the motion used to do so. The news channel it was on last night as background noise resumes, running another story about the escaped convict.

I bet no one was expecting something like that to happen here. A proud chuckle hums its single beat. *There's a lot going on in this town the people aren't prepared for.*

My smile spreads at the hand I've played in it so far.

3: Geoffrey

Purchase cattle. Haul cattle. Unload cattle. Repeat.

Working on the road is not for everyone, and it is rapidly losing its appeal to me. Farmers are cheap to pay while my expenses continually increase—stockyards, fuel, keeping the truck and trailer in service all costs me an arm and a leg. Then the ingrates bitch about forking over a finger in comparison.

"My life has become a joke," I grit.

Throwing the shifter into the next gear bogs the rig down as it struggles to catch up. Smoke shoots from the stacks, casting wispy shadows along the highway beside me.

Left alone to my thoughts on the road all day every day didn't used to bother me. It had been a nice reprieve from the monotony of working a nine-to-five. I could spend all day driving, without a care in the world. Enjoying the open road used to be the epitome of freedom.

Crackling voices chime through the CB radio. I don't hear my call sign, so they're easy to tune out.

Unfortunately, I can pinpoint the exact moment it all went to shit.

The night my family up and left had to be my wife's idea. I can't fathom either of my kids coming up with the plan to pack while I was on the road or leaving while I was passed out at home so they could sneak away with the keys to my pickup, too.

My pickup.

It wasn't enough to steal the car I bought my wife for her to be able to run errands and get the kids where they needed to go when I was gone. I had my pickup to drive in my off time to avoid navigating the big rig through town. Residential and side streets of Alva aren't made for it. They just had to take that too.

As if them leaving wasn't already a stab in my back, I receive divorce papers somehow. *This is all bullshit.* She doesn't get to run off, taking my truck and my kids. My rightful property.

At first, my marriage was great. She was a cute little thing who swiftly learned how to be a good wife. My two kids followed her lead. They were submissive, as children and wives ought to be. Life was perfect.

When the kids were older, she simply had to get involved in extracurriculars, had to have her own hobbies and interests. It became bothersome to stay in and keep house while I was on the road all week. *Well, dammit, what else could I do?* I made the money to put food on the table. There was plenty to keep her and my kids fed and clothed. Then, it wasn't enough.

In recent years, I noticed her submission start to falter. It was almost imperceptible at first, growing more brazen over time. Where she used to drop her eyes to the floor and backpedal if her tone rose, or tremble as my steps drew closer, leading up to her deceit, her gaze would linger higher, her voice rose without hesitation, gaining more sass during arguments also growing in frequency. Her stance would tense, muscles tighten when I got close rather than quake with anticipation.

Something she used to tell me was she thought she wasn't good enough to be my wife. All the years we've been together, apparently that was a lie. Well, joke's on her. I'm not giving her the out she wants by signing any damn divorce papers.

My foot eases up on the throttle as a band screams incoherent lyrics to pounding drums, diverting my concentration. The stereo is cranked up so loud, instrumental notes vibrate the cab around me. Sore muscles attempt to relax against the seat.

One hand rakes absently through my overgrown beard as brighter notions arise in tandem with the intense music. Like how things started to look up once this Casey kid approached me.

He offered a way to direct my anger. Something my wife complained about me needing to do. *Not that she's here to appreciate it.* Fucking ungrateful bitch. Probably whoring herself out at truck stops for money to get back at me. If I ever find her, she is going to regret this whole charade. I will make sure of it.

A small voice chirps, *I could probably be persuaded to forget all this deceit, be merciful if she and the kids return.* After I make them see the error of their ways.

The last hill stands between me and my first stop of the day at Alva's stockyards, slowing the truck's momentum.

Monday means it's time to pick up merchandise the farmers bought at auction over the weekend.

Separating and loading cattle takes most of the morning. Last night's chill minimizes the worst of the stench radiating off the beasts. A lack of swarming flies and hot dust settling into my clothes reminds me how far we are from summer. Winter takes stifling heat, where sweat clings to every pore and replaces it with the freeze that infiltrates any number of layers donned to thwart it.

Still managing to break a sweat by the time every head is loaded up, I'm sat and running down the road before anymore wayward thoughts nag at me.

Nothing is glorious about this job. Somehow it made me happy for a long time. Now every day is a battle to keep going. *Here we go again.*

In an attempt at mental silence, I crank the radio all the way up and zone out to the highway, numb as the miles fly.

For a while, it works. Minutes pile into hours, speeding by like only several moments pass before I arrive at the first delivery location. The farmer immediately tries to undercut me. My rational reaction is threatening to sell the fuckers elsewhere if he's going to play stupid games. Not wanting to be cowed, he heehaws around some more, huffing and puffing.

Already over this shit, it becomes a struggle to hold the balled fists at my sides until he's ready to pull his head out of his ass. *Since the sun is shining directly in his eyes, he'd never see my swing coming.*

The next few deliveries go better, nothing exciting or upsetting aside from intermittent nausea. Nothing I can't handle.

At the end of the day, my route puts me close to a truck stop I know has a late-night bar and grill. Of its own volition, the truck points that way.

Although it adds a few extra miles, this place is worth it. No one else is logging my miles, anyway.

Navigating through the rig-friendly parking lot, I hardly get mine to a stop and shut off before I'm out of the seat with the cab door swinging haphazardly behind me. As my feet hit the gravel, I don't wait for the click of the latch to echo across the lot.

Without a single stumble, determined steps get me inside. The bar entrance flies open under my heavy hand.

Banging against a stopper, it draws every patron's attention.

I holler, "Somebody get me a whiskey and burger. I'm about to I keel over!" into the dimly lit establishment.

A weathered bartender sighs as his face drops in recognition, already starting to make my drink in front of an empty seat.

Shakes rattle the arm I use to pull out the stool. I didn't realize how bad they'd gotten. *Good thing I'm getting it handled.*

Downing half the glass in a single pull, my periphery catches motion from the bartender already pouring another.

A couple more drinks disappear in the time it takes my burger to get to me. Nausea that reared throughout the day is beaten back by each new round of liquor. Hands stop their shaking once the warmth spreads through my body. Shooting pain, already building inside my skull, recedes as conscious thought catches onto its presence, mostly noting the vacancy it leaves.

It isn't long before the familiar, fuzzy feeling takes over. Floating away from myself, all problems dissipate, now irrelevant in the wake of soothing liquid that never lets me down.

I barely remember licking burger grease off my hands, the lights growing dimmer, when the next thing I know is a slap stinging my face, wringing me from the darkness I'd fallen into.

Pressure pushes against my shoulders and down my spine. Coming to from a blackout, an upward heave of my torso gains me a sitting position. A rough shake rouses me enough to confirm I am, in fact, on the floor.

Next item to note is all the lights are on. The high-pitched ting inside my ear canal fades in replacement of the bartender yelling for me to get out.

Something wet trickles out of my nose.

Another fact to register is I am on the opposite side of the bar from where I sat down to eat. Standing in front of me is a biker-looking type, rubbing his fist and glaring at me as he swears.

Rage clears the residual fog when my hand returns from my nose, bloody. *Oh, this motherfucker.*

My body hurls itself up of its own accord to lunge toward the guy. Too late, I think to myself how sluggish my reactions truly are.

The scene unfolds in slow motion. One of my fists swing toward his face. Without hesitation, he ducks down to attack from the side.

I don't even feel his punch make contact. Everything just goes dark.

While my vision is out, someone spouts, "Not a-fucking-gain with this guy."

A moment later, my upper body goes weightless as the lower half is dragged across the floor. There is no gliding across the stickiness. Jeans and boots cling to whatever substances coat the heavily trafficked wood.

My half-asleep mind can't be bothered by such triviality when the real concern is how I got across the bar and into a fight in the first place.

After a large hump, and sans ceremony, my body is dropped in the gravel to be left out in the cold. *Thank goodness I have my flannel on. Damn, my nose hurts.*

Pain is good; that means consciousness is close. An arm twitches on command. Legs pull in and kick out at the rocks and sand. Lying still a little longer, sharp pebbles dig in to try and break skin. I give myself a few more minutes before pushing up to a sitting position.

In plain view is the exterior of the bar, though it is much darker out than when I entered the establishment. Night fully descended makes the neon signs pop in contrast to the building's silhouette. Their harsh brightness blurs my vision.

Mechanical movements pat at my pockets in search for my phone and wallet. Both are there, so either they kept my card on file, or I got a free ride. My bank will let me know.

Slowly, I haul myself up and stagger across the uneven lot to my truck. It's parked farther away than I remember. An eternity passes as I climb the steps, slipping once to stumble over the driver seat and fall into the bunk of the sleeper.

Ah, this feels more like home than my house in Alva. Maybe I'll sell it and live out of the truck. This idea has surfaced in the past. Tempting as it may be to really do it this time. *Then where would my wife and kids know to search for me?* No, I need to hold onto the house so they know where to go when they come to their senses.

Yeah, that's why I haven't done it. They'll be back. They have to.

This train of thought leads me into the void of dreaming I never remember in waking.

Then at last, abysmal nothing.

4: Lizzy

Wow, first day at the new job, and students are already messing with me. One trying to ask me out. It would have rattled me even if he hadn't been obnoxiously joking. Then the other completely embarrassing the both of us with his slip of the tongue.

Sheesh, if this is a precursor for how the rest of the year is going to go, I've already had enough, I think to myself as I finish toweling off from a shower. Wrapping the coarse fabric around me, steam settles against my skin or floats throughout the room. A thin layer covers the mirror where I'm not facing my reflection.

In my present state, there's a high risk of picking myself apart, asking, *What makes me so special?* This is not a rabbit hole I want to spiral down at the moment.

Thank goodness for the small favor that no one passed along any condolences today. Whether it didn't click who I was or they were too busy to care, either option I am okay with.

I figured the students could call me Ms. Lizzy to prevent any possible recognition. Plus, it's a little less formal since it is only an art class. Most of the people are in there for an easy A or some down time between other classes. I get that. *Doesn't mean I'll allow any slackers, though.*

Realization strikes that I'd sat on the edge of the bed and remained there while losing myself in thought. A low growl bellows from my stomach as though I haven't eaten all day.

Donning oversized sweatpants and a T-shirt for pajamas, meaningless ideas track across my mind as I creak down the stairs. Ideas such as if the concept of tutoring might be applicable for an art class.

Darkness floods the house in these early evening hours. It's quickly become a habit to keep the lights off and blinds closed. I can't be broadcasting my presence and simultaneously hoping no one comes to the door to talk. A shudder racks my shoulders, pulling my elbows in tight at the thought of entertaining company.

Upon inspection of ingredients in the fridge, scanning in search of the easiest meal to put together, I rest some of my weight on the door. Leaning in amongst the bottles and containers might help decipher what it is I'm looking for.

Nothing jumps out at me when all of a sudden headlights sweep across the living room window. Impulsively, my knees drop to the floor to minimize the risk of being seen. The linoleum strongly disagrees with the impact to my bones, but there's nothing I can do about it now.

Pride at keeping my head from smacking the fridge on my way down is short-lived. Shame instantly replaces it at having completed this action at all. *I am ridiculous.*

Yet that isn't enough to pry me off the ground while the lights are still aimed into the living room. Several irregular breaths pass.

Eventually, they pull away.

Relieving my knees from the ground, my mind continues to chastise. Physically, I continue to throw together a snack.

My brain understands Mom was loved. A lot of people know this house. They probably recognize me or see the resemblance and want to be nice, but I can't handle a bombardment of strangers I don't know or hardly remember for the sake of courtesy. For some, it might be helpful in a time of grief to have those who knew her pass along well wishes and share memories. For me, I want to sort this out without being menaced by niceties and faking my way through reminiscing on the last few years of her life when I wasn't a part of them. Does that make me selfish?

Arguing with myself doesn't let up until the stairs creak underfoot once more. Tears spring to my eyes at the comforting shrieks of protest from each step. Deep breaths temporarily stave them off, who knows for how long.

Although the spiral is short, my snack has grown less appealing. The rumble in my stomach quiets to an upset gurgle.

Settling into bed, I crack my laptop in search of something to watch. Something I can fall asleep to. In the time it takes me to get some movie pulled up and started, my spiral recommences. Jumbles of incoherent images flash in and out of focus before I can stop them. Some of Mom, others of my old apartment, a little of Dad. Tears reignite to slide down my cheeks. There's not much I can do to stop them.

Defeated, I lie back and permit the salty traitors to persist as the movie plays. Listening to the dialogue only detracts from my own inner monologue if I intentionally funnel my attention. *I'd rather put extra focus into that than anything else.*

I almost forgot to check if my alarm is set. One hand blindly reaches over to the bedside table. Chapstick rolls under my fingers, and a bottle of lotion topples in my search.

At last, a bright screen shines into my face, illuminating the tears holding on. There's a banner notification flashing from my news app. Squinting against the light, it reads as a reminder for locals to be on the lookout for the escaped convict. An abrupt exhale somehow imbalances me to the point of nearly dropping the device onto my face.

The advisory tacked on states everyone should be wary of strangers. A whimper, balled into a groan, escapes at the notion. *Good thing everyone is basically a stranger right now.*

***

No progress is being made. Though my legs pump as fast as they can, there is no ground beneath my feet to put behind me.

A figure looms out of the shadows, lurching closer. Without a clear face to identify whoever it is giving chase, the most prominent feature to note becomes an incessant grin, spread wide. *There have to be extra teeth in the mouth because it looks like it sports far too many.*

Pushing that to the side, fatigue shortens my breath. Irrational panic rises over the distance between us shrinking. Not making anything better, it adds jerking motions to my already mechanical movements.

Familiarity taints the empty void we're inhabiting, begging to be addressed.

I've seen this face before, but I can't put a finger on where or who it belongs to.

An intermittent beep grows louder. After several pauses, it disrupts my disjointed horror.

The annoying cadence, repeating at timed intervals, solidifies my suspicion. *Thank goodness, this is just a dream.*

Acknowledging the realization doesn't rouse me from it.

Whether a conscious decision or not, my legs stop pumping. My form falls still. Shadows catch up to me first, stretching long beyond where I stand, followed closely by the figure. Right as arms reach toward me, I am released.

Pajamas and bedspread cling to me as I shove up from the mattress. Air itself chokes me trying to get in and out of my lungs. Sweat drips off my brow and runs down my body, suffocating me with its slick heat.

Clear of the dream fog, my alarm drives me crazy. Several shaky attempts are needed to slam my finger down in the right spot on the screen to make the noise stop.

My breathing slows to a more regular rhythm. *At least it was my first alarm, so I have plenty of time to try to get over this icky feeling.*

Any chance of finding more restful sleep eludes my grasp while remnants of the nightmare remain tangible.

Times like these are when it would be nice to not live alone. *Not this again.*

I keep telling myself, *Either I'll find my person, or I won't.* I'm trying not to go searching for a relationship. The last time I tried to force something, I found a real lemon of a guy. *Although, a lemon is at least a body to be there alongside you so you're not experiencing the nightmares alone.*

Too many problems are surfacing with nowhere near enough solutions. Before I overload myself on *what ifs* and *potentialities*, an idea comes to mind. A temporary solution is available.

One hand reaches for the pillow behind me. As calmly as I can manage, I raise the floppy support to gently rest against my face after drawing in a deep breath.

On the exhale, I release as much pent-up tension as I can. My hurt, anger, and doubt manifests as a muffled scream into the pillow. The yell itself goes on longer than I intended. A raw throat and slightly lighter soul is my reward once the sound cuts out.

Dropping the cushion from my face, I skip the part where I ask myself if I'm proud of that outlet. It worked. *It's not stupid if it works.*

Covers flying, they land at the foot of the bed, damp and matted. Exposed to the room, shudders move in at the cold of the morning meeting the sweat beading on my skin.

Next thing I know, I'm dressed and ready as I'll ever be.

Kitchen cupboards stare at me with their blank faces, and daylight pools in through the rear-facing window. It provides a comforting warmth and blinding view of the sun rising on the field behind the house.

Removing the mix from its home in the pantry, the milk and eggs out of the fridge, and producing a bowl from somewhere, I whip up some quick pancakes. I even remembered to buy chocolate chips at the store so this really will be a breakfast of champions. In short order, the aroma of melted butter and chocolate fills the house.

Runny batter bubbling into individual cakes is an extremely silent ordeal. Over the silence and opting for some musical background noise, I switch the boombox on, resuming the classical station. Not knowing a single song that plays manages to get the job done of soothing and distracting until the pancakes are ready.

Plate in hand, occupied by several cakes and tons of syrup already soaking into the fluffy goodness, hesitation halts me mid-spin. Taking a seat at the empty dining room table, among uninhabited chairs screaming their vacancy more loudly than the radio, becomes too overwhelming a thought.

The counterpoint that surfaces isn't any better. Many lonely meals were had standing in the kitchen of my college dorm and apartment shortly to follow.

An impasse stems from not wanting to continue unhealthy traditions here, while also not wanting to be intimidated or hindered by my own ideations.

Trembles overrun my hand. Syrup comes precariously close to spilling over the plate's edge. Pushing all reasons away, I ease back to let my hip dig into the cold counter. My focus shifts instead to enjoying the food I made.

Intentionally tasting the different flavors, noting the consistencies between pancake, chocolate, and syrup, reminding myself to use more butter next time, these details help to occupy my mind. At least, enough to get me to the end of breakfast without another breakdown.

Food being a mediocre reset, I return upstairs to grab my laptop and bag. Even after some dawdling and marching down the stairs, there's plenty of time to spare before I need to be in class. Wonderful smells linger as I double-check the front and rear doors to make sure they're locked.

My car takes its sweet time to warm up. Foggy breath fills the air between me and the lightly cracked windshield while I wait. Shivering my butt off, waiting for the heat to catch up, the idea arises to stop for coffee or hot chocolate.

The gas station on the way to campus would be perfect, I tell myself as another shiver rattles me in a full-body twitch. As soon as heat trickles through the vents, my car rolls out of the drive and chugs onto the highway.

Rumbling across the railroad tracks upsets my hold on the steering wheel. For a moment, intrusive thoughts butt in, teasing me to let go of the wheel completely and allow whatever happens to happen. Obviously, I don't listen to them.

First, the sign at the road, then the gas pumps, followed by the building itself come into view. Someone walks up to the door as I pull into the parking lot. Noting no other parked cars, they must have come on foot. *Awfully cold to be doing that.*

I make a judgment call to leave the car running. There's always a nonzero chance it could get stolen, but since I've got a spare key and can lock the doors, I'll risk those odds to keep this sucker from cooling down on me.

Heaving the glass door open, it clicks in my mind that the person who walked in ahead of me is one of my students. Of course, it couldn't be just any student. It has to be the one who said he left his pencil in my class. Along with a very different version he presented first.

Blush colors my cheeks as I remember his wording. At the same time he turns to see who came in the door behind him. *Hopefully he thinks the blush is from the cold because wow, I do not want him to get the wrong idea.*

I nod in recognition as our eyes meet. He reciprocates it, visibly more flustered than he was a second ago. *Shit.*

Beelining to the cappuccino and hot chocolate dispenser, the largest size cup winds up in my hand. Usually hot chocolate makes my stomach hurt. As a kid it would never, but my adult stomach doesn't seem to be on the same page. Still, I have to put it to the test once in a while, to make sure.

Hairs rise on my neck as a feeling of being watched settles over me. The button lights up, pressed under my finger. Warm liquid chocolate dumps into my cup, splashing up the sides.

I blank on how to stand normally, becoming extremely aware of how my legs are positioned. Shifting uncomfortably does nothing to ease the sensation.

Goosebumps scatter down my neck and arms as I peer over my shoulder to catch the student mid-argument with himself about something. One of his hands rubs at short stubble spreading from chin to cheeks. His eyes shift back to me, widening before he rotates completely around to continue battling himself.

My attention falls to the cup. Cutting the chocolate stream right as it begins to overflow, residual drips splash out into the catch tray.

The lids never want to sit on these properly. I use this as an excuse, making a show of trying to get it situated so he can collect himself.

Walking to campus is going to suck for this poor guy. Rolling my eyes internally at the thought of offering him a ride, I chastise myself on the kind of situation I could be putting myself in. *It would give him a chance to say whatever is plaguing him, or he can decline the offer, and I won't feel so bad.*

Having completed my task in an unnecessarily complex manner, my face returns to him at the tail end of his regaining composure.

Apparently winning one side of his argument, he stands upright and smiles more broadly. "Hey, Ms. Lizzy. I was wondering…"

Oh dear.

"Do they have tutors for art classes?" One eyebrow ticks up ever so slightly.

Well, that is not what I was expecting.

A response exits my mouth without being approved. "Actually, I found myself wondering that too." I stop to shift the warm cup between my hands. "I don't want any of my students to think they can slack their way through my class. I thought I might threaten them with tutoring if they try it."

Seems clear enough. I'm referring to them as students and maintaining assertion as a teaching professional.

His smile relaxes further, accompanied by a chuckle.

As I walk past him, stepping up to the counter to pay for my drink, I rip the band-aid off. "Are you walking to campus? It's pretty cold out if you need a ride. Nobody needs to be transforming into a statue out there."

Was that weird?

Mindful to give the cashier my attention, I am handing over my money when he takes up the space beside me. His form towers above mine. A granola bar and bottle of milk end up placed on the counter in front of him.

Ah, another breakfast of champions.

"Normally, I don't mind the walk. It grounds me and gives me time to think." He very nearly sounds nonchalant.

I suck in a quiet breath at his words, hoping I've gotten out of it.

"Although, the weather is colder than I thought it would be this morning, so I won't refuse a ride if you're offering." This time, his tone betrays a strained steadiness.

Grabbing my drink off the counter, my body and gaze shift to the door to refrain from making eye contact. A couple steps away, I toss, "It's Casey, right?" over my shoulder with a sideways glance. *I really hope that's right.*

He nods to the clerk, scoops up his breakfast using one hand, and stepping around me, sweeps his other arm out ahead as if to usher us on a journey. "Yeah, Casey. I was wondering if you'd remember me. I'm still really embarrassed about the mix-up yesterday. Let's start over, if you don't mind."

His hand splits the distance between us.

We stop in front of the door. Smothering my nerves, I grab his hand warily and give one pump. "Let's never mention it again," I state on the down swing.

Releasing each other, we push open the doors to reenter the wintry Oklahoma morning.

I alternate already chilled fingers in front of the vents during the short jaunt to campus. Initially, my main concern is he might try to make more small talk. When his silence throws me off guard, it quickly becomes appreciated.

Pulling into a spot not too far from my building, my nervous chatter takes over. "Alright, made it in one piece. I'll see you in class if there's anything you need to go off and take care of first." I grab my bag and push the door open.

A nod in agreement precedes, "Thanks for the ride, Ms. Lizzy. I appreciate it," and another pause. "So do my toes." His former, relaxed smile is replaced by a wavering one once more.

He hardly waves before sauntering off in the opposite direction.

A sigh of relief escapes me.

Hot chocolate warming my hands makes the walk to my building more pleasant. Wind still penetrates the openings of my sleeves or any other crevice available. Clouds looming close urge me to reach up and touch them. They look close enough to do so.

Only a few steps away from the door, one of the other instructors stops me to pass along their condolences. Thankfully, they are short and sweet.

She and I used to go to high school together. Her face is unmistakably familiar, though her name escapes me for the moment. Funny that we're instructors at the same campus now. Not that there are many opportunities around here.

As she prepares to walk away, she stops to ask if I've been to the dunes recently. It takes a moment to remember what she's referring to because I haven't seen the Little Sahara Sand Dunes in years. We used to go all the time when I was younger and Dad was around.

We'd go out on the dunes almost every weekend, either for us to ride along with someone or drive ourselves. *Wow, that was a long time ago though.* I haven't had any reason to since.

I tell her it's been a while, and she asks if I want to go with her and her family next weekend.

"Isn't it a little cold to be out on the dunes?" is my attempt at a joke, though it goes right over her head.

"That just means there are fewer people to worry about, and the heavier vehicles can run better on the sand." She tosses a hand towards me as if it were a ridiculous worry. "We like to take an old, beat-up suburban on the sand so we aren't too cold, and the kids can ride inside without any issues."

"I appreciate the offer, but I have plans this weekend. Thank you." It is nice to be invited to things, even if I don't want to go.

Spinning toward the building, I hightail it to my room before I can be stopped anymore.

5: Casey

Holy shit, plants itself squarely at the forefront of my brain. The only reaction allowed to process at first.

Hardly an acknowledgment of sensation returning to my extremities breaks the hold this single phrase has on me. Needles stab underneath the skin of my fingers and palms.

Annoyance shifts to pain as the glaze over my eyes recedes enough to comprehend that I'm seated in the campus cafeteria. I didn't realize I'd already made it inside and sat down. Restoring my connection to reality, somewhat, opens the floodgates for more than just those two words.

I can't believe we were so close and I didn't end up with my foot in my mouth.

I don't understand why I get so giddy and tongue-tied in front of her, as if I can't form coherent sentences like the relatively intellectual person I am.

How am I supposed to woo her if I can't keep from tripping over my own tongue?

We both questioned the notion of tutors being utilized for an art class.

Without any consideration to the growing flow of students around me, my gaze holds on an open space in the floor. Whether it becomes occupied by someone or not, I bore a hole into that spot as the tangle of words in my head pull apart.

Bites of granola disappear, the bar shrinking in my hand. Milk grows warmer by the minute, no longer chilled. Yet I have no recollection of intentionally eating or drinking any of it.

Just as easily, I could've gotten food here, or made something back at the apartment. *But no, I wanted to go to that gas station to get something. There has to be meaning.*

She did make sure to call me a student.

Damn the luck.

Worse comes to worst, I'll only be her student this semester. *As long as I don't take any more art classes she could teach.*

I don't think that'll be a problem.

Fountain of thoughts running dry, it dawns on me that the din of passing students has quieted. The act of chewing finally becomes apparent as my eyes truly focus to take in my surroundings. A cafeteria mostly empty.

Remnants of granola and milk stick in my throat during the agitated rush to sprint out the doors. Limbs flail and fail at coordinating until cold blasts sober me completely from daydreaming.

Barging through her classroom door, just in time for the period to start, I disguise my ragged breathing under a cough. It doubles as an attempt to clear debris clinging to my windpipe.

Ms. Lizzy does a sweep of the room in quick attendance. Noticeably, her gazes skips right over me.

The sharp inhale her miniscule action evokes is unexpected. *I'm in her head, too.*

This idea brightens my grim expectations of the semester for approximately three minutes. Until I squirm in my chair as class drags on from there, mundane as before. Light, at the end of the cross-hatching and shading tunnel, dims.

Her voice, slightly authoritative, commands my attention. Rising in excitement over the material she's explaining, then tempering once she catches herself. I could listen to her talk all day. The subject itself, I care little about.

Hopefully the semester flies by and this purgatory can be over soon. Although, what if I don't have any way to see her outside of this class?

Shouldn't this morning be a shining example to disprove such a theory?

A sobering thought shuts down the butterflies nipping at my stomach. *I can't let anything get in the way of my other priorities right now.*

Promises I've made and goals laid out for achievement don't disappear because of a new hyper-fixation. *Don't refer to her as a hyper-fixation. She deserves better.*

Previous engagements can't be so flippantly set aside when they are, quite possibly, far more important than a potential flirtatious fling that might not even make it to fruition.

An agreement with myself reached, the rest of class is easier to bear.

After her, no other instructor can hold my attention for a second. Their voices drone on in a droll monotone or irritatingly fake enthusiasm. Both pick at the wrong parts of my brain.

Another distraction overwhelms any and all mental capacity to learn: whatever Geoffrey and I will end up doing this weekend.

On the subject, I send him a quick text to verify he'll be back Friday evening. He takes over an hour, eventually affirming his return.

Either driving or sleeping off a hangover, I muse.

I'll do some legwork myself and be ready for him when he gets back into town. *It'll be fine.* Since this was my idea, he can't be too upset about it. *Might soothe the itch I've already developed.*

Why did I feel the need to involve him in the first place? I don't know why I bother asking myself the question. My initial encounter with Geoffrey plasters itself behind my eyes.

The horribly lit dive bar was where I decided it would be a good place to think. Somewhere I could be surrounded by people yet remain alone. Where I could blend in and simply exist.

The clinking of shot glasses and pool cues, yells from excited patrons, conversation and reactions to TVs playing some sport or reality show, bartenders shouting to be heard—all this noise helped to drown out my inner demons screaming at me. Impossible to ignore any longer on my own.

A burly man, silently staring into his own tall glass of poison, caught my attention. Hunched atop a squeaky barstool beside me, an impressively disturbing array of empty glasses accrued in front of him. When he caught me staring, his bloodshot eyes widened, and he lurched up.

As suddenly as he reacted, his face and body fell back into lethargy. After a few moments of silence, he told me his wife and kids had recently left him. That was his explanation for the "blubbering mess" he'd become. No tears traced lines down his cheeks, though his face was puffy and red.

Pity sent my hand out to his shoulder in consolation. Going through my own vulnerabilities at the time imbued me with an extra pool of sympathy to draw from. *Or would that be empathy?*

Word vomit of his circumstances was my reward. I'll admit, his tale of being a hardworking man, stuck out on the road all week long while his wife got to stay home and be present for the kids until she up and took them away, was compelling.

Maybe if I hadn't been so close to the edge myself, I would've never approached him, never would've extended an offer. I was mostly pleased my own tears stayed dammed behind clear eyes rather than spilling over. I'd also had significantly less liquor than him, by the way he smelled. It all seemed a good idea at the time.

Shaking off the memory of how quickly he agreed to my *kindness*, my mind is made up. All I have to do is get through the rest of today. Then I'll do some work on my own tonight.

Eventually, ready to crawl out of my skin, the last period ends.

An illusion of warmth skitters across my skin as the dipping sun peeks between the clouds.

A pep creeps into my step during the walk home.

Normally, I don't feel any special type of way towards my apartment. It's a place. To eat, sleep, rest, and hold my belongings. Today though, as I take the final steps toward the brick building, I am brimming with excitement.

Inside, down the hall to my bedroom, my regular clothes come off. Swapping instead into all-black jeans, sweatshirt, and sneakers. *I don't need anyone able to pick me out of a line-up.*

Dredging the depths of a closet, muffled tinkling emits through the coarse fabric of my satchel I use for these special projects. *It wouldn't make any noise if I'd cleaned it out.*

On the tiny dining room table, upending the bag spills its contents every which way. Anything not reusable is transferred to a plastic bag to be stored under the kitchen cabinet, for disposal at a future time. *That time better happen sooner rather than later, if I know what's good for me.*

Slinging the strap across one shoulder, the other hand pulls out and unlocks my phone to run a quick news search. Specifically checking for any updates on the escaped convict, no leads or updates on his whereabouts are mentioned. At least, none they are passing along to the public.

A soft latch of the door dissipates behind me. Down in the garage, my car comes into view exactly as I left it from the weekend. The sleek black sports car is nothing too crazy, blending in fairly well. Even muffled, the engine roars to life at the turn of the key. *Okay, it is a little loud.*

Easy pedaling pulls me out of the drive to exit the complex. Wanting no wayward attention, I allow the vehicle to grab and propel itself forward as my foot lifts off the brake.

Only a few miles lie between me and Hopeton. Already, that brief landscape is enshrouded in growing darkness.

I know where the easy targets live. Tonight isn't for scoping or scouting. Tonight is for action.

6: Geoffrey

Nails grinding on the inside of my skull make it difficult to focus on the road.

Snow piles along the ditches in lumpy, wind-blown groupings. Nowhere near enough to be a hazard, several cars drive as if it were negative thirty-two degrees and ice were coating the entire roadways. Others fly around me in plenty hurry, uncaring that they're skirting so close to a big rig.

Everyone forcing me to be so vigilant pisses me off.

How does nobody remember what courtesy and speed limits mean? A couple of the idiots flat out try to cut me off, ignorant to the fact I'm operating a screaming metal death trap capable of fucking up their world in a hurry if they want to play stupid games.

Actually, if I had more inclination, I could end a lot of problems for several of us here and now, if I really wanted to. The idea is tempting before reason has to ruin the fun. *Eh, I care more about the livestock I'm hauling than the precious few idiots I'd be saving the world from if I did anything right now.*

All that can be done is blare my horn less than I want to and shift gears a little more efficiently to not agitate this already piercing headache.

My frown deepens at the memory of finding out the bar and grill did manage to charge me a one-hundred-and-thirty-five-dollar tab after they tossed me out on my ass. *I can't believe they left me in the gravel just for getting in a fight.*

Shoving the thought down with the rest of the bile attempting to escape my stomach, I have to admit the first couple of deliveries this morning went pretty smoothly. Especially considering I wanted to hurl all over one farmer's snakeskin boots.

Somehow, I kept it together.

My stomach quit trying to flip so much once I settled into the truck for a long haul and stopped moving my body. Every now and then, bile still creeps up my throat, threatening to make me pull over.

Local deliveries done, I'm now heading halfway across the state to load more cattle and bring them this direction. I don't get why people can't buy more locally instead of going outside their county to have them hauled in. *Whatever. Lines my pockets.*

Cresting a particularly large hill for Oklahoma, I get stuck behind a minivan full of kids in sport gear. A ball bounces between the seats, containing identical colored uniforms.

Out of nowhere, nausea strikes again. Memories arise of my own kids in their old sports gear.

They haven't played sports in years.

That sidenote does little to stop their team photos from clearly painting themselves in my mind's eye. Photos stuck to the fridge ever since.

Something races to fill the cracks in my soul. An emptiness claws through every tendon. My muscles tense and relax, fingers flex from fist to hyperextension, joints pop and shift at the loosening and tightening happening all over, outside of my control.

These physical reactions distract me from the road. As well as the accompanying brain fog swiftly taking over.

I yank the wheel in order to stay off the rumble strips along the shoulder.

Sweat beads on my forehead while I try to think of anything else.

Casey messaged me to make sure I was going to be in town this weekend. *Who does he think I am?* I guess it is kind of nice having someone checking to make sure I'll be back, since I don't have a wife to anymore.

Oh no, here it comes again. Time for some emergency fluid.

Releasing the wheel with one hand, I reach under my seat to feel for the flask stored there. After fumbling around and hitting the center-line rumble strips, my fingers find the cool metal. Little effort is needed to pull the container loose.

Fluid sloshing inside instantly lowers my erratic heartrate. *At least I made sure to refill it before putting the damn thing away.*

Practiced ease unscrews the top and dumps a mouthful of whiskey to coat my raw throat. Warmth spreads across my chest as the liquid settles within me. A couple more swigs follow before soothing waves touch the sharper edges of my headache.

Over another hill, it's me and this minivan left in sight, still driving at a lackadaisical pace. Only a few feet separate our bumpers since we're going under the speed limit, and I've about had it.

Accepting the consequences, I pull the cord to my horn. Reverberations that shake the cab don't rip me apart like I thought they would.

Though the minivan swerves because the driver was caught off guard, she slows down even more, making me slam on my brakes to keep from rear-ending the stupid dumbass. A middle finger appears in her rearview mirror.

You're going to have me sitting in that van with you if you're not careful, lady.

I let off all pedals and put the shifter into neutral to coast down, nice and easy. The highway junction I need is coming up anyway.

To make matters worse, the minivan slows down too. *She better not be going my way.*

My rig screeches to a halt on the road, waiting to see which way she chooses. No signals flash for either of us.

Arriving at a dead stop too, her hands throw up in the air. *What the fuck is she waiting for?*

This is stupid. I flick on my left turn signal. She must see it, veering left herself and continuing on slowly to hold me behind her.

I imagine the smartass smirk she's wearing right now. Even though I can hardly make out her face in the mirror, the thought alone is almost enough to make me forget the kids she has in her care and do something drastic.

A chuckle wipes the frown off my own face as I jerk the wheel to the right and take off in the direction I actually need to go. *Stupid bitch, trying to get a rise out of me.*

At first, it crosses my mind she might throw her van in reverse and see how far she could go, just out of spite. She must think better of it because after stopping again, the van hauls ass. Taillights disappear beyond the bend, and I breathe a sigh.

Getting up to speed, part of me wishes for the chance to go toe to toe with that broad. Especially in front of those kids. *I'd have taught her a thing or two. Equal rights means equal fights.*

The fire clenching my jaw shut the remainder of the day only fizzles when it's pitch black out and I'm rolling into the next truck stop where I plan to do my overnight reset. With less blood pumping to keep me motivated, my eyelids droop as a tremble enters the fingers no longer white-knuckling the wheel.

What perks me up is realizing I've made it to my stop. I rally until noting most of their signs are off and their bar area is closed up tighter than a DOT checkpoint. *Fuck.*

A handwritten sign plastered in the window renews my faith in the place, stating alcohol sales go until midnight.

One hand rubs down the length of my face, disappearing into my beard. Fingers stick in the mass of hair before wrenching at the knots starting to develop.

The truck shudders and shuts off once I find an unpopulated corner to occupy.

Every thud of my heel against the asphalt risks shattering the thin barrier of protection holding back the agony, but each step is necessary to gain me the solution to this problem.

No liquor, only beer to choose from, three cases of different varieties load down my arms. I take as much as I can carry in one trip. Much more makes them a little uneasy to sell to me.

Walking to my rig, having delivered the last of the herd earlier, there is now a quiet spanning the lot with the truck shut off. No moos echo off the inner panels of the trailer to escape out the scattering of holes. No dirty hooves bang against the metal walls and floors to send a ringing through the air. There is near-perfect silence.

The crisp crack from my first beer as I settle into the bunk almost makes me forget I have time to sit alone in my thoughts.

Memories of arguments with my wife flood me like they are happening in real time. My blood boils, and the hold on my beer tightens, partially crushing the can.

As the kids grew, they became bold, peeking out of their rooms whenever we'd fight. I'd try to ignore them because yelling at them to get back to bed didn't work anymore. They'd argue if I engaged them. If I left them out of it, they didn't usually butt in.

Seeing the change in my kids too, it makes sense now where they got it from. My wife had to be conniving and planning for some time. Turning my own flesh against me.

That last night blurs at the edges of my mind. *I would've been out faster with liquor. Beer eventually does the trick.* The final fight was over her trying to take my pickup out while the kids were already running around in the car.

She forgot a few things at the store and absolutely had to go back before they closed.

I asked what was so important it couldn't wait, but she wouldn't tell me. I told her I didn't need anything, so who cares if it waited until tomorrow?

Then she kept yapping. "I just need to go to the store for a couple more things. Why am I getting the third degree?"

Her hands were firmly seated on her hips by this point. Not too often did she do that anymore. Not since we first started dating.

"It's too cold to walk and carry everything. The kids are already gone in the car, and I told them they could stay the night with their friends." A quiver in her voice betrayed her false bravado. "I want to make them breakfast in the morning and have everything here all ready to go."

I wasn't buying it. *Guess I was right about something.*

Her hands dropped from her hips when she saw I wouldn't give, the short moment of her old boldness gone as quickly as it came. I found myself disappointed.

That was when she started getting fidgety. Arms crossed and uncrossed, weight shifted off one leg to the other, one foot tapping. Or she'd twist and pop her fingers, constantly moving, twitching, fidgeting. She's only fidgety when she's hiding something from me. I found that quirk out one year for my birthday when she tried to throw me a surprise party.

I ignored her then, continuing to sip my whiskey.

But with that last argument, I knew there was something else going on. The way she kept pushing, more so than usual. Her movements extra twitchy.

She was going to tell me what was up.

"You keep lying to me, and you're not going to be able to fidget anymore," I warned her.

"Just let me have the keys, and you won't have to worry about me fidgeting because it will be handled." Her hand stuck out between us, implying I would actually hand them over. It was the closest she had come to back-talking me in a long time, and it pissed me off.

The buzz finally starts to erase the memory of me walking towards her. To either shut her up or teach her some manners.

Then, it's gone completely. Her shoulders that were gripped in my hands disappear as if I were holding shadows.

Ah, oblivion.

My sweet mistress, who can never escape me. She can run, but she can't hide.

7: Casey

Engine whirs send vibrations running up my leg from the accelerator.

I periodically remind myself to check my speed. Even the short distance I'm going, it's easy to forget and let a little too loose since my car stays stored away most of the time.

Running down a mental checklist helps to steady my excited nerves. Though it does make me wonder if Geoffrey would be proud, indifferent, or angry at me not waiting for him on this.

Not that it matters too much, hopefully he isn't angry. *I hate having to talk him down from a temper tantrum.*

My head shakes thinking about it.

Beast of a man that he is, he does have his uses since I am able to get through to him.

Plenty is planned after this once he's back in town and considering we have our escaped convict in play. *Now that was an ordeal.*

There wasn't a ton of useful information I could dig up on many of the inmates housed at the correctional facility outside Alva. Martin was one of very few with the right type and amount of disjointed family left in this area. Some inmates had many close relatives or friends near who would watch out for them, whereas most of Martin's actual family moved out of state after his sentencing.

His girlfriend owns an Airbnb in Dacoma while anybody else left wouldn't be promising him favors, as far as I could tell.

He happened to be the one we thought would hold the best chance of hiding locally, without actually being aided and abetted. If he were to actively have people helping him, that would create more work for us and increase our number of witnesses.

I need to stake out his girlfriend's place, confirm whether he is or isn't taking refuge there. Either way, these are thoughts and a task for another time.

Trees lining a creek along both sides of the road dissipate as I slow to cross the bridge right before the intersection into Hopeton.

A silhouetted grain elevator looms against the star-studded sky, blocking out those shining behind it. Slight curtains of moonlight cast enough glow to outline the lonely figure.

My headlights reflect across the first houses, sweeping over barren trees that hide nothing with their empty limbs. I switch them off to continue in hopes of evading notice.

The first couple of homes have an abandoned appearance. Shuttered windows and junk-strewn lawns speak loudly to disuse. Strange shadows cast through the misshapen yards, indicating objects forgotten or left to rot.

Eyes adjusted to the dark make it easier to pass by these and on through the center of town. Neon signage beckons my attention to fall on a flyer in the post office window. Since it's after hours, the empty lot provides ample space to pull up and inspect, though it does leave me exposed.

Pulling a black beanie onto my head, I bring it down over my eyebrows for maximum coverage. Slightly more at ease, I step out of the car, leaving the door ajar. No overhead light shines on the interior. That attention attractor was removed long ago.

Beautifully illegible font requires me to practically shove my face into the window before I am able to even attempt reading what the sign says. "Winter Block Party" is the headline stating a date for this Saturday. More discernable text below reads the event will be held at the church across the road.

Isn't January a little cold and late to be throwing a party? I scoff and roll my eyes at small-town trivialities. Although, the more I think on it, that could actually be a great opportunity. Residents might have enough gossip spread by that time, or they may start getting defensive.

Satisfied, albeit underwhelmed, chills penetrate my layers more noticeably while standing still. A shiver rips my gaze from the offensively bright signage to rove over the surrounding houses.

I peer beyond the immediate neighbors to focus on one farther down, sporting a lit window. Blinds betray a dim glow muffled behind them. Too faint to attract other interest, it's perfect for me.

Weightless footsteps carry me across the street. No gravel crunches or twigs snap under my careful tread.

A gap between the cheap plastic blinds and faded trim allow glimpses of my target: the slumped form of a middle-aged man occupying his recliner.

Whatever show is playing, unable to hold his attention, bathes him in flickering light. Losing the fight against falling sleep where he sits, a TV dinner tray perched empty in his lap, he is exactly what I'm looking for.

Another assessment of the immediate area yields no hint of any other presence. My pulse flutters knowing I can move forward, unencumbered.

Stealthy footfalls guide me around the house. To no surprise, a back door is unlocked, squeaky knob twisting with little issue in my hand. *Trusting small towners.*

Bracing the old wood as I inch it open, the growing span hitches my breath each amount it gives, begging to squeak and creak. Yet the old thing remains silent under my tense grip. I maintain an agonizing pace until there is enough space to squeeze inside.

Upon entry, a playroom appears to be my access point. Decorated with colorful pictures and posters that hang above shelves full of nostalgic children's books, toys, and games, the space creates an anomaly for the man who lives alone.

Beyond this is a kitchen in such a state, the appropriate response should be to call in a maid service. An impulse to gag overwhelms me before passing.

Through a formal dining room, containing far too many chairs set up for a single guy, I'm finally deposited into the sparsely furnished den.

There doesn't appear to be any other presence in the house. *It's just me and him.*

Entering the room behind his chair, any noise I make is swallowed by thick carpeting.

My knife appears from the bag, sheath sliding into my waistband for quick access. Several lengths of rope wrap around my hands. They easily pull taut for a controlled grip.

I take the time for one deep inhalation, holding it for a moment in preparation.

Without further hesitation, allowing impulse to reign, I reach over the top of the recliner and down in front of the man. My feet plant into the carpet to ground me in place.

Quicker than I can mentally process, my muscles retract, bringing the rope tight against his neck. Too slow, he tries to yell and lean forward, attempting to pull away from my embrace.

A choked gasp manages to squeak out, despite the pressure I apply. The sound is so silent, I can barely hear it above the low television volume.

He scratches ineffectively at the rope, fingers unable to find purchase on any slack.

Since he'd already been close to sleep, the man is easily subdued before realizing the full extent of what is happening.

Taking in the room while he fades away, an enlarged picture reflects the distorted scene of my creation back to me. I didn't realize I was smiling. Flashes from the TV cast flickering shadows across my face, bringing it in and out of focus.

When blurred into the reflection, the photo underneath becomes clear. Several kids are frozen in time as they run around one of the local playgrounds. The black and white photo appears as innocent as the children within it.

His silent gasps transition to bubbling gurgles as the last of his air escapes. Over the following seconds, they become fewer and spread farther apart.

Long after all noise stops, I hold him on the slim chance he's trying to fake me out. By now, my muscles scream to be released. Only once I'm sure do I loosen the strain enough to check his pulse and confirm he's gone.

Departed from this realm, any problems the man was facing have become meaningless.

Geoffrey and I discussed leaving bodies behind. Now that we have Martin, they don't all have to resemble accidents. Debbie's death was the last one absolutely needing to be perceived as unintentional. At least, until Martin is caught.

A few of them ought to be moved, dispatched, disposed of in some manner. In theory, that would create more chaos anyway.

It sounds less horrific, makes less of an impact if they're all discovered. If word got out several people are missing or were never found? That's where you get next-level panic, pandemonium, and fear. When imagination can run unchecked and questions are forced to remain unanswered, the potential is limitless.

I may feel trapped by Woods County and small-town life, but they're trapped here with me.

If I can't escape, I'm going to bring down as many as it takes to lift me up.

At least until I'm done or I can figure out how to move on.

Since I'll be taking this poor sap, I retrace my route through the house. The journey is faster, requiring less stealth and care.

Under cover of darkness, my car blends in alongside the house. Reversed to the door, it's nearly impossible to pick out unless someone has reason to stare.

Not many windows point into this bare backyard. Extra effort to keep my head on a swivel dawns on me as a tad drastic.

Trunk open and ready, I tread through the silent house again to retrieve my prize.

Cracks of protestation escape my neck and shoulders while I stretch to loosen up. Suppressing a grunt, I haul his heavy ass up from the recliner. Practiced movements bend my knees, dropping me into a static squat as I throw him over my shoulder. My balance readjusts to the additional weight in a smooth rise to an upright position.

One final trip room to room has me smiling. Even bogged down by my heavy load, I'm beaming at the successful incorporation of my workout routine in the form of this manhandling.

Tarps stashed in my trunk on the chance they're required come in handy to keep my friend's DNA contained.

I expected him to be more of a fighter. This works out better, no blood or messy cleanup to worry over. No attempt at conserving dignity is used as I drop him in.

Numb peace radiates through me. Confident this has been a successful endeavor, my heart rate and breathing slow closer to normal.

Sweat accumulated during all this exertion leaves me in a damp shirt now sticking to my slick skin. Sliding into the driver seat, a shiver shakes my unfeeling shoulders.

Dwindling houses along one side of the road give no signs of life, attributing an almost desolate quality to the town.

Except for one house on the very end. Visible through the mostly dormant tree branches and sparse evergreens, one second-story window exhibits life. Another dimly lit orifice, obvious to me because I am quite actively seeking it out, mocks with its existence.

I know you're there, Debbie Dern's daughter. You can't hide from me.

My eyes remain glued to the faint beacon until I'd have to stop in the road to continue staring.

At the intersecting highway, my brain doesn't think. A jerk of the wheel points me away from Alva.

The following silence, surrounded in an enclosure of darkness broken only by my headlights penetrating the first ten feet in front of me, allows me time to admire certain aspects of life again. The engine is a constant pulse, thumping along with the blood in my veins. Pounding rings in my ears as the blushing face of Ms. Lizzy flashes to the forefront, rising above everything else.

I briefly contemplate her potential reaction to my current state. *Would she turn away from me in disgust? Maybe my unexpected craft could cause her heart to flutter, leading to a another one of those flushes. What if she saw a reflection of this same darkness inside her?*

The whispers in your ear, tantalizing calls from the intrinsic depths of your subconscious, requesting you to do the unspeakable. A haunting temptation lures with tastes of impulsive and intrusive thoughts, abhorring you in the next instant once rationalization shatters the illusion.

Most people retain the capacity to tune those thoughts out or ignore them, assured in their ability to hold them back. While others, those who barely contain them under the guise of emulating a decent person, struggle to their very core. Daily questions arise to torment: *How could I ever consider those things? Why does my brain allow these thoughts to exist? I would be a psychopath to give in to such concepts, right?*

I know we're all susceptible to them. Some people solely require a nudge, their supposed decency hanging in the balance by a thread, to become complacent in darkness. With that little assistance, once they initiate acting on them, it quickly devolves into a second nature to follow through. Continuing to listen to them in the future requires less hesitation, if any.

A grin tugs at one corner of my face.

After a few quiet miles, the road curves toward where dying rays of sunlight clung to the horizon not so long ago. As memory races ahead toward the next town, a clearer outline of a plan formulates.

Although night has mostly settled, the time is too early to rid myself of my new friend. Dark and cold enough to minimize passerby interference, I need the slightest possible amount of people out and about.

Over one last hill, the road curves again, depositing me at the edge of Waynoka, home of the Little Sahara Sand Dunes.

Barely inside the border of town resides a quaint bar and grill where I can kill some time.

If they didn't close early.

Rounding the corner onto a nearly deserted street, my hopes drop as the place appears vacant. My car halts in the middle of the road so I can concentrate. Lights are on inside.

Doing my best to exude indifference, I grip the door handle and prepare myself to be in the presence of others, relaxing my face without allowing a frown to settle.

Inside, the chill falls away, stripped by the warmth of both the atmosphere and furnace together. A couple of tables continue their conversations after a glance up at the new arrival. Overall, the small place isn't crowded.

Quick calculations run through my mind over what seat I should choose. My options are the bar itself, regular tables, or mid-height tables. Each have their own list of pros and cons to go with them.

Foregoing a seat at the bar, where I'd potentially be expected to make more conversation with the bartender, and a regular table as that would put me right at the window for anyone who walks by to see, I take up residence towards the center of the room at a middle height, four-top table.

Eventually, a gal comes over to take my order. She flashes a genuine smile. *If it isn't genuine, she has an amazing customer service persona.* Not even pretending to write anything down on her notepad when I speak, she disappears. Her chipper form remerges to deliver sauces and my drink before fading into the background again.

I appreciate her infrequent presence allowing me to contemplate the events of the evening, as well as what is still required of me.

It is an odd sensation to enjoy being alive again. Acknowledgment of existing as an entity, rather than a thread woven into the backdrop of life, is freeing.

Mid reflection, an extreme self-awareness infiltrates every thought, *Appear normal so as not to draw attention to myself. Can't have people remembering me or leaving any impression, good or bad.*

The feeling of eyes being on me can't always be acknowledged. Jerking my head up at every perceived stare my way would make me appear shifty.

Wandering eyes straddle a fine line between sincere curiosity and creepy staring.

Relatively quickly, yet far too long to leave me alone in my paranoia, my food comes out. Juice from the burger runs down to pool in a rounded corner of the wax-paper-covered basket. Melted cheese hangs off one side, a wayward meat blanket.

Saliva fills my mouth, rendering speech impossible. Thank goodness, because I almost automatically respond to the waitress with *you too* when she tells me to enjoy.

Hyper-vigilance of my movements translates into step-by-step instructions spelling out in my mind. *Squirt some sauce on the side, dip one fry at a time. Chew. Take a bite of burger. Enjoy it. Chew like a normal person. Sip, don't slurp the drink. Don't make unnecessary eye contact.*

Everything tastes more flavorful. The ranch is zestier, fries crunch the perfect amount, even the ketchup quality is unmatched tonight.

I do have to marvel at how this evening has progressed from confidently snuffing a life, to self-consciousness overwhelming the simple act of eating in front of people. Such an impact comprised from existing too closely among others has to indicate a mental issue. *My brain has to be broken.*

On that note, I cannot shake the sense of being watched.

Daring a look around, my gaze meets that of a cowboy-hat-attired gentleman standing behind the bar. At receiving my attention, he asks if there is a stronger drink I might need.

In a rush to finish chewing, I clear my throat before offering a measured response. "Not tonight, but thank you."

He smiles, accompanied by a buoyant nod, then returns to cleaning glasses and talking to the other patrons seated in front of him. A white rag, draped over his shoulder when not in use, makes the pearl snap buttons of his shirt pop more brightly. Without the smile and bubbliness, for a second, he reminds me of Geoffrey. The rugged country, blue-collar appearance is resemblance enough to send a shudder up my spine.

Crazy to think one unexpected, miniscule encounter with the wrong person could potentially screw everything up for me.

Thankfully, I don't waste too much time pondering this detail when the waitress comes by to drop off a check.

This place is inexpensive enough I could really wow them, leaving a well-deserved tip, but then that would make an impression. *Can't be too cheap or too gracious because they would remember it.*

I spare one more glance to the room, pushing up from the table. After that, I keep my gaze focused towards the door. Before another word can be exchanged with anyone, it's shut tight behind me.

Cold air rushes to replace any trace of warmth I retained while inside.

Pulling the driver door closed onto silence reassures me in a way I didn't realize I needed. I find myself letting out a held breath.

Since winter is an off season for the sand park, there aren't many tourists roaming these small city limits.

Locals seem to almost disappear alongside the lack of seasonal traffic and fanfare. They blend in the dormant landscape of yellowed grass and leafless branches, waiting for the promise of warmer weather to bud. Not dead without it, merely slumbering until more ideal conditions present themselves.

On the other side of town, towards vacant cabins, campgrounds, and sand-sport-related stores, a shed Geoffrey owns sits adjacent to sandbar roadways. Where pavement gives way to gravel down side alleys, these backroads transition to sand at other, similar structures. Those in the know built storage off the beaten path, allowing direct access to the Little Sahara State Park a mile or so down the way.

One such dead end deposits me in front of his small shop. Rock bleeds into sand from this side of the tin building to the other.

In addition to personal buildings full of vehicles, empty rental houses and lots comprise this section of town. So much potential lies in wait for just the right times of year.

A soft pop signifies the trunk release. Barely open, the gap created allows a stench to claw from its depths. Another reason I use the tarps: defecation. It happens. Perfectly normal.

Still a nuisance.

While that airs out, I use my kit to unlock the shed. Geoffrey probably doesn't even remember mentioning this place to me. An asset is an asset. I couldn't pass up on the possibility of its usefulness.

The small door tries to creak in protest. What little sound does escape is limited to a line of evergreen trees across the gravel road.

Inside, one window faces these trees while another points directly toward civilization. Switching on any lights could possibly draw attention. Opting instead for stealth, I creep through the shed by memory. My shin only takes a hit once during this process.

In front of the far garage door sits an old pickup built for ramrodding across the dunes. Fully expecting it to put up a fight, I am surprised when the key left in the ignition turns with ease. The old girl rumbles to life after hardly any hesitation.

Exhaust rattles and engine surges send waves of reverberations throughout the small shop. Tin walls shake as the space quickly fills. My muscles pulse in tune as echoes ring back and forth, wall to wall.

I navigate outside to prep my burden for travel. Tarp already beneath him, it's nothing to finish wrapping the body.

Lifting him from my trunk turns out to be the most difficult part. Once he's slung across my shoulder again, transportation is easy.

A pause as my eyes linger on the pickup bed. I instead drop him to the passenger floorboard. Pulling away brushes my arm against a worn-out saddle blanket currently in use as a seat cover. Laid out, the rough fabric hides any trace of my copilot.

To conclude my itinerary, metal scrapes metal as a shovel slides into the bed. *That's the most normal thing about this escapade.* My head shakes.

A garage door opener clipped to the visor has enough delay from when the button is pushed to when the door lifts to bring into question its functionality.

Once clear of the shed walls, inside the cab becomes more manageable. I do wait on the door to finish closing before heading out onto the makeshift roadway.

Ruts and tracks riddle sandy lanes. Holes and bumps drag the tires one way then shove them the other. My steering wheel is never straight in the fight to move forward.

White knuckles anchor me since my butt is unable to stay in the seat for more than a second. No matter how slowly I dare to go, any divot or hop sends me catapulting about the cab.

Over the noise, I can still barely make out the shovel scraping around the bed. Metal grating irritates several of my nerves. *I'm a one-man band with all this racket.*

Shaken to my core by the time I get there, the park entrance comes into view. An overhead streetlamp bathes everything in harsh, white light. Without leaves to cover their branches, dormant trees allow illumination to extend far beyond its summer reach at this opening onto the dunes.

There doesn't appear to be anyone manning the gate for payment. A small wooden hut sits empty.

Driving under the arch, a comically long antenna protrudes from the hood to whip the wooden entry as I go by. Normally there for safety, no neon flag waves from its top to announce my presence to other potential riders.

This first stretch of sand to deposit motorists onto the main area is intentionally dipped and wavy. Similar to a dirt track.

My head narrowly avoids making contact with the roof as I bounce along the rough road. So close to my destination, with fewer obstacles in my way, it becomes fun. For a moment, enjoyment takes over. Laughter fills the cab.

Officially on the dunes themselves, there are steep rises, drop-offs, hills, bowls, and straightaways. Not to mention the wayward trees growing up through the sand at irregular intervals. Clawing free of their sandy grave, limbs protrude at all angles.

Vigilance is key, especially at night, in order to not find yourself nose down in a drop. Driving straight or up means nothing out here. Drops hide everywhere, and flat doesn't mean flat for long.

Dim headlights barely breach the first couple feet in front of the truck to shine a path. Light from the entrance attempts to spread to the far reaches of the park. Cut off by the dips and rises, it merely adds to the disorientation. Clouds blotting out stars add to the confusion of not being able to tell sky from sand.

Angling and weaving to keep on the path of least resistance, I follow the map in my head of the dune layout. My goal is the trails on the far side of the main park area.

Many drop scares, dips, and zig-zags later, the undulating sand levels out as flora takes over the landscape. Underbrush rises to surround me.

Limbs scratch and scrape both sides of the pickup. Aside from a shiver at the screeching it creates, I continue without care in search of the ideal spot. Several more hills, dips, and drastic directional changes deposit me to a place desolate enough to stop.

Shoving open the door grinds more unforgiving branches into it.

One foot sinks into the depths, unable to find balance in the sliding terrain. Nearly twisting my ankle slams me against the cab to keep from falling further.

This close to the outer edge of the park, patches of firm ground are interspersed throughout the sand. None of it necessarily contrasts the other. It all blends together into a seamless playground. Each step holds a potentially different outcome depending on which you hit.

At random, I choose an area beyond the bushes lining the trail. There's nothing significant or eye-catching about it, precisely why I'm drawn that way.

Shovel in hand, I weave a path to it.

Staggering strides catch my feet among the branches ripping and tearing at myself and my clothes. To remain upright, the specific patch I'm headed for slips from my vision as focus shifts away.

I have no idea if I end up at the same spot.

Sifting more easily than I anticipated, relentless, fine granules attempt to slide back and fill the hole with each scoop removed.

Moonlight casts faintly through the clouds. Enough to see by, it reflects white off the sand, causing it all to resemble snow.

Tiny cuts down my arms and legs sting once sweat beads on my skin again. Ragged breathing is the only sound to accompany scrapes of the shovel.

Hours go by, leading to the decent-sized hole opening before me.

With only a brief pause to catch my breath, I trudge toward the pickup.

Weight once again gracing my shoulders, the door slams shut behind me, ringing out into the open air.

Cautious steps navigate me back through the entanglement ready to trip at each placement. The extra time and energy spent carrying him have my legs threatening to buckle under his load before I get him down.

Uncomplaining, his new home accepts responsibility of my burden with plenty of room to spare.

Somehow, taking the same amount of time as digging it, the hole disappears. Level ground eventually covers the area again.

Leaning on the shovel holds me upright for a moment to admire my handiwork.

All the noise of redepositing the shovel and slamming my door shut rattles my ears after recent hours.

A final glance to where I spent most of the night reveals even I can't pinpoint the exact spot I'd chosen. Staring longer doesn't change the fact.

I smile to myself, despite the exhaustion, and tear out of the trails as if I were out here enjoying them like anybody else.

In the distance, the light pole guides me to the gate. Atop a dune, it draws me in such as a moth to a beacon. Dipping below ridges, it disappears, waiting to be found again at the top of the next.

By the time I make it back to the shed, I'm bounced out and near the end of my strength. *I desperately need a shower and change of clothes.*

Parking the pickup as I found it takes a couple of attempts to get it right. Once more shaking the walls, I shut it down as quickly as I can and lock the place up.

Thank goodness my trunk has aired out and doesn't reek of death or defecation.

My own engine coming to life is where I reach the extent of my energy. In my own familiar environment, fatigue washes over me.

It was worth it.

Before I can comprehend how I'd made it this far, the sign for Hopeton appears. This restores some energy. A sleepy grin pulls at the corners of my mouth. *There's a good chance I will be the only one who ever knows the truth of what happened to that man.*

Another near lapse in consciousness transports me to my apartment, stashing my car in the garage and giving it a quick once-over to make sure nothing is out of the ordinary.

Inside, willing myself to walk by my bed, I strip and hop in the shower. Attempts to keep myself awake long enough to get clean send my thoughts striking off in all directions. Many of them circle back to how pleased I am with how this excursion went.

Finally lying down, amid drowsy confidence, my thoughts pivot again to Ms. Lizzy.

8: Martin

It's been over a week since my escape.

I figured the people behind my preemptive release would've reached out by now. No one has come to find me. *At least, no one I know of.*

Hiding at my ex-girlfriend's place maybe isn't the best idea. Although, it has kept me out of sight, hopefully out of mind.

The first few days of waiting nearly rattled me out of my skin. Every sound or shadow elicited a jump. I thought for sure someone would come barging in using a key at any moment.

It hasn't happened yet. Not too many people knew we were dating, so the rational part of me knows there wouldn't be much reason for them to come investigating here. She definitely didn't broadcast our involvement once the story broke.

Mostly empty cupboards are all that welcomed me, except for a couple cans of nonperishables I'd rather not attempt to identify since the labels were long gone. I've been making do. Whatever the cans contained has been enough to keep me going.

Staying so close to Alva gives me the willies, but I'd rather not be picked up walking on the side of the road or through a farmer's field. A pedestrian wandering the countryside is cause for suspicion right now. I'm lucky I made it here unscathed.

The question of *why someone would break me out* constantly echoes in my mind. I can't make any sense of it.

Maintaining my position on the hallway floor has left my back numb. Cold seeping through the thin fabric of my jumpsuit, coupled with remaining still for so long, has my body slowly giving up.

I chose this spot for its inconspicuousness. Out of sight from any window, there is a small area where I am positive I can't be seen. Such a tight perimeter does require me to lie motionless, left to think and ponder. Things I do not do well. I've been left alone with my thoughts for far too long.

A gurgling grumble roils from the pit of my stomach. *Not much I can do to remedy that right now.*

As the last echo of a growl dissipates into my intestines, a car engine shuts off. Muffled by the walls, I initially believe it to be a neighbor's vehicle down the street.

Only after the latch of a car door resounds do I realize I can hear it plain as day in my otherwise silent world. For me to pick it up so clearly, it has to be right outside.

Pressing flatter against the floor, I will myself to forfeit no movement or sound.

Leaves crunch and crackle like thunder beneath feet stomping around the side of the house, falling silent at the back door. A lingering pause stretches on until I find myself twitching in anticipation over this interloper's next move.

At long last, there is a quiet knock so hesitant, I almost miss it drowned out by the roaring in my ears.

My heart rises in my throat. After several beats, another knock quietly echoes, yet I remain in place. I swear the knob jiggles, though considering the state I'm in, that might be in my head.

Silence fills the space again until the trampling of leaves resumes. A car door creaks, and the engine comes to life before fading away, disappearing down the street.

Fighting to remain motionless a while longer, I force myself to wait. Sweat trickles out of my hairline when I do roll over and crawl to the back door.

Leery of any potential view from outside, I keep low and stare down any window I pass by. At the door, I clamber upright enough to peek through the sheer curtain. There's nothing to see except the backyard where sunlight streaming in hurts my eyes.

Gasps heave my chest as I tentatively unlock the door, easing it open at a speed snails would complain is too slow. Cracked enough to peer between the gap, a bag of groceries unveils itself on the stoop.

This has to be a trap, my mind warns.

Apparently, the message doesn't travel to my stomach as it growls again, with more gusto. One shaky hand reaches out, nabbing the sack handles.

Whoever it was, they were thoughtful enough put it up against the door so I wouldn't have to step out for it.

It dawns on me, as I resecure the door, that this could've been whoever helped me escape.

A slow crawl back to the hallway proves more difficult with my wobbling arms.

Returned to safety, the bag opens easily for inspection on hopefully my next meal. Inside are cans of pasta and beans, cheese sticks, meat slices, and cereal. *They have to be involved somehow, or this is an elaborate trap.*

The last item in the bag is a typed note:

No fear, I bring food.
Will continue if you stay.
When safe, I come back.

Huh, okay. Aye, aye, captain. I salute to the empty house.

There is no name, no other information on the paper.

Without further ado, a can of ravioli appears in my hand and cracks open of its own volition. The smell alone is enough to put me at ease.

I still really hope this isn't a setup. *What else can I do?*

The original plan was to stay here until the heat was off anyway, figuratively. The actual heat has been off since no one stays here outside of tourist season.

If this person wants to feed me, who am I to complain?

Snarfing down the first can, I'm halfway through the second before it crosses my mind to slow down and make these last. *I have no idea when this person will be back with more.* Second can polished off, I add the empties to the pile forming.

I'm okay to stay right here for now.

9: Lizzy

Classes fly by without incident the rest of the week. No more students try to hit on or make fun of me, and only a few more people pass along condolences. Mercifully, they were almost painless. *Almost.*

Now that it's Friday, I can look forward to a weekend of nothing.

Maybe I will make an appearance at the block party. *Not that I've talked to anyone about it.* There was no mention on the flyer about bringing a dish or drinks. I think it's safe to assume whoever is planning it will handle everything in that regard, and we're just expected to show up.

My last class for the day twitches in their seats. Crossed arms and strong grips clasp their belongings tightly against them to eliminate any slack or drag. Every single person appears ready to spring as soon as the clock strikes. They're all packed and engaged in a staring contest with the clock or their phones, counting down the minutes. Someone's restless leg taps out a short rhythm before falling silent.

A bit selfishly, I dismiss us a few minutes early. Minimal rejoicing escapes them as they rocket to depart.

In a hurry clearing out, as if I might change my mind, most leave hardly mumbling, "Goodbye," or, "Have a nice weekend." My own chuckle fills the now empty room in collecting my things.

Snow, brilliant as the sky it descends from, falls in slow motion. Brighter than my future, glaring white covers almost every inch of ground and flat surface where soft flakes have built into untouched piles. Their serenity alleviates a bit of the seasonal gloom. Even as I tug my sleeves farther over my hands to keep some of the bite off, my mood lifts at being able to appreciate this view.

Classes officially still in progress leave me a clear path to the parking lot. My students disappeared so quickly, an empty lawn crisscrossed with vacant sidewalks already pocked with tracks allows for a peaceful moment alone. Feet sink in just enough at every step for snow to reach the top of my shoe. No ice in the air yet, they do not make a crunch.

Cars slosh through wet, salty buildup congesting the streets. Shiny clouds hang low, filling the sky as far as I can see once I get past all the blinking. Sunlight breaching the thin cover reflects off every wet surface. Leafless trees do nothing to hinder the wayward rays casting glare in every direction.

An echo on the wind gives me pause. Grinding to a halt as I reach the car, I nearly slip in sand spread across the plowed lot. My head tilts and ears brace to listen for any repetition. *I swear I heard someone call my name.*

Whatever I heard does not repeat.

Uncontrollable shivers twitch muscles throughout my body. My head drops to one side at a drastic angle while my chin wrenches to the other. A shudder ripples my shoulders, flailing my arms out like opposite polarity magnets forced apart.

This entire motion completes within the same second of starting, most aptly appearing as some kind of spasm to anyone walking by.

I hold my breath and dare to glimpse around. No one is nearby who might've noticed. The lawn is still mostly vacant. Nobody fills the windows facing me. *I think I'm in the clear. Whew.*

As my car warms up enough to take off, more students and faculty drift into view.

For some reason, my subconscious focus shifts to Casey. Unwelcome impulse draws my eyes to scan the oncoming flow for his familiarity. Darting from one face to another, disappointment settles into my stomach as each one fails to belong to him.

Once I realize what I'm doing, I attempt to squash this impulse and ask myself, *Why?* He's no different than anybody else. There's nothing special about him that should result in my thoughts turning to him, let alone searching for his face in a crowd.

Intentionally redirecting my attention towards driving does help to distract from the idea of my insanity, until it doesn't.

Slush lining the roads only requires a little extra care. Everything is wet, not icy. It allows the mind to wander again once adjusted, and it feels safe enough to use less concentration.

I almost miss the grocery store drive. Jerking awake from passive daydreaming, an empty lot in front of the store is a refreshing sight after my last trip here. Existing among others sounds much too difficult right now. *I've peopled enough this week.*

Of course, the cart I grab has a squeaky wheel. Knowing I'm the only person in here does nothing to ease my awareness of the high-pitched note periodically announcing my movement all the way up and down each aisle. I do my best to tune out the annoyance, although it quite nearly sends me into a burst of sarcastic laughter.

For over ten minutes, decision paralysis leaves me stranded in the cereal aisle. Stuck glancing from the box I automatically reached for in my hand, to several others I tell myself would be better options, an ongoing debate plays out on whether I even need any at all. If I do, which one? And why?

Fed up, I slam the box back down on the shelf and wheel away.

Catching on to the dramatic shift in my mood, it becomes apparent that I ought to leave. Unless I want a breakdown to hit me in the middle of the store.

Okay with purchasing whatever is already in the cart, checkout is a breeze. The cashier smiles and makes minimal small talk. It's nice not having too much expectation put on answering.

Preparing to be infiltrated by cold again, bags shuffle in my arms while I brace for the short walk outside. My face lifts to watch where I'm going when Casey saunters through the door. Catching me off guard, some of the slump creeping into my shoulders lifts.

Did I summon him by thinking his name?

He must've seen me long before I clocked him because he doesn't trip over his words at all. "Hey, Ms. Lizzy, do you want some help?"

The number of bags weighing me down is obvious and numerous. His question compels me to change up my grip.

"No, but thank you. I ain't no two-trip chump, and it'd feel like cheating if I got help." My ridiculous response flows far too easily.

He smiles. "I get that. Well, have a good weekend. See you on Monday."

I make to mirror his smile when it hits me I already have. *Shit.*

"Thanks, you too," spills from my lips as he circumvents me.

Bag straps dig into my fingers and arms more, their weight suddenly increased. It's a miracle I get everything settled in the car by the time they give out.

Behind the wheel, my hands rest on the cold material, waiting for warm air to exit the vents again. My brain shuts off completely for this drive. No bombardment of thought hits me like I expect. No questions pipe up or tangents come forward to pull me in any and all directions. I sit in silence. The singular sound my mind acknowledges is the car running, barely loud enough to drown out the low radio. I had lowered the volume so I could concentrate on the road. *Because that makes sense.*

Fewer people driving now gives the town a deserted atmosphere.

Headlights shine behind me on the highway out of Alva. *Hopefully they don't mind going slow or passing me.*

Snow falls faster and thicker now. Coupled with January's early onset of night, there is a higher chance of it being icy, so I'm not taking any chances.

Each mile slowly rolling by, I wait for the lights to grow larger. I expect the car to get closer and eventually pass me, but it never does.

On a clear day, Hopeton's grain elevator is visible from the edge of Alva. Today, I'm well inside the tiny township limits before it appears from the white fog. Heartbeats thumping against my chest contradict the relief I'd begun to experience getting closer to Mom's house. *Er, my house.*

Only after I'm parked in the driveway do those headlights come around the curve into view. Nothing about the vehicle catches my attention aside from the lights sweeping by because for some reason, I don't get out right away.

That crushing weight beginning to threaten me at the store is back in full force, holding me in place. Though I know I am physically capable of movement, telling myself to does nothing. Focused on chastising myself, I lose count of the minutes where I am unable pry my hands loose of the steering wheel.

My eyes bore through the windshield, taking in nothing. The garage door returns a stare as blank and ineffective as mine, as if it too wonders why I haven't moved. We stay locked in this position for…I really don't know how long.

A ragged breath drawing in—I'd apparently stopped doing that—finally cracks whatever spell gripped me. Pressure stiffening my shoulders dispels enough for me to flex. Released of my frozen mind, physical numbness has since crept into my fingers and toes.

Shakes rattle up and down my stiff arms as I retrieve the groceries. Concern over being debilitated again at any moment clumsily rushes and fractures my actions. My own feet become tripping hazards, weighing twice what they normally do.

These unexpected issues leave me woefully unprepared for how difficult getting inside the house turns out to be. Tears spring to my eyes in frustration over my sudden weakness.

My only consolation is less snow falling here than in Alva. The driveway is mostly dry, clear of the same precipitation only miles away.

At last, I manage to juggle everything just right in order to get the door unlocked and open. This is when my grip on the bags finally fails. Some tumble to temporarily rest on the living room floor.

It's okay. There isn't much that would break or spill, is my attempt at allowing for patience, while at the same time trying not to actively lose my shit.

Wintery chill rushes inside to replace any heat it can before the doorway is cleared and shut. Deep breaths do nothing to ease the vibrations still twitching different muscles as I step over the bags to take off my things from the day.

Everything retrieved and relocated into the kitchen, dispersed to its proper place, drains the remainder of my energy. I am ready to be cozy and watching a movie.

My steps marching up the creaky stairs destroy peaceful silence through the still, dark house. Comfy pajamas hang loosely off my body to allow room to breathe more easily, upon descending.

While I scan movies lining one of the rare shelves not occupied by books, the same selection in the same place they've lived for years, wind whistles against the house.

I didn't really get to watch anything Christmas-related this holiday season, is my justification for withdrawing a childhood favorite that has followed me into adulthood.

Nostalgic previews emit from the TV nearly as old as the film. I keep an ear open so I can listen while preparing snacks and whipping up some hot chocolate.

Soon, title screen music blares at me on repeat, loudly proclaiming the movie is ready.

Shuffling across the floor in fuzzy socks is a bold choice with my history of clumsiness and my arms loaded down. A cup and snacks make it to the coffee table unscathed, just within reach of the recliner.

After I verify curtains are all closed, front door is shut and locked, and the lights are off, I am ready to settle down into the chair.

In a basket beside the chair lies Mom's stash of extra blankets. Taking up one of the thick, fuzzier fabrics and tucking it in over me and the chair, I am the most comfortable I've been in a long time.

Remote in hand, selecting the play option ceases the repetitive title screen music that will live in my head for the next several days. As it diminishes, I brave a sip of the hot chocolate. Yep, scalding. *But soon it'll be too cold.*

Opening credits commence, and I resist the urge to sing. *I don't know why I would resist; there isn't anyone here to keep the weird locked in for.* This is all the permission I need to belt out, singing along to the catchy tune and dancing in the chair, shimmying my shoulders so as not to disturb the snacks conveniently located in my lap.

I try to backburner any problems or complaints of the world outside my door as I relax and immerse myself in the movie. Any cars, people, noises, other what-have-you no longer exist to me. Except for snacking, which thankfully doesn't require any thought.

The next thing I remember is darkness consuming me.

***

Aw, I fell asleep during the movie, is my first waking thought. It couldn't have been much later than seven o'clock when I started it. *I must be entering my grandma era.* Or I was way more exhausted than I realized.

Title screen music blaring again makes it difficult to pinpoint exactly when I fell asleep. Rubbing my eyes, loose popcorn rolls around my lap ready to spill as I straighten up. Beside me on the table sits the empty hot chocolate cup. Numbly scanning the room for answers, the remote and some popcorn falls to the floor.

"I'm a mess," I confirm out loud.

I can't believe I fell asleep so fast. I bet I didn't even make it a quarter of the way into the movie. Rolling my eyes at myself and groaning out a yawn, scene selection opens in front of me in an attempt to figure out where I ended consciousness. In wondering what time it actually is, I fumble for my phone only to remember I left it upstairs.

Another groan follows as I force myself out of the coziness and warmth of the chair. Creaks echo louder into the darkness, knowing how late it has to be. Blurry red lines on the alarm clock adorning my dresser read 10:43. Wow, what a way to spend a Friday night.

Hey, I can't be too mad. I've got a lot going on right now. Yeah, I'll just lean into that, I tell myself, grabbing my phone and heading back downstairs.

Returning to the chair to see my blanket draped off one side and snacks strewn about elicits a sigh as my head shakes at the sight I must've made.

A creak sounds from the kitchen while I start cleaning up some of my mess. My spine straightens, and my head snaps to peer through the dark doorway. Obviously, I don't see anything out of the ordinary. *Because why would I?*

The mess picked up or thrown away puts me at ease in again retiring to my cocoon to finish the movie. I find where I believe I fell asleep and start watching again at the previous scene.

By the end of the movie, I'm ready for my actual bed. Up and out of the recliner, stretches and groans exalt sleepy frustration.

Mine refolded and placed with the others in the basket, the blanket pile resembles exactly how Mom always wanted them to. *You have to fold and stack them just so. Nice and neat, Eliza, so they don't topple.* Her voice and accompanying hand gestures towards the heap are as clear in my head now as the last time I experienced them in person.

Tears flood my eyes. A yawn I was working through decides to choke me instead. *Damn.* Sniffles overrun my nose as I check the front and back doors. I don't remember if they were locked.

Blurry vision doesn't matter when creaks of the familiar floor guide my steps. Mostly the tears are silent; only a couple times do I shudder and breathe more heavily under the weight of this unexpected grief.

Dammit, Mom, why did it have to be so out of the blue? We hadn't seen each other in a long time. There were quite a few unresolved issues between us that neither reached out to continue working on anymore. The failed relationship was both our faults, but I'm the one left to handle the fallout of it now.

Curled up in bed after disabling my morning alarm, I try to ride out the sorrow barreling through me. It takes some time—I have no idea how long—before I finally feel sleep come for me as tears still stream down my face.

Teetering on the edge of consciousness, something wipes at my cheek.

I scream.

10: Geoffrey

Stupid kid. I swear, I will lay into Casey like one of mine if he doesn't show up or answer his phone.

He said he'd meet me in the superstore parking lot at ten, right after I got back from my route. Now here I am, waiting, and he's nowhere to be found. Then to top it off, of course he isn't answering calls or texts.

I'm gonna teach that kid some manners. He should know better than to pull this kind of stunt.

"Uuuggghhh," I release into the lighted lot. Echoes carry on past the bright perimeter, dying somewhere in the darkness beyond.

He's lucky this is where I was going to park my rig for a reset, anyway.

I only wait so long before the walk home entices me. At least there, I've got beer.

It's not the cold that bothers me; my flannel is all I really need. Mostly, I feel ridiculous standing here resembling a date, unaware she's about to be stood up.

Taking one last sip from the flask leaves it a little too light sliding back under the seat. *Damn thing needs to be refilled again.*

The empty lot is easy to cut cross once my feet get moving. My hands stuff into the front pockets of my jeans to give them something to do.

If he gets ahold of me before I make it home, then I might let this go.

Empty streets throw back every little noise I make tenfold. One porch I pass has a light flickering to mark its impending burnout. At one point, footsteps echo down from some other street. Their maker never crosses my vision. Though none of these details matter, they are something to note, something to detract. *Distract?*

I make it all the way to my block when buzzing shakes my pocket. Wrenching the phone out illuminates a name on the screen: "Kid."

He told me not to use his actual name. *Should've done it just to piss him off.*

For a second, not answering sounds fun. Maybe it'd give him something to think about. Then I answer despite the notion.

"What," I bark, not posing it as a question.

Blowing right along, like I hadn't said anything, Casey delves into his spiel. "Sorry for not responding sooner. I thought we had a problem requiring further attention. It won't be an issue after all. Where are you?"

"I walked home since you couldn't be bothered to answer me. I'm almost there now." A shiver punctuates the statement, though it isn't from the cold.

"Well, stay there. I'll come pick you up down the street." He hardly finishes talking before cutting off the call.

Guess I don't get a say in nothing. Maintaining some modicum of composure, I restore the phone to my pocket and chalk it up to him owing me in the future. *He's got a lot coming his way if we ever split.*

Several minutes tick by as I grumble to myself. My fingers flex and retract, wishing for a beer or a bat to hold onto, when his black car comes around the corner and slows to a stop at the curb beside me. Automatic locks click as he drops it into park.

Hesitating a moment, I throw open the door and plop down into the passenger seat. It isn't even shut behind me before he's pulling away.

"Jeez, you can let me get in first," I spit at him, facing the window instead of his direction.

"I don't want anyone to see us together. I'll drop you at the same corner when we're done talking," is all he says, taking another too fast.

I brace myself to not slam against the door. "Can you cool it with the evasive driving? You're gonna make me hurl."

I'm almost serious. My truck is bigger and handles differently than this little car.

Ignoring my threat, he moves on. "I contacted our friend, Martin."

I'm definitely going to have a cricked neck tomorrow with the way my head snaps to face him. Dashboard lights faintly illuminate his eyes and mouth through the gaps in his steering wheel.

"For real? Are we going to pick him up?" I ask, searching his dim features for any signs of deceit. This kid isn't the easiest to get a read on. An additional glow reaching his face from the passing streetlamps isn't enough to distinguish anything helpful.

"He's good where he is for now, hiding out and hopefully a little paranoid. I think he knows there aren't many options," Casey says, a glint flashing in his eyes.

Is it deception? Mirth? *Who knows when it comes to him.*

Unsure where he wants that topic to go, I switch to another. "So, did you make progress while I was gone?" I wouldn't be mad, unless he were to try to cut me out completely. He's the one stuck here all week long, whereas I get out at least for a moment on the road.

"I did make some discretionary moves. Nothing that should affect anything we do moving forward…" He trails off, giving no further detail.

"Are we still doing one tonight?" I ask, my voice steady as I realize he's driving aimlessly up and down the streets of Alva.

"It's already late—" he starts, cutting himself off.

My fingers curl into a fist on my knee. White-knuckled, I wait to see what this little shit decides.

"—but you deserve to have some fun."

Some tension in my hand releases, though the fist stays in place.

He keeps driving as I sit back and attempt to cool off.

We pass the outskirts of Alva. Now nothing except some prairieland separates us from Hopeton. Those miles drag on so slowly in the dead quiet. The radio hasn't played since I got in, and I am in no mood to make idle conversation.

Part of me thinks he's doing this on purpose. *That's okay. The silence doesn't unnerve me. It's just annoying.*

The black expanding nothingness of night, swallowing the rest of the world outside this car, provides me a backdrop to use in tuning out my thoughts. White noise droning in the background of my brain are replaced, focusing on the operation of Casey's engine instead. I succeed at clearing my mind until the car begins to slow, lessening the rhythmic vibrations.

Trees and buildings take shape in the darkness at this slower speed. Despite the radio's glare in the window, several lawns go by as Casey drives past the first couple of houses. He continues toward the railroad tracks before pulling over and cutting the engine completely.

We take in the small neighborhood, assessing if any night owls might linger. Calm stillness welcomes us. No one else appears to be lurking.

In this final moment of waiting—really, I've waited all week—my muscles twitch their resistance to not immediately throw open the door. A patient façade, not reaching further than skin deep, holds me steady until Casey gets out.

He comes around the front of his car, stalking across the street. Aimed at a rundown, two-story farmhouse, we blend easily into the night.

Shivers of anticipation run along my spine. Adrenaline seeps into my veins as we come up next to the chipped and flaky siding. Controlling footsteps consumes my concentration as we hit the backyard.

Knowing the highway is only a few feet farther momentarily gives me a start. Eyes adjusting to the lack of light reveal a cluster of trees blocking most of the view to anyone who might drive by.

They'd be going too fast to see anything, I remind myself.

Casey holds an index finger to his mouth as he ascends the back porch stairs. *No shit, Sherlock.* Even though we're already silent, I make a show of trying to be extra quiet to make the fucker happy.

Of course, that moment is when my big ass squeaks one of the steps behind him. He rounds on me so quickly, yet so soundlessly, I almost topple over. All I can do is make another show of shrugging and throwing my hands in the air.

Eyes wide, his attention returns forward. Darkness aside, I see his head shake. *Fucking asshole.*

We reach the door, and I am far sweatier than I anticipated. I cross my arms and wait while he gets to work on his lockpicking magic. In the deafening stillness, a creak emanates inside the house. My hand thrusts out to stop him, finding he's already frozen.

An eternity passes waiting for another sound. Breathing gets in the way of listening, so that comes to a halt. One icy breath fills my chest and rests there as I ponder if our presence might be known or if it was normal settling noises of an old house.

Faintly, running water trickles through the plumbing as if someone is getting a drink or taking a piss. The breath releases, and I create a wave motion using my hand. Casey raises an eyebrow at me before it relaxes in understanding. Confirming this, he makes his own gesture of tilting his head to drink from a cup. I nod, and we wait again. Another creak sounds somewhere deep inside the house.

Quiet sighs escape both of us in visible puffs. Allowing him to continue, my eyes sweep the back and side yard. They come to a stop at a sign sticking out of the ground almost too far away for me to read.

A light click marks the door unlocking. Casey takes the knob in his hand, preparing to give it a try right as I make out the logo of a security company.

My hand reaches out again to stop him, hoping I'm not too late.

He releases the knob, shrugging my hand off, and turns to look at me as if I've lost it. Annoyed myself, I point out the sign. Squinting to read that far, his face relaxes.

As if consoling a toddler, barely above a whisper, his voice manages to remain full of sass. "Fake signs."

Smug smile in place, he slowly opens the door. No alarms or sirens go off. All remains quiet. *It is so aggravating how much of a know-it-all smartass this guy is.*

As he makes a sweeping gesture with his arms, akin to a magician performing a trick, I refrain from banging his head against the doorframe. It is a difficult task. Fists shake at my sides, holding out for more intentional use.

Casey leads us into the kitchen, down a hall to the living room, and works his way soundlessly up the stairs.

I hold back, lacking the same confidence he has that we are alone aside from the targets. One glance around conveys the house seems under-furnished. No obvious places to hide call for further inspection. Knowing this, I am satisfied we should be alone.

By the time I get to the bottom of the stairs, Casey is already gone. Slow steps up elicit as little noise as possible. The time it takes me to ascend allows my heart to pump faster, fingers to twitch and curl, and shakes to rattle my arms and legs. This has nothing to do with fear. It's anticipation. *I'm so fucking ready.*

A partially open door at the end of the hall is my singular clue to where he went.

Two body-shaped lumps lay still, spread out in a bed. Casey takes up residence on the far side, motioning me to the other.

Walking across the bare floor and trying to remain silent proves difficult when my body is primed and ready to engage. In position beside the bed puts me close enough to see Casey's chest rise in a deep breath and hold. I prepare myself, waiting for it to fall.

As his breath releases, we carefully lift the covers away. Folding them down to the foot of the bed, two twenty-something-year-olds are revealed. A man and a woman, probably either married or close to it.

Poor bastard. He's lucky we're here.

I'm on the woman's side, and Casey is on the man's. Covers removed, shivers begin to draw our victims nearer to consciousness, rousing them from their slumber.

Before she can stir anymore, one of my hands clamps over her mouth. The other I use to gather her wrists. Scrawny and bony, they both fit easily into my one.

Her eyes flutter. Sleep blurs any chance for sight as they pry open. Confusion crinkles her features. She can't open her mouth to yawn or move her hands to rub her eyes. Though she tries, my hands keep her still. Blinking repeatedly—*since that's really all she has left to do*—she awakens enough to gaze up and notice me, taking in my shadowy form hovering above her.

A smile pulls at my face as her eyes open wider. Her muffled scream dies in my calloused palm. Pulling at her hands, wrenching with all her tiny might, she attempts to shake my grip loose.

I'm not going anywhere, little lady.

Veins bulge in her neck under the strain of trying to twist her head, wanting to look away from me and toward her fella. I allow it. She is rewarded with a face full of Casey over his side of the bed. A giant knife protrudes from the man's chest.

Jeez, Casey. Revel in it a little, why don't you?

The sigh escapes me before I bother stopping it.

Angling her face back to mine, I accept the potential risk and release her wrists. This hand comes up to wrap around her neck, right over those bulging veins.

She wants to scream so badly. *But we can't have that, darlin'.*

My grip grows tighter until I think any sound would be inescapable. Only then do I let go of her mouth and bring the other hand around her throat as well. Not that I need both of them to do the job—it's simply more satisfying.

Her face shifts from ghost-white to pale blue. Ever so slightly, my grip relaxes. Merely to prolong this euphoria, not to allow for recovery. As the blue lets up and she attempts to drag in a ragged breath, I tighten once more.

A glance spared to check on Casey shows me he's made several cuts after the initial, dramatic plunge. Blood is pooling all over their side of the bed.

Little lady's feet eventually stop kicking. My grip holds a while longer for two reasons: because I can and it's a nice feeling, and I want to make sure she's not holding out on me.

Any chance for a lingering pulse is long gone when I release her.

Casey appears to have given up on whatever game he was using the man to play and is preparing for his next step.

Taking a moment to rub some of the tension out of my arms, I gasp at the prickling sensation it evokes, drawing my gaze down to fresh claw marks.

"Ah, dammit." The swear cracks, grating on my throat from disuse.

Casey looks me over, whispering, "I'll be right back."

He holds up a gloved finger, telling me to wait here. Keeping my reaction suppressed as he disappears down the stairs is a feat I did not think I would manage.

Alone in the room, I take in my little lady again.

Her eyes are set more deeply into her face, sunken in to wrinkles and crow's feet emerging upon closer inspection. Where before her skin appeared flawless and porcelain, she now gives the impression of being significantly older than the twenty I had guessed.

Silent moments fill in the gap between Casey's return. A bag is slung across his shoulder.

Foregoing whispers, he outright asks, "Did you touch anything?"

What kind of idiot does he take me for?

"No, I didn't touch anything. Little miss sure as shit *touched* me, though." It comes out snarkier than I intend in presenting my bleeding arms and hands. What a dumb mistake.

Surprisingly, he doesn't berate me. He just nods and pulls several items out of his bag. A pack of cigarettes, lighter, and a bottle containing some kind of liquid. My gaze lingers on the unlabeled glass.

"Grain alcohol," he explains, lifting it.

My face snaps to his. "Wait, I thought we weren't covering these up anymore?"

His answer is cool. "This one we should keep open to interpretation since your massive hands left marks on her and your DNA is under her fingernails. Fire will handle all that."

Condescension tints his tone. I don't entirely blame him. *Though it still pisses me off.*

Casey doesn't hesitate. He sets up a cigarette in the dead guy's mouth and lights it. After pulling the covers over them, he pours some of the alcohol out on the bed. Placing the bottle between them, the last thing he does is rig the lighter to stay engaged.

Ushering me out of the room ahead of him, he finishes his setup. The lighter ignites in his hand. When laid down next to the man, everything catches instantly. Fire overtakes the bed, spreading to the curtains and anything else in reach.

Heat created by the eruption hits me in a wave. One hand reaches up to check my eyebrows, hoping they're still on my face.

Flames beat us outside, casting yellow over the entire backyard. The flickering glow grows brighter each second.

Getting clear of the house, I was ahead of Casey. Now, pausing to admire the heat and light consuming so quickly, destroying easily, without bias or care, I slow. Crackles and snaps hypnotize my ears the same as the lapping of the color-changing blaze holds me at attention.

Entranced in place, strong hands have to pull me away.

Torn from the light begging to be noticed and appreciated, my gaze unwillingly rips. Falling into the car to watch as smoke and flames become visible at the road, I am a bystander within myself.

We've closed most of the distance to Alva before my nerves settle and relax. Control yields to me, leaving me left inside a better version of myself. Adrenaline subsides to be replaced with a contentment I was hoping for. Tension in my muscles ease as I settle in the seat, breathing easier. Heartbeats thump loudly in my chest, reminding me I am alive.

No firetrucks or sirens pass or flash in the rearview mirrors. The possibility of them responding so quickly sends an extra tingle down my spine. Part of me wants the whole house to burn by the time anyone finds it. Another part wants them to show up and be able to see our work in action.

Miles doused in silence fly, depositing us back onto my empty street.

Not another word is exchanged between us. Casey's face remains forward while I remove myself from the vehicle. As the door shuts, all that's left is to face my empty house.

I need a drink. A sigh accompanies the thought in relation to tonight's events, also because of something I'd done a long time ago. Something still haunting me lurks within the house. *I made the mess. It's time I get to cleaning it.*

My hand reaches for the knob.

Casey's car rounds a corner, fading off into the night, headed to whatever cave he resides in.

Bitter musk fills my nostrils the second an opening is cracked into the dwelling. If I weren't prepared for it, already acclimated to it, the smell drifting out probably would make me sick. The air is denser and more difficult to breathe once I'm across the threshold.

I leave the entry unlocked behind me. Darkness most people have reason to bolt their own doors against already calls this place home.

Stumbling through unlit rooms, carpet snags at my boots until tile provides for lazy steps to reach the fridge. Empty cans and bottles litter every counter. Light filtering past me illuminates the clutter while I grab a fresh beer.

Cracked and half gone in the first chug, two more cans tuck nicely under my arm as the door closes. Fabric rubbed smooth from years of wear hugs me like a second skin as I settle into the couch.

Procrastination roots me firmly in place. Ever since the night my wife left, there's been a…situation I've put off handling.

At the bottom of the third drink, motivation rallies. Tossing the empty cans aside, I hit the basement stairs willing and ready to finish this dreaded task.

My momentum falters at the last step. Something akin to regret gives me pause. The stench is far worse down here.

I wait in the smothering darkness, adapting to the lesser air quality. So long I stand in the dark, I'm almost convinced I've fallen asleep. A bite to the inside of my lip confirms, *Nope, awake.*

At the flick of a switch, one bare bulb overhead chases most of the shadows away into the unfinished corners. Squinting does nothing to ease the harshness of it. Slowly cracking them open, the scene I knew would be waiting for me appears, more grotesque than I remember.

Blood stains dried into a section of carpet tossed down over the concrete floor discolors an originally eggshell hue to a deep, rusty red. Furry patches cluster in sticky wads or thinly coat red or off-white areas of the ruined rug.

The dog my wife and kids begged me for as a puppy, the one I didn't want and wasn't going to get stuck taking care of, lies in pieces among the mess.

Killing it was supposed to be the first lesson after I found out she took my pickup when I told her not to.

I'd woken up the next morning to find my truck and wife both gone. Left alone knowing that, and with the dog barking in the backyard, something snapped.

There was nowhere else to put my rage. I went outside and picked it up by the scruff. *Fuzzy fucker stopped barking then because at least something living here knew who the alpha was.*

Carrying it down to the basement, I wondered what exactly I planned to do. No formulation of a plan came to mind. Around the edges, my vision wavered and blurred, vibrating with the need of a precedent having to be set. Anything else was unimportant; details were trivial. All that mattered was how big of an impact it had to leave.

I still don't know how the hunting knife appeared.

Not a bark or bite did the dog try to turn on me until it was too late. It was a submissive creature. How the rest of the house was supposed to be. *Too bad this cooperative beast had to be punished for the actions of others.*

Everything went numb when the slicing started.

Whimpers permeated my haze. I was aware of these and the exertion it took to hold the thing down to enact its punishment. Aside from the amount of blood being striking enough to remember, not much else is discernable out of those minutes, hours, however long we spent together.

Sitting back, admiring the myriad slices accumulated on such a small creature, I truly regained my senses.

Revulsion, remorse—neither of these were present in the wake of what I'd done. I was in awe at the horror it would instill in those who sought to disobey and question me.

Hours I waited, contemplating and anticipating the reaction of whoever made it through the door first.

Dismembering it happened later that night. When no one came home, my gut knew the situation went deeper.

I ripped those bedroom doors wide open in search of answers.

Upon first glance, everything seemed normal. Beds lay made, waiting for the return of their owners. Boy band posters clung to the walls. Books were left on the shelves. Trading cards lay scattered as if the players would walk right in to pick up where they left off.

Then I realized the rooms were half empty. Anything tucked away was gone. Cleaned-out closets and vacant dresser drawers were hiding beneath the decoy.

That's when it dawned on me: they planned it. I had been their stooge, a damn fool.

If blood could boil, my skin bubbled and popped while the deepest rage I had ever experienced distorted my vision.

Furious steps brought me to the scene of horror I'd cultivated for the traitorous ingrates. Shocking as the visual was, it became apparent the stakes needed to be pushed higher. With this greater deception as motivation, it was easy to sever limbs and sprawl them out like confetti.

Fur and blood mixed together to continue painting the already stained carpet. Some bits were tougher to hack apart than others. Eventually, there was nothing left attached to remove. Time passing did little to faze me in those moments until nothing remained to destroy.

In the months since they ran out on me, I'd left the mess down here in case they returned.

It's not that I regret doing it. Causing such a mess to deal with now sucks. *Apparently, a mess I made for nothing since they haven't come back.*

Enough time has passed. This gore needs cleaning up.

By the time I get all the pieces scraped together into an old boot box and dirt covers a fresh hole in the backyard, daylight spreads across the sky. Tendrils from the smoking carpet stretch upward to meet it.

Leaning on the shovel to catch my breath allows my mind time to rest and questions to arise, such as if they forgot to take the dog in their scramble to get away? Or did they think leaving me the mutt was a mercy? Spit is my last contribution to the grave.

I hope they worry about that damn dog every single day, their concern going to waste.

Exhausted, a smile manages to grace my lips. Cleaning up the mess was definitely the right call.

It is unfortunate my message was not received by its intended audience. I'll find another way to show them. I just have to wait.

They'll see.

They can't stay away forever.

11: Casey

Shit, shit, shit, is on repeat after dropping Geoffrey off near his house.

Driving away once he's clear of the door, darkness surrounds me inside and out. It's all I can do to exist apart from my disbelief.

Ms. Lizzy is Debbie Dern's daughter.

Finally alone in my thoughts to process this revelation is a waste of the rush since we went out tonight. I should be exhilarated and on top of the world right now, reeling at the euphoria of our conquest, yet all I can think is, *What the actual fuck?*

Fingers grip the wheel tighter while my mind falls into itself, replaying the evening.

I had hoped to sneak a peek at Debbie's daughter in order to know who we were dealing with. Instead of some random person, Ms. Lizzy was who I found in that damn house.

Curled up under a blanket so soft, the idea of crawling into the recliner beside her became a difficult one to ignore. She was out like a light. An old Christmas movie blaring title screen music indicated she'd fallen asleep well before I'd snuck into the house. *A very time-consuming task to minimize all the creaks and groans.*

Glued in place, I found myself awestruck once I realized it was her my gaze had fallen upon. She began to stir. Her movements froze any residual composure willing me to escape. There was nothing else to do without alerting her to my presence except stay hidden until she went to bed. Waiting for her to rewatch the movie and ascend those janky stairs took every ounce of patience I no longer possessed control over.

Her sniffles and tears beckoned for someone to provide comfort. I think that's why I didn't leave right away.

Once she'd been quiet a while, I followed up the stairs as irritatingly slowly as I could manage. Her steady breathing released me from some of my shock-driven focus.

The only light source in her room was an alarm clock. Red glowing numbers shone brightly toward the bed. Illuminated in the harsh glow were tear stains running down her cheeks. Before I could stop myself, my hand was gently wiping them away.

At my touch, she rolled and moaned in her sleep, re-instilling some incredulousness—toward myself and the situation. Hastening a retreat, I bolted and got the hell out of there.

Only in the safety of my car, driving away from the darker pit of hell my life had fallen into, did I remember to call Geoffrey. It was stupid of me to waste so much time there, allowing him to slide to the backburner. *He doesn't need help getting riled up.*

Part of me hoped he and I going out tonight would ease some of the reality crashing in. All it truly did was hold off the wave of questions and concerns now threatening to drown me.

Of course it's the one girl who claims my attention. She's the one who moves into the middle of our target group, plants herself smack in the line of sight to a danger I instigated, a problem I now am forced to handle differently. There is absolutely no way I can make this work. *Or is there?*

A tiny voice at the back of my mind won't stop chanting, *If anything happens to her, it'll be on your head.*

Thanks, brain, what good does that do me?

I can't warn her of the danger except to show my part in it. Maybe I could explain everything to her, and she would understand? Or she has a firm grasp on her morals and wouldn't hesitate to turn me and Geoffrey in once she knew. *Damn the luck. Damn my luck.* How did I let myself get this distracted?

Thankfully, for most of this internal conversation, I'd somehow made it to my apartment. Not that I remember arriving or taking a seat. My physical form may be perched on the couch, but my mental presence is anywhere other than here as I question every single one of my life choices leading me to this exact moment.

Darkness loses its depth, fading into receding shadows as sunlight forces a new day upon me.

I've got to snap out of this. Plans have not changed. Hopeton is going to be weeded out. Once the evil in the town is taken care of, the killing will stop, and everyone can find out the truth of those who are gone. People are going to drive by on that highway, unaware of what has happened until it's too late. Then after, maybe they shiver a little when they think about it, wondering who or what town could be next.

No one else might ever know what I've done.

I will. So will Geoffrey. Maybe Martin, maybe Lizzy.

Eliza. I am an idiot for missing such an obvious connection.

Sinking against the couch, cool pleather soothing my feverish skin, I attempt to revel at least a little in the kill of last night. Eyes closing to bar out the growing rays allows snippets of memory to take up the forefront of my mind. The woman turning over to see a knife sticking out of her man's chest, unable to scream or put up a fight due to Geoffrey's grip, was priceless. A smile twitches at the corners of my mouth as I am drawn under by exhaustion.

***

Hours later, an alarm pounds on my skull. Groaning into the ether does little to relieve any pressure until I cut the droning short.

Sleep was dreamless, yet possibly more satisfying than if I had dreamt. *Probably gave my mind the break it needed after going a thousand miles an hour.*

Rubbing my eyes raw inside their sockets, my body rises to relinquish its spot on the couch, trading it in for a shower. Shivers rattle me at the temperature change as hot water cascades down my back. Steam rises to fill as much of the small space as it can. The scalding liquid washes over me to rinse away my sins.

Long clean, I remain in place under the water, enjoying this small pleasure. This steamy warmth won't last long once these rivulets cease.

Another shiver hits me while knotting a towel at my waist.

Fog covers most of the mirror, showing a blurry reflection of my general shape. One hand swipes away the moisture to create a fragmented trail. Warped and misshapen still, it appears all too right a way to view myself.

Throwing the door open, any lingering dampness along my skin clams up from the coolness permeating other rooms.

Vague plans hint at taking shape. Hopeton's block party is tonight. There may lie a chance to make another move. *Or it could end up being a bust.*

In preparation for any circumstance, an inconspicuous outfit would be smart. I prefer to blend in when I can. All black attire sometimes does the opposite.

Perusing through my drawers and closet, a navy-blue T-shirt and black jeans call to me.

Refreshed and clean, spending an idle moment at the table to solidify some of the steps swirling in my brain makes looking forward to the evening attainable.

I'll stop in at the party and check it out. Either it'll be packed with a ton of people, or there will be absolutely nobody there. When I know which for sure, I can possibly head to Lizzy's and attempt to keep my wits about me this time to see what she has going on. Maybe there's a normal way to check in on what she's doing. Unless she isn't home. Then I'm not quite sure what I'll do.

Stop thinking. I just need to wait and see what happens.

If something does end up going down tonight, Geoffrey will want in on it too. Eyes rolling of their own volition launch me into the next thought: *What if Lizzy ends up at the party?*

My fist slamming down onto the wooden tabletop sends a sharp pain tingling up my arm, relieving no stress. Now I get to worry over her presence so close. I don't want that son of a bitch to have reason to go anywhere near her. *He can stay out of this for now.* At least until I'm confident enough to where he won't fuck something up. *Inadvertently or purposefully.*

Speaking of *fucking something up,* I almost forget the remnants stashed away in a cabinet, waiting for disposal.

Chair legs screech in my rush to stand.

Fist relaxing only enough to retrieve the bag, it wrings the strap, clenching tight again having something to constrain.

Ready for action instead of endless questions and scenarios, I head toward my car. Many preoccupations pick me apart, taking off out of the lot. One problem at a time draws into focus. First: where to rid myself of this burden. Instinct points me south out of Alva.

Muscle memory knows this way. It's too easy to drive aimlessly. I force myself to focus and decide on a specific location. The closest I get is a suggestion of, *One of the local cemeteries.* Somewhere there shouldn't be any people and I can be alone.

Several litter the countryside to choose from. Landing on one at random, it doesn't take long navigating dusty, red roads to get me there.

The graveyard is empty when I arrive.

These back road burial lots don't come with designated parking. Instead, I pull over along the road and let myself out in the grass.

Half-melted snow coats most of the area while some patches remain dry and untouched. Careful steps navigate around the wetter areas to take me toward the far corner of the cemetery. Sparse cover of needled evergreen trees creates enough of a barricade to carry out my business in peace.

Dropping into a crouch completely removes me from sight of the road and the graveyard itself. I use my trowel to dig a shallow hole, upend the bag into the freshly vacated dirt, splash a little lighter fluid over everything, and set the tiny pile alight. Significantly smaller and less consuming than the blaze of last night, this fire hardly puts off any sound. Minimal smoke rises to draw attention.

When smoldering ashes are left, the hole fills in easily. Some leaves and needles spread through the area add a nice touch. Unless you're looking, nothing is out of the ordinary.

Remerging from the shadows does nothing to replenish the warmth I'd lost standing at the dwindling fire. Although the sun is shining, there is no comfort in its light.

Faded grave markers line the path. Farther out from these trees, they become easier to read. Names rattle in my head as I silently take them in.

Walking to my car, my pace slows, weighed down by my interest in headstones. *How easy it would be, for my name to adorn one of these rocks.*

All focus centered on mortality, my own recent close call, and other less prevalent issues means there is no attention spared to my surroundings. Rather, the other car now parked behind mine. Any dust long settled after its slow cruise down the same road that brought me here.

None of this catches my notice until a door closes. Echoes of the single sound fade into the silent countryside.

While I recompose myself, having nearly jumped out of my skin, the chastising begins at being so caught off guard. *Idiot.* It takes a moment to register who is approaching me. Because of course I know who it is.

There is no fucking way this is happening to me right now. Lizzy Dern enters the cemetery, walking slowly towards me. The place where her mom is buried. *Fool. How could I be so stupid as to pick this one?*

"Casey?" leaves her mouth. One hand rises to shield her eyes. "Is that you?"

Part of me is touched she remembers my name. *Try to keep cool, you imbecile.* "Hey, Lizzy, what are you doing here?"

Her footsteps falter at my informality. Oops, I forgot to say *Ms.* Lizzy. *Complete and total imbecile.*

"This is where my mom is buried." Suspicion enters her voice, only to be shaken as she inquires, "What brings you out this way?"

Scrambling, trying to disguise it as my usual flustered self, my brain finally spits something out. "This is one of the closest cemeteries to town." *Cause that's not a weird statement on its own.* "I wanted to come out and ground myself, you know, get a little more in touch with my mortality." My words begin to shake. She waits for me to proceed after catching my breath. "Plus, I needed to get out of Alva for a minute. Sometimes the place can be suffocating, you know?"

Her sigh eases the nerves ready to vibrate me right out of my skin. She picks it up from there. "I definitely understand. That's why I came out to see my mom's grave. I'm hoping to get a reality check. I've had a weird week. I know she just passed and hasn't been gone long." Tears force her to pause in order to move forward. "It's really weird living in her house without her there."

She's showing weakness in front of me. *A good sign. Don't start celebrating yet, you dunce.* Ignoring myself, I shove onward. "That has to be difficult. It must mean you're pretty strong for being able to endure."

A smile threatens to break out, despite her grief. *Oh, there's a gut punch straight to my heart.*

Wet eyes bounce back and forth between mine until something snaps inside her. The mask falls away. Shoulders slump and arms drop from where they gripped each other across her chest.

Now those limbs rise toward me, followed by a soft plea: "Would it be out of line for me to ask for a hug?"

Her words so quiet, their meaning contradicting everything I know, my mind convinces me I didn't hear them correctly.

Sniffles accompany her repeat request. "I know this is kind of forward, but right now, I really need another human, if that's okay?"

She's drowning in sorrow.

The freeze staying my movement, stilling all motion, slacks enough for me to nod. My arms open toward her in response.

Allowing her to take the lead, she closes the distance separating us, wrapping her arms around my middle. Mine drape over hers and tense.

Sniffles emit from her form as the squeeze to my gut tightens. Heavy breaths rasp into my chest. Shudders shake her shoulders, eventually lessening as the tension eases.

I maintain a tense grip to maybe help hold her together. It's all I can do apart from overthink the placement of our hands and bodies leaning into each other.

My cheek rests near the top of her head. An urge to deeply inhale becomes difficult to ignore. Floral scents do grace my nostrils unintentionally. I will claim this little reward for myself.

At last, she breathes a final sigh, pulling away her tear-stained face.

I let up as soon as she does.

Releasing me, she goes to swipe at a cheek while I gently take the other, brushing away the streak trail with my thumb.

A wet smile shines up at me. I don't know if she knows she's doing it or if she means to. Either way, that's another victory I will claim.

Dropping her gaze to the grass, she stumbles on. "Sorry. I've felt so cut off and alone. I don't really have anyone to turn to except people who'll tell me they knew my mom and are sorry for my loss. I swear, if another person tries to pass along condolences, I am going to take a toaster bath."

Even though the phrase is facetious, a darkness behind those tears and twitch inspires confidence she doesn't contain much hesitation in following through on such a declaration.

That is exactly the darkness I was hoping for.

The corners of my own mouth tick up. "Well, I'll keep my sympathy to myself." Worry of overstepping haunts me. "Do you want me to sit with you, or would you rather be alone? I can wait at my car if you want someone nearby?"

Unsure if I come across too eager, my hand slides into a front pocket for something else to focus on.

Teeth gnaw at the inside of her cheek, hindering an answer. "I think I'll be okay."

If this is where her statement stops, so will my heart.

She stares somewhere behind me. "I won't say no to you sticking around to wait though."

Whew.

Her face jerks back to me, flushed. "But you don't have to."

"I don't have anything planned," flies off my tongue too quickly. "I'll hang out if you need me." My head gestures toward our cars, not trusting the hand to be steady.

I flash her another smile, letting it drop to a smirk as I walk by.

Pushing my luck, I squeeze her arm during my sidestep. There is no recoil. She doesn't wrench away. *Man, today is a win overall.*

Propped up against my hood provides me a great vantage point to keep watch over her as she kneels beside one of the headstones. Who knows what she might be confiding or asking? Maybe some of it is about me. Fat chance.

Don't push your luck, Casey, I try to tell myself. *Not too much, too fast. Keep it cool, calm, collected.*

Yeah, right.

She maintains this position a few minutes before wiping at her face and standing.

As she turns this way, it strikes me I've stared at her the entire time. To remedy this, I busy myself glancing either way down the road. You never know when a car will blow by and coat everything in that fine, red mist.

The closer she gets, the more her gaze pierces me, requiring my best effort to resist meeting it until she is almost upon me. Only then do my eyes drift to hers.

A flush colors her cheeks. "Sorry again. I guess I needed some extra grounding myself. Thank you for being so nice."

How could I be anything but with you? is what I think to myself. "Of course, I'm glad I picked this cemetery to wander. You're not putting me out any."

Giggles rise from her face pointed toward the ground. Then, looking straight into my soul, she asks, "Were you going to try asking me out on the first day of class? If the other guy hadn't beaten you to it?"

Her not beating around the bush is contrary to the intense thumping currently happening in my chest. *A woman after my own heart.*

My eyes widen as a blush heats my own cheeks. Coughing into my hand does nothing to quell the reaction.

She sees.

"Maybe," chokes out of my constricted throat. "I didn't want to assume you were single. I also didn't want to miss shooting my shot if there was a chance." A hand nervously rubs at the back of my neck.

Her tone maintains its usual seriousness. "I really can't mix my work and personal life." Hands on her hips fidget from one placement to another as she ponders her own words.

In this pause, it comes to my attention I'm holding my breath as I wait for her to continue.

She eventually lands on, "How old are you?"

Like a proper idiot, I test my luck. "Old enough."

Her face reflects the joke is not appreciated. A frown begins to develop. Laugh lines smooth and disappear as the skin pulls taut.

The swift reaction causes my quick concession. "Kidding," I say as I throw my hands up in supplication. "I'm getting close to thirty. I'll be twenty-nine next month."

This response must please her because the lines reappear. As quickly as it formed, the frown disintegrates. "Okay, well, that isn't so bad. I'm recently thirty, so you're not far behind."

Silence descends while we search the other's face, waiting for one of us to make a move.

I make mine. "Well, I'd enjoy the chance to take you out if you'd be up for it. I definitely don't want to make you uncomfortable or get you in trouble, but I want to get to know you more."

Deeper pink floods her cheeks. She struggles to maintain eye contact, flicking between one of them to the other, then off behind my head. "Well, if you can agree my job comes first and it won't be weird…" Here, she truly lets her vision wander as her inside thoughts spill out. "I might still look into getting you transferred out of my class, if only to make myself feel better." Then her full gaze shifts to me. "Would that work for you?"

Even providing me the chance to converse with her, enjoy her presence, and on top of everything, to extend to me an opening to ask for more…

The fact she is negotiating, continuing to question herself and possibly let someone else take advantage of her good nature—I cannot allow this behavior. She deserves someone who will prop her up so she can stand on her own two feet unquestioningly. *I could be that.*

"Those sound like appropriate requests. Though it may destroy my willpower to make it the rest of the year not getting to listen to your voice discuss art." A smile, as big as I feel, elicits a giggle on her part.

Laughter aside, she raises an eyebrow at me. "I didn't think you paid any attention in class."

Her dangerous smirk sends a shudder down my legs.

Subduing an entirely different train of thought, I power through under faux innocence. "Oh, I am very attentive to your voice. The subject doesn't necessarily make an impact the way it should."

Shrugging at the jest incurs a playful slap for my trouble.

"That's not productive," is all she can muster in meek retaliation.

"Maybe this will be. Can I get your number?" An eyebrow of my own rises.

Pretending to think on it, she chews the inside of her mouth again. I can only assume the pause is to try to get a rise out of me. *It won't work—yet.*

Giving her as much time as she wants permits me to resituate against the car. Arms crossed once I'm comfortable, my attention returns to her, expectant.

Without breaking silence or eye contact, her hand appears between us. My phone ends up in it before any better judgment processes.

Her fingers close around the device I normally care nothing for. Right now, it is the most important item I own.

A glint makes me wonder if she'll actually add herself or do something to mess with me. *Do I really care which?*

Swipes and typing completed, she half smiles, handing it back over to me. One of my eyebrows is already up again.

"It's under Lizzy," is the confirmation to send my stomach aflutter.

Ooo, this woman is going to be the death of me. The eyebrow drops as a shaky hand deposits the phone in my pocket.

"Do you want me to wait to contact you so I don't come off as abrupt? Or…" I peter off, waiting for direction.

She leans in close to me. Unexpected proximity tenses every muscle. Any breathing I was in the middle of ceases, her eyes peering directly into mine.

"I'll save you the trouble. There's a block party in Hopeton tonight. Would you want to go with me?" Punctuating her question, she stands up straighter.

Her form retracting retrieves my stymied breath. Conflicting goals war inside me. On one hand, there were potential plans for the block party tonight; on the other, she is offering this up as a date, and I don't think I'll be able to refuse it.

Choosing deflection for now, my hope is to dissuade the notion of the block party altogether. "So you'll have someone to protect you from more condolences?"

Color drains from her face, chin hanging slightly askew. A swear sneaks in under her breath. *Naughty.*

She groans. "I forgot all about that. I've been hiding out in the house all week so they could rip the band-aid off all at once. Now, I don't think I'm up to facing so many potential sympathizers."

As the anxiety creeps further into her tone, dragging her voice higher, her hand movements increase. Finding different resting places on her hip, arm, cheek, and then finally, she deposits a finger into her mouth, chewing one of the nails.

Such a bad habit looks cute on her, makes it easier to see the wheels spinning in her head. Though, I can't stand the expression of consternation terrorizing her features.

It pains me until I offer a solution. "How about instead we go see a movie or something? There's a small theater in Alva we could check out?"

Red returns to her face as worry melts away at the prospect of having anything else to attend besides the block party. Breathy and shaky, she agrees, "A movie sounds nice."

This is when it hits me how unprepared I am. "Do you know what's even playing right now?" *Cause I sure as shit don't.*

She doesn't skip a beat. "I'll look it up and figure something out. Then I'll text you what time, and we can meet at the theater. So uh, you'll need to text me first."

Stomach still aflutter, my hand bridges the gap toward her. At first, she hesitates, then understanding, clasps it in a handshake.

Barely containing my giddiness, I somehow manage, "It's a date. See you tonight, m'lady."

She stumbles once while walking away.

I pretend not to notice. *Good to know I make her a little nervous, too.*

Her car is well out of sight by the time I'm able to move. A small victory dance may or may not take place on the side of the road.

Plans reforming for the evening, I pull up the newest number in my phone: "Lizzy Dern."

I grin like an idiot starting a text to her: **See you tonight.**

Headed back to my apartment, in greater spirits than when I left, thoughts surface of Geoffrey and the block party. Too elated to stand for anything else, the decision is simple to hold off on any further attempts on Hopeton tonight. It's easy to fire off another text to Geoffrey to let him know we won't be meeting up.

With him temporarily handled, I can focus on preparing for my date with Lizzy.

12: Lizzy

Dummy Dern, the chastising commences. *Why would you agree to this? Especially since you narrowly avoided him asking you out in the first place?*

My head smacks onto the wheel. In the safe solitude of my driveway, I wonder repeatedly, *What the hell is wrong with me?*

Vague attempts at justification clatter through my head. *It was a moment of lonely weakness. He really is a sweet-seeming guy. What's the harm if it doesn't go anywhere? I'm not a tenured professor, and this isn't a major credit for him.* Reasonable answers slowly begin to assuage the guilt and embarrassment pooling in my stomach.

If it were to go anywhere, the semester will be over in a few months anyway. We're both adults, not kids or teenagers. There can be maturity here.

Says the lady pressing her head farther into the stitching of her steering wheel.

Really, the most it'll do is potentially make the semester a little weirder than it already would be. *Or we might have a good time, and it'll work out for the best.* Who knows unless we try, right? *Right*, is what I'm going to tell myself, anyway. *Until I am presented a reason not to.*

Plus, this is the first time I've been excited regarding something new in I don't even remember how long.

A heavy grunting sigh releases the tiniest fraction of pressure as I drop back in my seat. *I'm acting depraved anyway. Might as well enjoy it.* Flashes of our hug transport me to the cemetery. Goosebumps rise along where his arms encircled me.

Casey's muscles, prominent under his jacket, cause a shiver reliving the memory of them. He doesn't look overtly muscular. *But oh, they are there. Damn it, Lizzy,* I say to myself, shaking out this audacity I've developed. *What am I doing with my life?*

It's fine. Everything's fine.

Shaky legs transport me from car to porch. Managing the stairs, remaining upright is a miracle.

The solidity of the door is perfect to hold me until these unreliable limbs give out immediately once it's shut.

In recomposing myself, it dawns on me I lack the little voice yelling at me to lock it. Then to double check and verify it's locked.

Inside my head is less cluttered, less heavy. It's nice. Maybe I've been cooped up by myself for too long, and it's good I'm going to try my hand at dating again. I am definitely too crotchety for how young I am.

Creaks from the stairs calm some of the jitters. A little shimmy shakes my shoulders at the reality of having a date. This starts another inner monologue tangent. *Jeez, I am lame. Hopefully it isn't obvious right away. Maybe he'll like it. I don't know. Either way, let's try and keep the weird to a minimum to start. Okay there, Lizzy?*

To conclude, don't scare the guy on the first damn date.

During my conversation, I catch a glimpse of myself in the full-length mirror. *This looks okay for a date, right?* Dangerous to ask such questions. *There lies a can of worms to be potentially opened.*

The dark grey crewneck sweatshirt hangs loosely over my blue jeans. *Eh, there's nothing special about it.* Slightly oversized, neither piece hugs me tight, just the way I prefer.

For a date, I guess I can throw something else on under it. Dual purpose—in case it gets hot inside the theater, then the sweatshirt can come off.

A brightly colored tank top in one of the drawers grabs my attention. *Best of both worlds.* The jeans stay. They're clean, and I hate doing extra laundry if I don't have to.

One less decision to make relieves more weight off my shoulders. *Now, to research movies and show times.* My bed groans in protest as I plop down onto it.

First listed is a scary movie fresh to the theater. *No thanks.* Second is a romantic comedy that's been out for a few weeks now that I've wanted to see. Then, there's a new superhero movie that might not be too crowded. *I'll let Casey decide between those two.*

Opening my messages, I go to reply to his text.

See you tonight.

There is absolutely no reason the words should give me chills. They do. *Damn, I gotta get out more.*

I type back, **Would you rather see an action hero movie or a romantic comedy? I am torn.**

Fortunately, I don't have to wait long. **So a definite no to the scary movie option? I think you could use some laughter and something upbeat, so let's hit the romantic comedy. We'll both enjoy it more.**

My heart flutters, sending high-pitched ringing to my ears. I can hardly hear myself think, messaging him, **Yeah, I'm not good at scary movies. They get in my head. Thank you. I could use laughs right now. Meet in the theater lobby at 6:30?**

Another notification vibrates as quickly as the first. **Understandable. Works for me. See you then.**

That's it. I am going on a date tonight. *Why am I so excited? I must really need this.*

To keep from rationalizing a way out of it, and so I'm not sitting there staring at the time, I busy myself cleaning random areas around the house.

It actually works better than I hope. Next thing I know, the old clock in the dining room chimes six o'clock.

Assuming either I myself or we together will get dinner after the movie, I tide the beginnings of hunger with a snack before heading out the door.

Several minutes of shivering, waiting once more for the car to warm, melds into anticipation on how the date might go. Shaking and overthinking riddles me the entire drive. Hopes of it all subsiding by the time I park are dashed as my breathing remains more ragged than it should and my hands throb.

Empty spots at the rear of the lot give me a target to focus on. Once I'm no longer mobile or a hazard to those near me, it becomes easier to manage my symptoms. *Don't be so in your head, Lizzy. Let yourself enjoy this. He's already embarrassed himself in front of you, so you know he's a goober too.*

During the process of calming down, my eyes bounce between the cars to see if I recognize any of them. *It's ridiculous I'm already this hooked.*

A few more beats pass where deep breaths are achievable and my hands shake significantly less.

Confident enough to stand under my own power, strength to open the door fills me. Amid agonizing steps, my phone appears in hand to provide distraction. I'm a little early. *Maybe I've got time to wrangle myself under control.*

Pulling on the front door at the same time a couple walks out, I pause to hold it open. This small moment is exactly how I reset.

An easy breath comes and goes as they smile at the gesture, providing time for me to spot Casey already lined up to buy tickets. *Sneaky guy was probably going to buy mine.*

More relaxed, walking comes easier. Playfulness infiltrates the lingering anxiety as silent steps bring me right up behind him.

He whirls, obviously prepared for me, because he's already got one of those smiles teasing his lips along with a sassy tone. "Nice try. You're early."

The cheeky fucker. I quip, crossing my arms, "So are you, and in line to buy tickets."

Of course, his response is something I am unprepared for. "Well, yeah. I buy first, and we see what happens next. Isn't that how it normally goes?"

Oof.

Any response I start to formulate falters. A long while has passed since I've dipped into the dating scene. I don't remember protocol and am none too embarrassed in admitting it.

"Honestly, I haven't gone on a date in some time, so I don't really know." My face contorts into a grimace for good measure.

His deep chuckle recaptures my attention. "It's okay. I've got us this time."

Warmth floods my cheeks. *This is fine.*

Quickly, our turn comes to buy tickets. Him acting as a gentleman, I won't interfere.

Instead, my gaze is drawn to the lights reflecting off the shiny floor. Striped bands of neon outline the walls and ceiling. Lights, bright in and of themselves, yet not so harsh as to repel prolonged staring, captivate me. The rest of the world blurs at the edges of my vision. *Pretty lights. Mesmerizing.* They remain the focal point to my existence as the din of everything else slips away. For a moment, even the ringing in my ears goes silent. Nothing else matters except for the neon glow entrancing every fiber of my being.

Casey calls to me through the fog. His voice isn't what drags me back, but the shock his touch elicits as one hand guides my shoulder, pulling me off to the side and out of the way of people in line.

Shaking myself, his voice is able to penetrate the white noise scrambling my brain. "You alright, Liz?"

Empty blinks are all I manage at first, slowly returning to myself. His face centers on mine, commanding attention. This is when I notice his hands gently gripping my arms.

Words are miraculously able to form in rapidly growing clarity. "Sorry, I must've zoned out. It happens sometimes. You just gotta reconnect me to reality." A giggle, manic to my ears, emits from the depths of my borderline hysteria.

He remains unfazed. Concern is the singular emotion showing on his face. Eyes bore into mine, as if to confirm I remain present and attuned for him to continue.

"Don't worry, I got you. I won't let you float away." A tighter squeeze reinforces his words.

Tears build behind my eyes.

His own go wide, searching the room for something. What would he be looking for? *An escape from me, probably.*

Whatever it is, he finds because the panic leaves his face. The next moment, we're flying across the room. Blinded by tears and self-loathing, I accept his guidance depositing us behind a pillar, out of sight and alone in a secluded corner. *Is this where he hightails it and runs before things get worse?*

To my surprise, no. The poor guy sticks it out. "Are you okay? Did I say something wrong? I didn't mean to upset you."

Shortening his stature, he gets eye level with me. Warm hands cup my cheeks and wipe away watery evidence the moment it accumulates.

My throat clears only to gasp, "Sorry—"

Do I know what I'm apologizing for? No other words make it. Sobs, barely holding in, overtake me.

Without hesitation, he wraps those arms around me, pulling me in for another hug.

Like dissociating at the neon lights, everything melts away except him. Just a guy letting me be vulnerable, helping to get through whatever current hell is punishing me. Not giving any implication of expectation or recompense.

My word, his muscles are exactly how I remember. It's as if he could squish the broken pieces of me back together and make me whole. *Jeez, I am on one today.*

At length, I realize the dread, grief, or whatever it was, has dissipated. All that's left are his arms, and a more familiar sensation. *Ah, I recognize this one. Shame.*

Removing my face off his now damp shirt, I begin the embarrassed apologies. "I am so sorry I keep doing this to you, and so much in one day. I need to get a grip."

His side of the embrace relaxes once mine does, arms falling to his sides as mine come up to wipe at my downturned face. Or so I thought.

Instead, a firm hand tilts my chin up. Sucking in the breath I nearly choke on almost drowns out his lowered voice. "Hey, you're fine. You don't need to get a grip right now. Experience your feelings. Don't keep them bottled up."

Ah yes. Breathe, please, Lizzy.

"If I can help by being here and rooting you, I am happy to. You tell me when you're ready to go in there." His nod towards the auditorium reminds me we are indeed, in public. He draws nose to nose for the last sentence. "But I do want you to speak more kindly about and go easy on yourself right now. Got it?"

Holy shit, is this a man or a dream?

He asked me a question. There is no hint of question to his tone.

His hand still gripping my chin, a fraction of a nod satisfies him enough to release me.

Breath flowing freely—*I can't believe how difficult a normal bodily function that is for me today*—allows me to shake myself off and confirm I am ready. *Ready to sit the fuck down.*

Less firm, he prods, "Are you sure?"

Another deep inhale confirms, giving me the chance to relay, "Yes, I'm good. Thank you."

My gaze holds his as proof. I guess he approves because his serious expression melts into a smirk. Offering me a hand, he leads us into the auditorium.

We take our seats minutes before previews start.

The dark atmosphere provides the perfect way for me to recover, existing blended into a backdrop. There is nothing casting attention on me, to pick me apart of any other shadowy forms occupying seats identical to mine. No reason to be perceived.

I laugh, he laughs. I cry, he squeezes my hand since he'd taken it into his again.

Breakdowns aside, I am more whole than I can remember being.

Something I've struggled to do better is opening up to others. Since Mom and I's relationship lapsed, lacking that, there weren't any other close friendships or family to replace the hole she left, even when she was alive. Unwilling to rely on anyone else for help, I've coasted on my own. It's been easy to stay closed off.

There are times the loneliness is welcome, preferred. Other times, I could scream at the top of my lungs if it meant someone would talk to me and let me escape it.

Almost never is there any middle ground. Either I want people to stay the hell away, or it is imperative someone notice and pull me off the brink of insanity. *Maybe I need therapy.*

Casey, in this short amount of time, has already provided more than I'd ever expected. Someone to simply exist alongside me. He sees me struggling, acknowledges it, and sits with me until everything passes.

It's called support, Lizzy.

Credits roll, and lights come up.

I don't think I'm quite ready to be alone yet. My heart thuds in the wake of parting ways already.

"Are you hungry?" he whispers while I think of a reason to stay together.

Hiding relief, I answer in similar fashion, "You read my mind."

All traces of sunlight are gone beneath the horizon, emphasizing the darkness waiting outside the theater. Streetlamps cast their glow. An orange luster, unequivocable of the same warmth.

"What are you in the mood for?" I ask beyond the lobby doors.

Our shoes grind in salt and sand mixture dusting the road. A chill immediately seeps beneath my sweatshirt. Crisp, night air sets my shoulders to tremble.

Uncaring how ridiculous I look, my steps quicken, practically running the length of the parking lot to my car. Victory is hardly mine as I pull a heavier coat clear of the backseat. Having sat inside the vehicle dictates the fabric is still cold.

Low snickers come from behind.

Whipping around, an eyebrow cocked at him, I hiss, "Is my shivering amusing?" between chattering teeth.

His smile stays spread wide. Smugness enters his tone. "No, just you suffering instead of letting me help."

My arms are crossed before I can stop them. Sass oozes out of every pore. "And how exactly would you have helped?"

He rolls his eyes.

Rude.

A couple steps separate us. Throwing his coat open and closing the gap, his arms pull me in, sealing around the both of us. Most of the chill closed out, warmth envelopes my upper body. *What an ass.*

"I didn't realize this was an option." The words disappear into his chest. Snaking my arms behind him, careful to keep them inside the coat, we stand there a moment. "Where did you park?"

My head tilts up to peer in his eyes. *Yeah, you keep smirking, shithead.*

Hardly remaining composed, "Right there," he says, gesturing with his chin since his arms are preoccupied.

Cold bites at my face peering over the edge of his jacket. There is his car, a few stalls away. *I had to be really out of it when I got here to miss that.*

"Ah, so what were you thinking for food?" I try again, shifting my legs to keep moving. Standing still is doing nothing to warm them.

No longer containing his laughter, it rumbles through his chest and my arms encircling him. "Somewhere close so I can get you inside before you shake us both out of our skins."

"Shut up," is my mature retort. "Chips and queso sound good. There are a couple of places to choose from if you have a preference."

While he thinks, my stomach decides right then to growl against his. Immediately drawing our gazes together, we descend in a fit of laughter.

Weaving words amongst his giggles, he leaves it up to me. "I don't care. You pick because I'm not the one who might be disappointed."

Being the decider stresses me out. In this moment though, I would rather pick than bicker, so I do. "Ugh, I haven't eaten at the one on the east end of town in a minute. Let's go there."

Without waiting for a confirmation, I extract myself from his embrace and jump in my car.

We make our way past the residential neighborhoods comprising most of town. Drool collects in my mouth when the sign comes into view.

First to park, I'm standing outside watching as he noses his car up to mine. Several semi-trucks litter the superstore's lot next door.

Shivers shake me as he approaches, joking, "I can't take you anywhere!"

It doesn't matter. I'm already making for the door, moving at a brisk walk, teeth clamped so they don't chatter.

Long strides easily overtake mine in his attempt to get to the door first. Our hands grab for it at the same time.

His tongue sticks out at me. I crinkle my brows. Neither of us let go.

Both of us pull on the door, pushing each other inside rather than holding it for the other.

My heart skips. I didn't anticipate how fun it would be to be openly weird with someone.

I give him one last playful shove. An unbothered hostess asks if it'll be two of us.

"Yes," we respond in unison.

Okay, this has to be too good to be true. The thought proves I've allowed my hopes for this date to soar far too high.

If my victory existed in getting the last shove, his replaces it poking me while we're escorted to a table. The hostess leaves us, probably thinking she sat a couple of quacks.

"You're impossible," I whisper to him across the table.

"Thanks. I try."

I use my menu to whack him as our server comes up and dives into her introduction.

Ordered and alone, Casey and I snack on chips and salsa as we work through the standard small talk. It turns out, he's going to college because everyone told him he should get some kind of degree. Sick of hearing it, he finally enrolled and has regrets.

"I think most people want the piece of paper proving they're more than a high school graduate. I don't require such validation."

His hands fold in front of him. A set look, eyes directly on me, gives the impression I hold every ounce of his attention.

Effortlessly, I tell him how I was doing in Oklahoma City. "I didn't know what to do after high school. I worked a couple of dead-end jobs to put food on the table, but I wasn't happy and didn't know how to change it. One day, I sat myself down and asked, 'What fulfills me? Something I wouldn't mind doing for work?' It started out listing hobbies, marking off ones I didn't want to do as a job. Then, I landed on writing. From there, I set out to seek any kind of writing work. I was getting closer to successfully doing it full time when Mom died."

Faltering on those final words, my gaze drops.

Casey's hand appears atop mine.

Always ready to criticize myself, I let slip, "Sorry I'm so blubbery today." His mouth opens, ready to respond, so I continue, "Not to disparage myself. I just wasn't expecting this emotional rollercoaster. A good relationship didn't exist between us."

Tense shoulders relax across the table, leaving a face still bothered. There aren't any prying questions; he merely sits and lets me unload the amount of information I am comfortable dealing.

Our food comes out, shifting conversation to where he lived before Alva. Then on to what we see for ourselves in the next couple years.

"I don't know what I want to do. I simply seek peace," he concludes, finishing off his dinner.

There is another meal's worth of food on my plate. Calling it quits, I muddle through a response. "Peace sounds nice. Now to figure out what will do it for you. I wish you luck, my friend."

Lifting my eyes quells the jovial smirk sliding into place.

Pain twists his mouth, dipping a brow.

I freeze, thinking over what I said to possibly upset him.

My panic spikes at his low response. "I want to be more than your friend."

The piercing gaze forces mine to drop faster than my jaw can fall in a race toward my plate. I'd be surprised if he didn't see the resounding blush.

Searching for my dignity, I sift through the possibilities of how to respond. Our server saves me the trouble by bringing out a check. Casey grabs it and hands her his card. She's gone too soon to process that I'm the loser in a race I wasn't prepared for.

Flattery forgotten, he receives the full force of my evil eyes. "Hey, I will not be bought and paid for. I can pay my own way, dammit." My arms cross, realizing I probably resemble a pouty teenager.

He rewards the action with another smirk, then flatters again, "I wanted to spend more time with you after the movie. You didn't plan on going to dinner, so I'm not making you pay for my selfishness."

His softening fumbles whatever curt response I was working on.

"Why are you being so nice to me?" is instead the big question on my mind.

It catches him off guard. "Because I really like you, Lizzy. I need you to understand this."

My mouth opens yet remains silent on thoughts not coherent enough for a response.

Since my flabbers are gasted, he proceeds, "Just let me be nice to you and show you a good time. If you want it to stop, say so and it will. Until then, I will treat you how I think you should be treated. Deal?"

His head falls to the side, eyes locked on mine, waiting for a reply.

All I can manage is a nod. I understand, but I don't understand. *Make sense? Yeah, I didn't think so.*

Apparently content with that as an answer, he asks the server for a box for my food while he finishes paying.

A hollow emptiness moves in on my stomach, leaving me numb sitting in this restaurant. I have no idea what to do with myself. The insane part of me wants to ask this man to move in right now so I am never required to spend another minute alone against myself. Then the logical part chimes in to ask, *What the hell is this guy's problem?*

Deciding to meet in the middle, I remain silent. Instead attempting to will appreciation to show in my face. For my eyes to reflect acknowledgement as his bore holes into them.

There's no way there isn't a catch. *And it's going to hit me like a ton of bricks when I find out what it is, isn't it?*

Well, for now, I force myself to stop questioning and let it happen. My internal struggle calms for the time being.

His grin returns. "Come on, let's get your car started so you can stay warm," he coos as a hand reaches for me once we're free of the table.

He opens the door for us to step out into the cold.

Shivers tease. I can't give in to them, or they'll hurt my stomach. This fact also forces me to walk to my car as a normal person instead of flailing across the lot.

Both vehicles started, I'm not quite ready to be done. I close my door and approach him resting against his car.

Accepting my form falling into him, he asks something I dared to hope he would. "Would it be very forward of me to ask the lady for a kiss?"

The question is accentuated by a slightly raised eyebrow this time, instead of him throwing it to the sky. It's nice, subtle, as if he's trying to be seductive. *Don't get distracted.*

"The lady is surprised you had to ask—" I barely finish before his lips are on mine, one hand reaching into my hair.

A long time has passed since I've kissed, and never like this.

He's forceful, yet gentle. His lips acting as if they know what they want and will take it, as long as I am willing. *And I am.* Leaning further into him after the initial shock, we stay locked for a few moments.

He draws back, releasing me from his spell. *Wow.*

"Wow, I was not ready," comes out far breathier than I intend. *Why are my eyes blinking so much?*

"Too much? I thought you wanted—"

This time, I cut him off as I reignite.

He tilts down toward me, keeping the hand tucked into my hair. The other arm ends up around my waist. Still, the moment ends too soon.

I break this time, smiling against his lips to reassure him, in case he doubts if it's what I wanted.

Breathy as me, he manages, "Well, I think we had a pretty good first date, if I do say so myself."

His head pulls away. Both hands remain where they are, hugging me tight to him.

Allowing a few breaths to refill my lungs, I find myself urgent for him to know how truly appreciative I am. "And you do say so yourself, though you're not wrong. This was pretty good. Thank you. Seriously. I needed this way more than I thought. Thank you for your gentlemanly behavior. It really helped."

Having retrieved his own breath, he takes me in. "Anytime, m'lady. As long as you give me the chance, I will do my best for you." Releasing my hair and waist, he kisses my hand. "Goodnight, Lizzy. Text me when you get home safe?" Another statement-sounding question.

He really is a gentleman.

Hopefully, the last blush of the night colors my face as I say, "I will. Goodnight, Casey."

Twirling, I break for my car. His stance doesn't change as I pull away, going my own way home.

A heavy sigh fills the quiet car in the best way. *Today was awesome. Maybe a little heavy thinking about my mom. Awesome besides that.* I'm as bad as a lovesick puppy, and I don't care.

I'm not going to look this gift horse in the mouth unless I have to.

Hopeton rises out of darkness. Scorched ruins on the edge of town linger after the fire.

Not many details have been released on the incident. The consensus, so far, points to a tragic accident. What a horrible time of year for it to happen.

There's never a good time for a house fire, Lizzy.

What if it wasn't an accident? *Maybe the couple started the fire together and didn't want anyone to think they could've stopped it?* You never know what someone is going through, what their mind is doing. Even if they act happy or appear to be in a good place, they could be right on the edge, and you'd never know. Then it's too late.

I always try to be kind. Silent battles rage inside every one of us. Sometimes our minds are our own worst enemy. A few harsh words could be the point of no return for someone, or a smile their saving grace.

A shiver, unrelated to any physical chill, rattles down my spine as I try to push the thought aside.

Ah, Mom's house. My house. I've got to stop calling everything hers and start calling it mine. This is how it is now, and I better get used to it. *Casey would be so proud.* Oh yeah, I'm supposed to text him I made it home safe.

Pulling out my phone, our conversation opens. **I made it home. Thank you, Casey. Goodnight.**

The front door locked behind me, my phone goes off. **Good. Thanks for giving me a chance. Goodnight, Lizzy.**

Butterflies war with the food weighing down my stomach.

My shoes fly off as I wonder what to do tomorrow. This weekend has already gone so unexpectedly.

I don't hear the stairs creak under me. Insanity offers up contemplation of inviting Casey over. *But for what?*

Waiting for the shower to get hot, my mind is made up. In the morning, I'll invite him here to watch movies. *Just movies. That's it.* Maybe some more kissing magic he worked on me, then that's it.

Steamy water beats back the chill penetrating my bones. Under its warmth, I hope for as good a day tomorrow as I've had today.

Then I hope it isn't too big an ask.

13: Geoffrey

Damn this kid.

Tightening my grip crinkles the can. Golden liquid rises to spill from my drink until another swig disappears.

My blood boils. *I can drink any damn time.* I was supposed to have a higher purpose, work in more of that stress relief before getting back on the road.

He tried to hold out on me last night. Then has the nerve to call off tonight. *What game is he playing?* Here all week long, doing whatever he wants, suddenly there's a problem when I get into town.

Casey better not be cutting me out.

The thought alone nearly sends me into a rage. *He's a smart kid, not telling me where he lives.*

Stir-crazy all afternoon since he cancelled, there are no longer any fucks left for me to give. I fire off my own message: **What's the deal? You do whatever you want all week just to pussy out when I'm in town?** I hate this texting bullshit. We can't say whatever we want. Any conversation has to be "vague and open to interpretation." *My ass. Vague enough?*

Last's night trance has already faded. Heightened senses, dulled. Additional strength temporarily lent, reclaimed. Confidence renewed in the shitty life dealt to me, drained. Highest of highs, followed by the lowest low.

Shaky hand tilting to get the last dribble, my body presses farther in to meld against the flattened couch. I've sat here most of the day, waiting until tonight so we can make our next move. It was nice to enjoy my time at home now that that mess is taken care of, but there's no fun in it if relaxing at home is all I'm going to be able to do.

As I prepare to haul myself up for a fresh beer, Casey responds, **Sorry to cancel because of the block party. Go without me if you want.**

What the fuck does he mean?

Opening a search tab, I type in "block party" and "Hopeton." Several unhelpful results pop up. Then, one link takes me to a social media post. Included is a bright photo, listing today's date under "Winter Block Party."

Now we're talking. Could be a chance to prove I can do this shit on my own.

My heart thumps faster. Final traces of evening light filter faintly through cracked blinds. *I can go now.*

Heaving off the couch, I hit the door wondering how I'm going to get there. The big rig is my first option. *Too conspicuous, and too far to walk.*

Out the front door, my neighbor's car is parked along his curb. Two facts coincide: he usually leaves his keys, and the bastard owes me a favor.

Crossing our empty street sends an elevated heart rate higher. Fingers curling around its cold handle, pounding beats shut out all other sound.

It opens. The door easily swings wide to show keys dangling in the ignition. *He's asking for it to be taken.*

A smile hides beneath my beard. This is the only sign of excitement I allow, taking a seat.

Behind the wheel, one town falls away to another faster than last night. Few cars reside in the church's lot.

Even less line the road. Nothing from its exterior screams *party* except several people entering as I pull in.

Decorative lights illuminate a brick façade. *A beacon drawing us in like moths to the house of the Lord*, or some other gibberish metaphor my wife would spout off comes to mind. Unwelcome, the notion disappears just as quickly in approaching the door.

My breath fogs during a pause to peer inside. Darkness fully descended provides an unobstructed view. A handful of people mingling are revealed at first glance. Scattered balloons litter the floor or are strung together to form decorative clumps.

This moment, I realize I didn't prepare a story or cover for anyone who might ask.

Brief plans spinning in my head envisioned a large enough crowd I could blend into. It relied on residents filling in the gaps. So far, this crowd resembles a work party nobody wanted to attend.

The urge takes over to pivot and run. Preclude any issues or *conversation*. Then, a voice taunts, reminding me why I'm here, *The rush, the hunt, the kill.*

I tug on the door, shoving down any doubt.

More people are interspersed inside than appeared. Still not adequate to easily blend in, most glance my way as I enter.

Swearing under my breath gains extra attention from a geezer next to me, who turns, mouth agape. *Oh, well.*

The small congregation is almost entirely made up of elderly folk. Maybe a handful are closer to middle age or younger, while kids of all ranges run rampant. Along the far wall, food covering a table wafts delicious aromas. To procrastinate inevitable small talk, I circumvent the group.

A loaded plate doubles to occupy my shaky hands. Positioned in a corner to keep my rear clear, no one pays me any mind after the initial staring. Most follow it up with a midwestern smile or nod.

Slowly, the space fills, becoming easier to fade into the background. Kids continue to run by. One teen catches my attention. Lanky, slumped shoulders and cropped, dark hair reminds me of a boy my son used to hang around. The lecture of times long gone transports me. *Your friends better learn to keep their mouths shut and heads down in my house.*

Sucking in a breath, I relax as my plate empties. Any lingering jitters are noticeably more manageable once my plate is dumped in the trash.

Eyes constantly rove to keep from staring, then train again on the teenager. He and his playmates file out the door after a younger adult scolds them for running amuck.

An opportunity.

Following the last kid, I emerge shortly behind.

Outside, shakes hit me again. My hands find pockets to stuff themselves into. Eyes adjusting to the dark scan for where they all disappeared to.

Light shines down on me alone.

No one yet visible, high-pitched voices carry from beyond the lit perimeter. Laughter stems from past the corner. Screams echo in the courtyard created by the building's horseshoe shape.

Mid-debate on whether I should approach or not, the familiar teen runs out from his own hiding spot for their game. In pursuing another kid, their chase comes to a screeching stop in front of me.

My silhouette swallows them. Casting such a deep shadow it's difficult to ascertain the expression on either face.

Any potential young adult attitude falters when he speaks. "Do you need something, sir?"

Being addressed as *sir* throws me off. I can't tell if it signifies this is the same kid I'm thinking he is or if he was taught to use *sir* and *ma'am* as manners.

To play it safe, I act dumb. "Do I know you from somewhere?"

His voice breaks. "I don't think so. We just moved here and haven't really met anybody. The town is nice. Quiet. Boring."

Ain't that the truth.

The other child runs off, having not been addressed.

Casey probably has a rule to not involve kids. It turns out, I don't.

As the boy relaxes at his explanation, I hit him again using my dad voice. "You look like one of my son's friends. He hasn't come home, and I'm starting to worry about him."

His feet shuffle in place before inching backwards once standing still becomes too much.

I follow, keeping close to continue, "My wife is really worried too. I didn't think he'd actually run away. It's been weeks since I've seen him. You'd tell me if you saw my son, right?"

Not paying attention to his steps, he stumbles over the lip to a garden bed. Falling on his ass, his head cracks against the brick wall. A grunt follows as he reaches up to check for blood.

Shaken, he squeaks, "Yes, sir, but I swear, I don't know your son."

I drop down on one knee in front of him. My hands placed to either side of the bricks around him create a cage.

Our faces are inches apart, forcing his gaze to mine. "What's your name?" The smirk spreads unintentionally while I await his answer.

He doesn't hesitate. "My sister is going to get our parents."

How cute. He thinks he's threatening me.

Despite the dark and his faux bravery, fear twinkles in his eyes.

Content in my control of the situation, I tease him a little more. "I can check you over. Make sure you didn't hurt yourself too bad."

Removing one hand so I can tilt his head down, the other remains in place as a buffer between him and the entrance. Quick inspection, despite his trembles, confirms blood trickling out of his hair.

Children carrying on with their play distracts me enough to almost miss his intake of breath. An exaggerated scream draws my attention for a second too long.

He pushes up from the raised bed, knocking me off kilter, and makes it several strides down the street in his panic.

His haste to put distance between us places me directly in the path he needs to reach the church entrance. Instead of weighing his chances, he proceeds south, toward the edge of town.

Recovering pretty quickly, if I do say so myself, my footsteps pound not far behind.

A single house lies on the west side of the road, our only blockade keeping us out of sight of the highway. No lights emanate from it, or any houses lining this side. We're in an alley of darkness, running farther from the lone streetlamp.

His pace frantic, he periodically yells for help. The effort wastes breath as continual shouts of other kids mingle with his.

My arms and legs pump in unison, closing the distance. Unsure where it originates, a push propels me forward. It catches me up to him right as he reaches the last tree keeping us shielded. Several cars speed past. For a split second, their headlights illuminate everything. The next, they are gone, driving on as if nothing were happening.

No consideration of consequence, I go for a tackle to bring him down. In the process, all my weight lands one side, and his foot collides with my mouth as we tumble.

Ragged breaths sound from both of us after hitting the asphalt.

Pain sears half my body. Blood pools on my tongue. I can't gather my bearings.

Scraping ourselves up further, squirming on the ground, he wriggles free.

Jumping up, full of an energy I no longer possess, he runs again. His path continues towards the far houses even though none of them show any signs of life.

Shoving myself off the ground, I weigh trying another attempt to take him down versus the odds of someone stumbling upon us. *The longer we're out here, the worse they get for me.* This kid isn't worth getting caught.

Lungs scream and fire ravages my left half from head to toe. *Tonight is a bust.*

Ducking between houses provides an alternate route to the church parking lot. Spikes shoot through every nerve ending at each step.

None of the kids sound hysteric or genuinely scared. They play on as they were.

Safely in the car, composure goes out the window. Heat floods my face as badly as the aches warming me. This drive home is longer, stewing in my massive failure.

A shout wrenches free. Directed into the steering wheel, it ceases only once my throat is rasping, unable to keep up.

My single consolation is the kid's head wound. There's a chance, whatever story he tells, will be chalked up to a concussion and wild imagination.

Parking along the curb where I found it, I am amazed at my ability to restrain further outbursts until I'm clear of the car.

Shakes take control in time for the couch to welcome me home. Beers appear, though no memory of retrieving them exists. Cracked and half gone, after the first, I make an effort to savor the next. To run through what happened tonight and see where it all went wrong.

My mind turns over every detail, again and again. *The entire shitshow happened so fast.*

Fuck it. Finishing off the drink in my hand, another follows. *I guess I'll enjoy oblivion tonight, after all.*

Resolved to lose myself in a stupor, an idea arises. *Maybe I'll stay home this week to get more practice. Casey can't make excuses all week, can he? What's another push of my luck?* It's not like he knows I went out tonight, anyway.

I'm taking this week off. We're going to do something since you left me high and dry. Words are typed and sent without further question.

A haphazard toss sends my phone across the room. *Tomorrow's problem now.*

Drinks appear, then disappear.

Pain recedes as darkness takes me.

14: Martin

I don't know how much longer I can stay here. *The walls are closing in.*

It would behoove me to stretch and get a change of scenery. *What if they find me?*

Plenty of time has passed. I should be able to move on from this hideout. *Has it really been long enough?*

Despite these contradictions, I remain sprawled on the floor. This hallway has provided my everything. Tucked away from windows and doors, it allows easy access to escape if I need it. Hopefully, I won't.

Limbs splayed loosely in corpse pose does not bring on relaxation as the yoga position implies. My muscles teem with energy begging to be dispelled. A mind racing past one potentiality to the next stokes the fire ready to burn me alive. One could say I'm beginning to get antsy.

No more deliveries of food or supplies have arrived since the turmoil caused by the initial drop. Stores are running low. *What if they forgot? Or decide to rat me out?*

Trains of thought such as these call into question, what was so bad being locked up? I got three hot meals and a cot every night to sleep in. There was never worry about making money, paying taxes, or acting as a productive member of society. All I had to do was exist. Everything else was handled on my behalf.

I mean, the other guys could get rowdy and took girlfriends sometimes. If you could avoid that, it wasn't too bad.

Of course, I'll never forget how I ended up there in the first place.

People are the worst, but you aren't supposed to do or say anything to change it. Turn the other cheek, be the bigger person, just walk away. There aren't any consequences for their instigating or goading. The "aggressor" is the one who simply retaliates once they've had enough. Nobody sees the buildup, how the other person starts it by acting aggressively first.

For me, it came to a head at the family holiday party. I, the sibling who didn't possess a steady relationship or as put-together a life, was a sitting duck. The easy target, teasing commenced. This wasn't out of the ordinary; picking on each other was practically our love language. Until it went too far. It usually did.

Well, the oldest had too much to drink. *Nothing new.*

What made that night different was he decided it'd be funny to start poking me in the chest. Taunting, "When are you going to find someone to love you? Huh? Stop showing up to family functions alone? Quit being weird?" Accompanying every other word was another prod thumping against me. Each tap put me closer to bursting.

It was always something with him. Talking shit about another's life choices, never a nice word to say unless a backhanded comment went alongside it, or pushing someone to the point they explode. Then having the gall to act like he did no wrong. He would get in your face to provoke, retreating only to prevent any retaliation. A big hen clucking and plucking, preening far beyond measure. Nobody could do anything right in his eyes. Nothing was ever good enough.

Yet I became the asshole when the last poke broke something inside me.

To the police, on the stand, over and over, I swore I blacked out.

I remember everything.

His final poke hitting me pulled a trigger. No hesitation hindered my actions, though I couldn't describe how it happened. The poking finger wound up in my hand. Bending it back to drive him away, his screams were exaggerated at first.

In trying to pull out of my grasp, he realized it wasn't a joke.

A *snap* clicked in my ears. Bones breaking under my duress took less effort than I anticipated. One moment I pictured it, the next, it happened. *Seemed perfectly fair.*

Silent seconds ticked between us before he tore his gaze from mine. Cries died in his throat as I released the limp digit. Words failing, sputters and half sounds garbled in their stead as he clutched the broken hand to himself. Not a peep breathed out of anyone else.

Adrenaline set my blood on fire. Electrified fingers tingled at my sides. Legs, made of mush, twitched and threatened to fail. Every sensation screamed for me to do something. *What else was there?*

Twisted features returned to mine. I don't know what stunned him more. He must've not approved of what he saw in my face because the next moment, he lunged.

Larger in build, his movements slower and lumbering, the man still formed a brick wall. Even his toasted state didn't diminish the hulking form he created. Ducking beneath his arms, reaching toward me proved difficult.

An answering fist I sent into his gut did satisfy on a level I wasn't expecting.

Unsure of its effectiveness, I didn't wait to drop and roll out of range.

His groan followed instead of retaliation. Arms failing to ensnare allowed me time to recover.

I couldn't believe I'd made it so far in a fight.

Rounding on him, I delivered a kick to his backside, sending him careening into the same counter he'd pinned me against. Cabinet doors caved in under his face, splintering under the weight. Pulling himself up, he spun on me as if to charge again.

For a moment, accepting the brunt of this assault to even the odds or backing down completely came into consideration. Then I asked myself, *Why?*

This man never let up on anyone else, never backed down if he pushed too far. He would only stop far beyond the point of no return and holding a list of excuses.

Why did I always end up stuck as the metaphorical bigger person?

So instead of taking one more hit, a sidestep requiring little effort sent his angry mass barreling down the stairs behind me.

It was his own fault for not seeing beyond his rage. He rolled a couple times, snapping his neck at the bottom. *Fucker finally got what he deserved.*

Apparently, it was considered a type of manslaughter. Everyone stayed silent or took his side over mine after his wife found his crumpled heap. She screamed to call the cops, repeating to anyone who would listen I tried to kill him. I did it on purpose.

He'd picked on all of us. Multiple family members saw him instigating, poking me in the chest. None of this mattered as the courts ruled in his favor.

One last middle finger to me.

It didn't matter I called it self-defense. The size difference separating us wasn't enough of a factor. Nobody else saw it that way. He was the victim and I the aggressor because he was drunk and I should've known better.

I was sent away. I waited dutifully for my parole hearings, and they sent me right back. Acting like a model prisoner didn't help, nor did my recommendations for the shortest stint.

Then I wondered, *What's the point in being a good prisoner if it doesn't get me anywhere?* I had kept myself out of the internal affairs of other prisoners, and it'd made me an outcast. Well, it wasn't worth it anymore.

Abstaining the first few years, eventually I joined in. I started choosing sides. I let the dark whisperings take the reins, same as during that fight. Giving in felt better and better each time.

Someone told me to stab. I asked, "Who?" and "When?" Someone tried to stab me; I stabbed them instead.

It became a game, one I was great at. Until paranoia crept into every waking and nightmarish moment. Each interaction or silent moment alone might transform into my due next.

Hysteria rose, instilling a fear I wouldn't be fast or smart enough to make it out of the next skirmish. I tried to withhold myself again, but by then it was no use. I'd put myself square in the middle, right in the line of fire. I'd become a target. The darkness wasn't a safe haven anymore, wrapping me in its warm embrace. A protective cocoon.

I could see the dark for what it was: a trap.

One day I received a note, similar to the one I got here, telling me someone on the outside required my help. The note said whenever I get out, to stay close. I assumed whoever sent it was as crazy as the rest of us. I didn't really give it any actual weight.

Damn, if they didn't make it happen. Less than a month later, I was running for my life, away from that hellhole. No one, not even myself, thought to stop me.

The escape happened so fast, I didn't pause to think if I wanted it or not. These days, weeks, *whatever it is now*, with nothing else to focus on, darkness has begun whispering again.

Why not enjoy it while I'm out?

They're going to hunt for me whether I do anything or not. Might as well make this freedom worth it since I've got it.

Slipping into evasive sleep is easier having reached this decision. I can't believe it took me so long to remember who I am, why I'm here.

Let's have some fun.

15: Casey

Worry over Geoffrey waits until after Lizzy and I's date. His text before we met at the theater annoyed me to no end. The hint steering him to the block party was supposed to keep him off my back.

Honestly, I shouldn't be surprised. *He is not going to ruin this.*

Settled in at my apartment, Lizzy and I's kiss left me experiencing the same euphoria I've gotten from killing.

I am thoroughly rocked to my core she agreed to go out in the first place. Dinner was another victory in stealing more time together. Then, to top it off, not only did I get to kiss her, but she also kissed me in return.

My body melts into the mattress, attempting to relive every second of our date. Replaying each moment becomes a lullaby to drift asleep to.

Scenes that successfully soothe lead up to one palm making contact with my forehead. A physical punishment for tainting mental pictures of Lizzy in this disappointment when all I want is to revel in post-date wonder.

Unfortunately, the fact requires acknowledging: Geoffrey has nearly worn his usefulness thin.

In relation to disappointment and killing, Martin plants himself in the front of my mind. An unwelcome reminder I haven't gotten him more supplies or figured out where to put him.

Dragging the hand down my face in hopes of rearranging the thoughts behind it does help.

Mental note made, to productively take action towards both problems tomorrow, makes it easier to direct my attention where I'd rather focus.

Her name, rolling off the tongue, brings peace. Yet, at the same time, speaking it stokes a fire I didn't realize was burning. That smile, especially aimed my way, is a balm on the cracks riddling my soul. Those eyes, reflecting a void as deep as the one in me, cause shivers. She is a magnificent conundrum on my faculties.

It pains me to assume her heart bears similar marks to mine. For who or whatever made them, I want to burn their reason for existence. The way she treats herself had to be learned, taught. My mission now is to undo it.

Whispers persist as loudly as ever, though under her gaze, they're different.

Killing is done in the shadows. Few others are privy to such an intimate act, fewer still to discuss or share in achieving success. This, whatever this is, I don't need to hide. I could scream about Lizzy to the world if I wanted to.

Simply existing in her presence elicits the same rush. Potential power electrifies every sense. *Why couldn't I find her sooner?* Maybe what's building between us might've been enough to keep me from setting these plans in motion.

Intrusive ideations most likely would've ensued no matter what, but perhaps been easier to ignore. I could have been in a better place to turn them down or channel such energy more effectively. I'll never know.

What I do know is I yearn for so much more of the way Lizzy looked at me tonight. I watched the internal abyss retreat after rearing its head. Light grew within her, replacing it. Her gaze fell on me as if I were a hero, the singular link keeping her fixed to this mortal plane. How easily I made her blush. How magnificently she could do the same to me.

The entire time spent in her company was exhilarating. Far better than the hollow fear in the eyes of victims. A similar darkness mirroring my own.

Her text to tell me she'd made it home brought it all rushing back. Flashes of our date refueling my purpose, fulfillment.

Selfish whimsy instilled hope she would ask me to accompany her home. For nothing more than to remain close. To place trust in something to cling to, someone to hold. *What must it be like to have someone hold onto me?*

Am I lonely? Is that what all of this is?

Don't go down the rabbit hole. Don't start questioning what may or may not be true. Hang onto tonight. Geoffrey, Martin, and any other problems or consequences can be handled tomorrow.

Tonight, I am going to enjoy being wanted, craved.

Everything else will be tomorrow's problem.

Sleep comes on these sweet notions.

Is this love? I hope so.

16: Lizzy

Darkness encircles me.

Whispers echo, unclear and faint through the void. Incoherent snippets taunt beyond my reach, capturing attention only to dissipate into resounding nothing. The sensation of my head swiveling ignites hope there is anything to be seen. Alas, all that awaits is more emptiness. No presence lingers in this hollow abyss consuming me.

Then it hits me. *Ah, I must be dreaming.*

Continuous spinning brings on an internal dizziness. Somehow, not rousing consciousness. Voices carry on their intermittent reverberations. No source or end to them is disorienting.

A vague notion allows acknowledgment of an attempt to pinch myself. To no avail. Racing heartbeats match the pace of my breathing, unable to wake.

Panic rises, drawing darkness closer. Insubstantial arms reach out from shapeless nothing towards me, grabbing at whatever they can in response to my agitation. I make to move outside their reach. This action puts me closer to the dark presence lurking behind me.

In search of any semblance of sanity, a deep breath forces the expansion of my lungs. A real deep breath, it immediately grounds me. Weight tugs where previously I was floating.

The pull draws my attention down. Light pools under my feet. Shifting them releases more, its source emanating within me rather than beneath where I stand.

This is a weird dream.

More of a concrete connection to consciousness lets me cling to its frayed edges.

Conscripting my eyes to close, whether they are already or not, is followed by another intentional breath.

Breathe in. Think about something happy. What am I happy about?

Breathe out. Experiencing my childhood home as an adult is nice. Don't delve further.

Breathe in. Objectively, I am doing okay in life.

Breathe out. The date last night was very nice.

Breathe in. On this breath, light creeps under my lids.

Dream eyes open to shiny brilliance glowing brighter. Golden rays illuminate and beat back the darkness. One arm extends so I can admire its shimmer. Fingers bend and curl, dazzling in their trance of opalescent fragments.

Breathe out. At this, the entire vision fades.

My eyelids flutter dramatically as I wake with a start, gasping for breath. *So much for the intentional breathing.*

Sunlight barely begins to outline my room. Thin curtains filter what little there is. Shallow shadows turn everything into an optical illusion. The blanket covering my feet melds into the end of the bed, blending into the wall and dresser seated somewhere along it. Any depth separating the individual surfaces is hardly visible this side of the morning where night fights to remain covering all that it can.

Too early to be awake, there's no way I'm getting anymore sleep at this point. A groan accompanies the upheaval to get myself to a sitting position. Half out of the covers, sweat glues my sleep clothes to any skin they touch at the same time chills infiltrate exposed limbs until enveloped again.

Light reflects a faint, dusty halo around the window identical to the one I used to sneak out of when I was younger. I'd sit on the roof and contemplate life, staring at the fields surrounding our house. Straight across the highway, I could watch the sun set on whatever season of crop there was.

A variety of light and dark green would span the miles to fade as it grew into golden waves, each contrasting against bright blue skies right up to when everything was brought in. Stubble left over from a fresh cut created a barren wasteland. Prior to the next planting, flat nothing expanded into the distance after those remnants were gone. The emptiness provided plenty of opportunity for dirt devils to spin up and sputter out several yards away in the gusts following harvest.

Those shingles were an escape from all the shouting and arguing. What started as fights between my parents, eventually—once they quit fighting each other—shifted into arguments against me. When I grew old enough to tire of those, stony silence resounded throughout the house. Unable to twist words I didn't speak, my decision was reciprocated. Implicit feuds to follow became too suffocating to withstand.

Our roof was always there to welcome me and provide peace. True quiet, no judgment or trap questions. All it did was exist. Everything I needed.

Mom would tell me, "Quit disturbing the shingles," and, "You'll break your neck." Not that it stopped me. I got better at sneaking.

There's no one here to stop me this time.

Bringing the blanket, I move the curtain aside and pull up on the old trim. At first, it sticks. After a good shove and screeches of protest, the window opens to the cold morning.

My covers stave off most of the bite. Taking care to avoid dragging on any rampant nails or splinters, I climb out.

Tentative steps make for a long journey to the roof's highpoint. This puts me closest to the sky, where I can see the highway to the west and wide-open fields stretching on toward the eastern horizon. Bare feet grip the gritty tiles, providing ease of movement at my slow pace.

Chills set me to shaking in the time it takes to get situated and rewrapped in my cocoon. Sunlight creeps higher as pink and orange gradients rise to replace the navy hue clinging to the sky. Similar shadows dot an expanse of overdue cotton reaching out of sight. White buds sprawl across this side of town, giving the impression of snow.

Hypnotized by the morning's beauty, a sizable gap separates sun and horizon when my blanket no longer keeps out the cold. Shudders pry me from thoughts disintegrating out of grasp as soon as the spell concludes.

A comforting idea does resurface to invite Casey over.

An exaggerated shrug fades into a genuine smile teasing at my lips.

Preparing to go inside and warm up, movement out of the corner of my eye stops me. My initial instinct is to disregard whatever it is as most likely an animal.

Another flash piques my curiosity, getting the better of me. I snap my head in time to catch a silhouette darting between neighboring houses down the road. Two-legged and upright, it's definitely not an animal.

Frazzled tendrils of my dream reignite paranoia. *Freaking out will get me nowhere,* is my effort to calm myself.

Whoever it is keeps to the shadows, scurrying from a row of bushes to a backyard window. An ineffective push up on the opening tells us both it's either stuck or locked.

Could easily be someone sneaking in after a late Saturday night out. This excuse doesn't slow my heartbeat trying to pound out of my chest.

Any doubt or justification is negated the moment the figure breaks glass.

My gasp escapes prior to a hand covering the orifice.

The form looks around.

A sitting duck in my current position, dropping behind the roof peak nearly sends me sliding down the sloped gable. By the time I stabilize and peek out again, they've already disappeared into the gaping window.

Roof-turned-obstacle-course stands between me and calling for help.

Luckily, the one fall I sustain lands me inside my room. Slamming onto the floor, my blanket does nothing to soften the impact.

911 is dialed, and a dispatcher is addressing me when my feet hit shingles once more.

"911, what is your emergency?"

Breathless, carefully retracing my steps across the slanting surfaces, everything comes out in a rush. "From my roof, I saw someone break into my neighbor's house. I don't know if anyone's home or if they might get hurt. I don't know what else to do."

"It's okay, hon. Tell me the address and we can send help your way."

Though my words answer, I am no longer aware of them as they leave my mouth.

The soothing operator's voice asks, "Can you stay on the line with me?"

Don't think that'll be a problem. She also advises to not engage or get involved. *There isn't anything I could do, except get in the way.*

Resuming my position is chillier this time, blanket discarded in my mad dash.

No movement or change in the house to indicate if anyone is home or in danger starts me down a spiral. *Damn it. I should have gotten to know my neighbors better. I'd know if anyone were home now or who to call if there was a problem. It's too late to be thinking about that.*

Hopefully, most people are gone for their early Sunday service or breakfast already. Burglary is nothing compared to some of the other options.

It's agonizing to sit and watch, waiting for something to happen.

On the edge of my awareness, a panic attack builds, threatening to strike as soon as I'm no longer operating on adrenaline.

A vibration shakes my phone, nearly causing me to lose the device to gravity. No notifications are going to distract or break my concentrated scanning for a sign, any indication of what's going on. Not knowing if someone's in there, hurt or otherwise, very nearly drives me off this roof, even if only wielding a baseball bat, to find out.

Sirens blare faintly in the distance.

I breathe a touch easier.

My hint of calm lasts for hardly a moment. Then the figure re-emerges. Nothing has changed in regard to their appearance, no burgled items in sight to weigh them down. Tears brim at what this presumably means.

I pass along the update to the 911 operator, voice ringing hollow to my own ears. She makes no comment from her end other than to inquire which direction they go.

Hands placed on their hips, the figure arches their spine, shoulders pulling up and back into a stretch. Taking in their surroundings, they stiffen as sirens grow exponentially closer and louder.

Teeth chattering reverberates inside my skull while I remain hunkered close to the shingles, waiting to see what they do.

Their features are indistinguishable at this distance. All I can see is their general outline. What is obvious, regardless of distance, is their gaze stops on my house. *There's no way they can see me.*

My heart falls out of my ass when the person raises a finger to point directly at me. *Fuck.*

Gasping, despite my mouth hanging open, broken sentences tumble out to the operator.

She says not to worry. *I wish her words could soothe the gaping hole gnawing away at my stomach.*

An eternity passes, their accusing finger shaming me before they lower it and take off running to the north. They disappear into the next yard, where I lose all visual.

Choked breaths escape past the frog taking up residence in my throat. One hand covers my gaping mouth in a feeble endeavor to contain whatever reaction is rearing to overwhelm me.

Opting to stay put until police cars flood the street wins out as the better choice, rather than climbing down too soon and risking a fall in this state. It allows just enough time for the panic to subside to a more manageable level. Several cruisers take over my driveway. The rest tear through town.

Robotic movements inch me off the roof to meet them.

A female officer graces my doorway. Gently prodding to talk inside, she accepts standing on the porch so I can watch the other officers.

She asks for me to repeat everything I told their dispatch. Heavily used, a pocket notebook appears in her hand. Produced out of thin air, her pen perches at the ready, waiting to scribble onto the next blank page.

Confusion must show beneath my hollow expression, prompting her to explain how they want to ensure their details match.

Reiterating information I already gave doesn't feel like helping.

Once her pen stops writing, the officer asks, "Is there someone you can stay with?"

I disregard her question in place of my own. "You haven't found them yet, have you?"

She shakes her head. "No. But, they shouldn't get far." Her face is apologetic, not placating. It's sincere.

"Thank you," dies on the tip of my tongue as another question demands attention. "Do you know if anyone was in the house and if they're okay?"

I have no idea if she can tell me or not. Selfish pride desires to know if someone got hurt because of my cowardice.

"I'm sorry, I can't comment on the ongoing investigation." Her mouth and eyes flatten, answering anyway.

A nod in return is all I can handle, and only that due to my neck turning to rubber. Long numb, now it hits me my legs are close to giving out.

I don't remember saying anything else to her or closing the door. My next flash of consciousness places me on the recliner. Not even in it—perched on the edge. As if falling into the fabric will catapult me beyond the other precipice I'm teetering on.

Blood flow reheating frozen limbs ignites an unbearable itching. At this, my body surrenders to the chair. This discomfort is all the push I needed. Tears fall as the wave of emotion rocks me. Silent sobs make up its majority. My mind blanks to all thoughts and questions. All of existence is this hell I'm currently living.

Another vibration of my phone dredges me out of the panic. Unfortunately, what follows is rage, and I'm deposited straight into the thick of it.

Yanking the device in front of my face to see who dares to bother me during such a shitty time, an older message shows from Casey: **Can I see you today?**

Flames spurred to life so quickly are as swift to perish into embers. Low heat smolders under my skin, embodied as another emotion entirely.

There isn't time to find a deeper meaning in his text.

The new notification is a 911 alert to be on the lookout for a murder suspect reported on the loose this morning in Woods County.

Murder.

Someone did die because of my inaction.

Tearful anxiety renews with a vengeance. *I don't think I've scratched the surface of my impending breakdown.*

Casey's contact information opens in a couple screen taps. *If it's late enough for a text, it's late enough for a call.*

Barely two rings in, and he's answering. "Hopefully that's a yes?" sings from the other end.

His faux ego would be more appealing in a better state of mind. Right now, at the sound of his voice, I experience a factory reset.

It takes entirely too long for me to choke out, "Casey—"

Immediately shifting to concern, his lightheartedness disappears. "What's wrong? Are you okay?"

I swallow panic bubbling up my throat. "Did you see the warning about a murderer just now?"

He doesn't hesitate. "Yeah, I saw it."

Thick silence follows while I search for some composure.

"Why?" he quietly prods.

I get the impression he wants me to proceed at my own pace, but the suspense is killing him.

Hysteria cracks my voice as everything spills out in one rambling wave. "Well, I saw someone break into my neighbor's house, so I called it in. Whoever they were saw me. They pointed directly at me and then ran off. Now, I don't want to be alone and I'm probably going to have a breakdown because I let my neighbor get murdered and I was too chicken shit to help."

Composure? Never heard of 'er.

Whatever his calm response is doesn't register right away.

"I'm sorry, what'd you say?" I ask, sitting up so I can hear better. This position also allows me to rock in place. My recliner elicits itching anywhere it touches my skin.

"I'll be right there. Are you okay?" he repeats.

Another fabulous rubber-neck nod is all I can manage.

Clearly, an answer not good enough for him. "Lizzy, I need you to breathe. Please breathe and tell me if you're okay. Can you do that?"

Commanding without demanding. *That's a nice feature.*

An unhelpful nod again accompanies a squeaky, "Yep, yep, yep."

I mistakenly believe my stomach couldn't sink any lower into itself, then it threatens to reject all contents at the idea of hanging up to be alone in my thoughts.

Reading my mind, he saves my gag reflex. "Do you want to stay on the phone while I drive?"

Didn't know that was an option.

Words are not my specialty at the moment. "Yep."

Jeez, Lizzy. Try to keep it together, please?

"You got it. I can babble, or we can listen to the radio together."

Whirring in the background drowns out whatever song is playing. He's already driving. *Thank goodness. This man is going to singlehandedly salvage my sanity.*

Relief in knowing he's on his way, normal speech flows more readily. "Radio is okay. Knowing you're there helps." A deep breath barely holds in another flow of tears. "Thank you," escapes as a whisper.

"Anything for my girl."

He says it so matter of fact. As if there is no discussion; it simply is.

Normally, I would rebuke, seeing as I am not a possession. *Except belonging sounds pretty good right now.*

The road noise lulls me into pacing the living room. Rhythmic steps aren't enough to refrain from biting my nails. They're at the mercy of however long it takes him to get here.

Several laps in, ragged edges are gnawed too deeply into the nail bed when engine rumbles match between the phone and outside.

I hang up mid-step and abandon the rut forming in the floor. Speed limits had to definitely be ignored for him to arrive so quickly. *I'm not complaining.*

Outside, balance is tricky to maintain since it apparently fucked right off. Stumbling across the porch and down the steps, Casey hardly clears his door before I launch myself into his arms.

They wrap around me immediately. We stand locked in an embrace, my feet scarcely touching the ground as he lifts me into him.

Too soon, his hold slackens.

Or so I thought.

My legs buckle, and the next thing I know is I'm in his arms, crushed to his chest, being carried inside.

Not permitting myself to enjoy the gesture, I sputter, "I can walk fine."

Again, using his stern voice, he says, "I know. But standing there, it seemed like you were going to collapse. It's okay, I've got you."

Following it up by hugging me tighter against him, his hold isn't forfeited until he relinquishes me to the recliner.

He's strong.

Giggles surface, thinking about his muscles. It takes every ounce of self-control available to keep them suppressed.

My butt safely in the chair, he kneels next to me. Eyes, level to mine, captivate. I almost miss him asking, "Are you okay?"

A simple question to renew the flood. Brief surges of giddiness at his presence fall to the wayside.

How does one answer when one is being ripped apart inside? Asking for a friend.

Apparently, I possess neither the capacity to see or to think. Both, especially cannot be done simultaneously. Coherency escapes me as my vision blurs.

In hopes of boosting thinking capabilities, my eyes close.

While grasping for something, anything to respond with besides *um*, Casey's hand appears at my neck. His palm cups my chin, thumb rubbing my cheek. Warmth guides me to a place where words are possible.

"I feel like an idiot."

The hand stiffens.

My lids pry open to see his face tighten in an urge to challenge. He remains composed to let me ramble, "I watched someone break into a house. I don't know who lives there or if anyone was home. I didn't want to get in the way, so I figured if I called the police and stayed on the roof to pass along information, it would be enough. I feel as if this whole thing is my fault."

Guilt forces my eyes closed again as I finish, unwilling to meet his gaze any longer. My head starts to pull away so I can lean into the chair. His grip holds me in place.

Expecting to be chastised, I am pleasantly surprised at his response. "What were you doing on the roof?"

That's the takeaway?

I let an exasperated chuckle slip. "It used to be my happy place as a kid and teen. I hoped watching the sunrise would clear my head after a nightmare. It almost worked."

His face is an anomaly. Same as last night, there is no judgment or scrutiny. Only eyes searching mine.

Then I open my mouth. "Sorry if I ruined your weekend."

I must enjoy getting a rise out of him. The stare, so open and content a moment ago, darkens. Laughter bubbles in my throat.

Dropping a couple octaves, he grates, "How dare you assume spending time in your presence wouldn't be the highlight of my weekend." Pausing to inhale through his nose before proceeding. "I, quite literally, asked if I could see you today."

Any willpower left fails as I let the laugh loose. "You're bad for my ego. I kinda like when you say nice things to me. Even if they are hard to accept."

He smiles in agreement. "You're not doing any wonders for mine. The way you look at me, it drives me crazy. Good crazy. I might be dangerous if I think so highly of myself."

Suddenly craving more of the comfort from last night, I lean in closer for a kiss.

He doesn't engage right away, as if giving me the chance to change my mind. When I don't pull back, he closes the distance.

Forceful, yet gentle.

It's freaking perfect. Almost enough to make me forget why he's here so early on a Sunday. *Almost.*

Pulling back, I slap a hand to my forehead and drag it down my face. "I'm sorry. I—"

He cuts me off, initiating another kiss. His hand ascends into my hair. We stay locked for a moment, until both of us let go.

"Don't. You. Dare. Apologize." A tug at my hair reinforces the message.

Received.

Untangling myself, he doesn't fight me this time. I fall against the plush in defeat. "I don't know what to do. It doesn't feel safe to stay here, but I can't let some weirdo, who may or may not come back, run me out of my own house, right?"

Looking to him for answers does nothing. His face is passive. *Concerned, but still passive.*

"I'm not going to tell you what to do," is what his mouth says, face falling as if it pains him. "If you want, you could come stay at my place. Or I could stay here with you, if it wouldn't be an intrusion."

Not telling me what to do is a nice feature. Focus.

Coherency again escapes me. Trying to think under his stare isn't working. Opting to pace instead, he trades places with me, taking a seat in the chair.

Bare feet smacking at each step on the cold floor accompanies my fractured thinking.

If it isn't safe to be here, this should be a no-brainer. *Why would I stay?* What about everyone else in town? Are they all going to up and leave? *Probably not.* Whoever it was might be long gone. They did murder someone. *Don't tear up. We're talking facts right now.* I can't live my life in fear, expecting the worst. *It isn't living.*

Knocking at the door derails me. My head whips toward the sound. Lips clamping together silence a shriek ready to tear free.

Casey is already up and bypassing me to answer it.

At least he stops to look out first.

It opens to a familiar voice. "Is Ms. Dern here?" The officer uses a professional tone when addressing him. She tries to inspect behind him in search for me.

"Here I am, Officer," I squeak out, brushing past Casey. "My…boyfriend came so I wouldn't be alone." Plastering on my best reassuring smile, I hope it covers up hesitating at the word *boyfriend.*

Casey's shit-eating grin is big enough to catch in my peripheral. *I don't regret it—yet.*

Her demeanor warms for me. "Good. I wanted to make sure you're doing okay and let you know that an officer will be stationed outside later tonight as a precaution."

Ignoring the smiley dope at my side proves difficult. Somehow, I manage without breaking, "Thank you for everything, Officer."

She nods and wishes us a good day.

Inside the living room is dark compared to outside's bright, sunshiny day. Shut out once the door is closed, this dimming does nothing to quell the brilliantly cheeky grin spread on Casey's face. *Okay, now I'm having regrets.*

Not an ounce of humility exists in him. "You called me your boyfriend."

Here we go. "Yeah, it sounded better than calling you my *friend.* Plus, I thought you'd appreciate it." Pause to direct a pointed glare his way. "Apparently, I was right. Hopefully it wasn't out of line?"

His smile infiltrates every other feature on his face. I dare say that his eyes even twinkle. "Are you kidding? I wanted you to call me your boyfriend the first time I saw you."

Too real, too fast. My cheeks are on fire. Redirecting... "We should go to your place so you can pack a bag." I make sure to use *we* because I am not ready to be left alone here.

That damn eyebrow of his shoots up again. "You do want to stay?"

Oh, I guess I never acknowledged anything out loud. "Yeah. I'm not going to be scared out of my home over *what ifs.* Whoever it was may never come back. If they do, I've got you and an officer outside." The words flow confidently, more than I actually believe.

No arguments or questioning ensues. "Okay. There are a few things I have to tie up. Are you able to keep busy in Alva while I handle some errands?"

One eyebrow is still up. *I'm starting to think it's his default face.*

"I could meander around the grocery store. Pick up a couple more things." *I'm definitely okay getting out of the house.* Not waiting for another word, I'm spinning away to go get ready.

Changing clothes is too much effort. Instead, I throw an oversize hoodie on top of my pajamas. Pairing together whatever shoes I can pull on, this mismatched outfit perfectly reflects my current mental state.

At his car, he opens the passenger door for me. *How the hell could I be surprised at this point?*

Reversing out of the driveway, he places a hand on the back of my seat to lean in close so he can *see behind us.* There is no one and nothing. This is the last house on a practically dead-end road. He's doing it to be closer to me. *Damn him. It's working.*

On the highway, every mile passing eases a little of the ache building in my gut. *Gah, I hope it doesn't return on the ride home. Then I'd probably cave and go to Casey's. I'm not saying it's a bad option. I'd just rather be in my own space. Or at least, experiencing his of my own volition.*

Too many problems yielding not enough solutions bleed out my ears, almost making me miss Casey's hand coming to rest on my knee.

Damn the blood flow to my cheeks.

The hand only leaves my leg out of necessity, reclaiming its place once its use is no longer required. Placed on my person, the weight is an odd sensation. Then, when gone, it leaves an emptiness behind. *Something is deeply wrong with me.*

At the grocery store, people are scattered across the lot, minding their business as if this were a regular morning. *I guess for most, it is.*

He parks front and center to let me out in front of the door. It reminds me of getting dropped off at school.

I know nobody is paying me any notice. This fact doesn't lessen the sense of being watched.

Leaning in, he locks my eyes with his. "I'll be about an hour. Please take your time. I'll text you as soon as I'm getting close, okay?"

My cheeks pull taut. *Into a grimace or a flat smile? Who knows.*

His car doesn't move. A wave out front isn't enough; he motions me inside before he'll pull away from the curb.

Arms crossed and eyes rolling, I oblige. Really, it is nice to know someone is looking out for me.

Wandering up and down the aisles, nothing comes to mind on what I need or what to get. Most of my time is spent window shopping or zoning out at different shelves, trying not to overthink.

Time flies to maladaptive daydreaming.

Items I don't remember picking end up in my arms, and I'm walking toward the front to check out as Casey texts that he's a few minutes away.

My place in line provides a front-row view to his flushed cheeks and wicked resting bitch face walking through the door. *There's an expression I haven't seen up to now.*

Immediately, his features transform upon finding me. A smile teases his lips, locked and loaded, ready for use. Dim eyes, set in a determined stare, literally light up in meeting mine.

An arm around my shoulders pulls me into him for a side hug where he can keep his voice low. "How'd the shopping go? Did you get enough to feed my ass too?"

"Fine. Hopefully you're not too picky," I exaggeratedly whisper.

"Not a problem. I'll fill up during the day or after classes if I have to." He doesn't even try to maintain a straight face.

Shrugging his arm off, I smack at his chest for the reminder. "You better amscray from mine." There is no way he can stay in my class now.

His hands lift in supplication. "Don't worry, I was going to drop it first thing tomorrow. It was a filler class, anyway." He punctuates the statement with a flutter of eyelids.

We finish checking out and reenter the cold. There's a sharper bite to it now, despite the sun shining more brightly.

In my haste to brace against the chill, I almost barrel face first into a burly man sporting a flannel shirt. Worn and torn, there is no way the fabric is warm or thick enough for how cold it is.

Our near collision provides ample opportunity to waft the pungent stench of alcohol clinging to his clothes and body. The stuff has to be seeping out of his pores.

"Oops, sorry, sir. I didn't mean to try to run you over." I sidestep, putting on a meek smile to compose the rest of my face.

Dazed, he mumbles, "No worries, little lady. You couldn't hurt me."

His eyes flash to Casey. After a brief stare-down between them, we depart.

Pulling ahead as he lags behind, I try to regain his attention. "Hey? Casey? Are you okay?" His trance remains. My steps angle toward him to ask, "Did you know him?"

This gets a reaction.

He shakes himself off to finally look at me. "Huh? Sorry. I thought I recognized him. The guy reeks. He smells worse than the inside of a whiskey barrel."

Most of the drive to Hopeton, we're both silent.

I utilize the time to focus around my building anxiety. *Why am I anxious, though?* Trying to dig deeper and ascertain what is causing it, I ask myself more questions. *Am I worried to stay in the house? Someone coming for me? Is it leftover guilt and shame from this morning? Is it about Casey and I being alone? Ding, ding.*

A light goes off somewhere in my brain. Casey. The maniac is either going to be a problem or not. However that situation ends up, I'll handle it. I'm nervous about putting undue pressure on Casey and I when we weren't even supposed to be a thing in the first place.

Maybe we fizzle out and realize it sooner. Or maybe it'll be a testament to the foundation of an amazing relationship. Either way, it's anticipation that's burning a hole in my stomach for an outcome I wasn't prepared to grapple with yet. *Hmm, sounds familiar.*

It still sucks. At least identifying the cause allows some relief. Enough to reach for Casey's hand.

He jumps at the unexpected contact.

I choke down a laugh. "Jeez, I'm supposed to be the skittish one."

His eyebrow rockets to the sky. "I was unprepared. Lost in thought." He trails off, picking back up. "How are you doing?"

Calm or numb, I am confident in my response. "Actually, I think I'm okay. Whatever happens will happen, no matter where I am."

Despite my ambition, heartbeats pound on my chest as we round the bend to bring mine and the neighboring houses into view. Thumping steadily increases until I can busy myself putting everything away, returning to normal as I collapse in the recliner.

Casey stands over me. A frown crinkles his forehead.

Scooting to one side and patting the cushion next to me, I admit to my original plans. "You know, I was actually wanting to invite you to watch movies today. Then this morning happened. So, I was already hoping you were going to be here anyway."

Why blush now? I think to myself, cheeks aflame.

Relaxing, his head shakes. "Good. I'm glad we both wanted to see each other." He eyes the recliner. "I'm not responsible if this breaks under us."

"It'll be fine. You should actually pick something for us to watch first." I wave off his concern, pointing to the DVD shelf.

Not making it very far into the selection, he guffaws and rips one down. "You've got *Tommy Boy*? This was one of my favorites when I was younger."

Movie deposited into the player, he squishes in beside me.

Even though it's an oversized chair, I end up partially sitting in his lap.

He doesn't act bothered. Although, I start to get self-conscious and wonder where the hell all of this audacity came from. I wish I could say I don't usually fall this fast or hard, but according to my track record, it proves I become obsessed quickly.

Previous guys I've tried to date found alone time with me wasn't such a pleasant experience. My hopes are already too high, but it doesn't mean I need to preemptively ruin this for myself. I resolve to enjoy whatever this is, as long as it lasts.

When I turn to him, Casey's eyes are boring into me.

"What?" I ask, unsettled, wondering what I did.

"You look very preoccupied, and I didn't want to interrupt. I don't know where the remote is." His shrug's effectiveness is reduced by the recliner and our strategic placement in it.

Oof, I'm zoned out like a psychopath while Casey's waiting to do the thing I said we should. Mechanically, very aware of my movements, I grab the remote and start the movie.

"You're fine," he assures. "I didn't want to disrupt whatever you were thinking about. If you're anything like me, it's difficult to get the train back on track sometimes so I figured I'd let you be." A squeeze of my leg adds to his reassurance.

When the movie ends, we pick another. Somewhere in between a couple more, a frozen pizza is made and devoured. Credits for our last movie roll as I groan my way out of the chair to clean up our dinner mess.

Returning to the living room, I find him preparing the recliner to sleep in. "Nu-uh, nope. You're going to ache everywhere if you sleep there."

He stops and directs a questioning expression at me.

"You can stay in the guest bedroom. It used to be my room." I pause, unsure if I should proceed in giving the next option. "Or, if you promise to be good, you can stay with me in my room. I mean it though. No funny business."

A teeny, tiny little voice hopes he'll be a true gentleman and take the guest room, no further discussion. Another screams for me to drag him upstairs before he can make the decision. Somehow, I ignore both and remain quiet.

His tone is borderline sarcastic. "Well, if you're leaving the choice to me." Wheels spin in his head as he unsuccessfully fights the cocky smile he's not hiding very well.

What have I done?

He continues to make me regret my decision. "I am here to protect you and make you more comfortable. Which sounds harder to do if I'm in a different room. I can be good—good is relative, by the way. No funny business. It sounds as if the best way to protect you would be to stay in the same room as you."

I swear, I am going to shave that eyebrow right off his face.

"Great rationalization," I huff, knowing full well I'm happy at this result.

He picks up his bag and ushers me in front of him. "After you, m'lady."

My head shakes, and an eyeroll flies to cover any obvious relief. *I can't encourage this type of behavior.*

Creaks and groans protest louder as he follows me up. At the top of the stairs, I wonder if this is a bad idea. *Too late!*

His bag drops next to the lounge chair shoved in one corner of my room as he takes a seat. "This is really nice. I wasn't sure what to expect in an old farmhouse."

Skirting past him, I grab fresh clothes out of the dresser to claim bathroom rights. "I contemplated being nice and offering to let you shower first, but you're already reaping reward enough for your *chivalry*." My eyes narrow at him. "There's a half bath downstairs if you need it."

Beaming from his chair, he draws a cross over his heart. "I will be good, I promise."

The door closed between us makes it easier to attempt to enjoy a normal shower. Scalding water rinses me in a burning cleanse to reset.

Dressed and opening the bedroom door, my gaze immediately searches for his. Still seated, I'm sure he thinks he appears innocent as an angel. *Really, he looks to be having the time of his life.* Credit where credit is due, he does sport a slightly less cheeky smile

"You don't have to be so pleased with yourself," I grumble.

"Oh, I'm not allowed to enjoy myself in this situation? I thought I was being good." He feigns innocence, shit-eating grin resurfacing.

My arm sweeps in a grand gesture towards the bathroom. "Sorry if I took all the hot water. I'm not used to someone else needing it too." I would feel bad if he got stuck taking a cold shower.

"I actually prefer to shower in the morning, if that's alright?" he asks like he would change his routine if it bothered me.

I nod.

Permission received, he removes clothes from his bag.

"There are a couple of empty drawers in the dresser if you want to put anything in there," I say, opening unused ones to distract my hands.

It dawns on me he hasn't changed yet. He waited to make sure not showering first wasn't going to bother me.

Clothes dispersed, he steps around me to get to the bathroom. One hand holds me in place as his body circumvents mine. The motion sends a shiver through me.

Under the covers, my phone plugged in and alarms set, I start to drift off when the door opens.

He walks out in sleep shorts. No shirt.

Oh, his muscles are defined when you can see them. I temper my eyes wanting to widen and clamp on a breath trying to suck in. *Get a grip.*

Appropriately tempered, my eyes are glued to him while he plugs in his phone and sets his own alarm.

His gaze meets mine as he lifts the covers. *Watching for my reaction to make sure he's still welcome?* Maybe checking for any hint I've changed my mind.

The only thing I'm trying to hide is my regret for asking him to be good.

Jeepers, his feet are freezing. They aren't even on me, and I'm chilled by the cold emanating off those bad boys.

Restraining myself, I kiss him on the cheek. "Thank you, for coming to my rescue and making me feel safe."

He accepts the cheek peck and in turn seeks out my lips.

Neither retreating nor leaning more into him, I let him close the distance. Taking my lips in his, an arms wraps around my back, bringing me closer. There isn't a push for more.

"Anything for my girl." His voice is low as he pulls away. It raises goosebumps everywhere our skin meets. A hand appears to cup my chin before he lies back onto the pillow. "Goodnight, Lizzy."

Today might have started out like shit, but it's ended pretty well for me, I'd say.

17: Casey

Sleep does not find me immediately. *And that's okay.* I've got plenty on my mind to untangle and process.

Once Lizzy's breathing evens, I relax.

A police cruiser stationed outside for the last couple hours has wracked my nerves from the moment it parked. It's unsettling to know a cop is so close. Of course, having one nearby does keep Lizzy safer.

Part of me wants the other murderer to try something so I get the chance to verify who the hell it is and put my own hands on them. *That's a selfish and stupid notion.*

At first, I wondered if it might be Geoffrey. He was hung up on me leaving him *high and dry* yesterday. I didn't think he'd really have it in him to do anything alone.

Technically, there is a chance Martin made his way here.

Regardless, whoever it was, they're lucky they hit one of the right houses. If they hurt someone innocent, I would've had to make them pay.

Rubbing my face hard enough to rearrange it does little to assuage my guilt. I scold myself for getting Lizzy into this and ruining our time together worrying about what I can't control.

Everything will be better once I know who else is causing a commotion here. *When I know who to tell to back the hell off my girl.*

She resituates in her sleep. Breath struggling a few beats slows again as she settles. Light snores weave in every so often, soothing me to continue.

The neighbor who our mystery murderer took care of was already a target for being in cahoots with the suspected child predator I strangled last week. Burying such a monster beneath the dunes was oh so satisfying. I'm only disappointed I didn't get to do the same to his friend myself.

We got lucky when the couple's house didn't explode after we set it ablaze. Their drug lab in the basement could've easily caught fire and done major damage.

Fake security signs they posted almost fooled me. If there were real cameras, they would've potentially captured evidence to be used against them. There's no way they were going to risk it on the off chance someone broke in.

Awful people believe they can hide out in these rural areas because they're more reclusive and out of the way. I'm showing them they can't stay hidden.

Geoffrey doesn't realize the type of people we've sought for targets. It's better he thinks they're random victims he can expel anger on. Telling him the truth won't make a difference. He'd probably turn on me if he thought I were soft in killing scum and creeps. He is ever increasingly panning out to be one of them.

Pounding in my head grows incessant. Whiplash from bouncing between all these thoughts. *You're losing it, Casey.*

Speaking of whiplash, too bad it doesn't stop here as my mind takes me back to where this entire mess started.

Research on the local community for one of those ridiculous college courses yielded interesting results once I did enough digging. With time, patience, and drive, I found out how some extremely shady people came to live in Hopeton. Trying to hide under the guise of small-town life, most of them did a pretty good job blending in.

There are good, regular residents in this town, among the monsters. I met some during my reconnaissance.

That's how I found Debbie. She opened up to me pretty quickly—*must run in the family*—and told me how her life lost meaning. No one left to live for and a withered relationship with her daughter, she wanted peace. They've now both told me they weren't close anymore.

At first, we discussed giving her something to live for, to get her out and find joy in life again. Over a few months, we talked. Since I recently found myself in the same boat, we tried to brainstorm reasons for her to want to stay. *Who would I be to judge her for admitting to the same thoughts I experienced?*

One day she told me she couldn't take it anymore, begged me to help her. Finally, I agreed, and it was the happiest I'd seen her. Unafraid of death, she was ready to welcome the release.

Sneaking into her house while she slept, I wanted it done quickly. An injection of air into her veins caused a heart attack.

She awoke for a moment, in this same room where I am so close to Lizzy now, and spoke her last words, "Is it over yet?" before she was gone. I smother a shiver to keep from disturbing Lizzy further.

Debbie supposedly wrote a letter as part of our agreement, not necessarily to explain the entire situation, but something so her daughter would be able to more properly grieve and have some form of closure. Estranged or not, a daughter deserves more from her mother than an intentional, unexplained departure.

Unable and unwilling to handle life anymore, she wanted an out where she didn't have to do it herself or see it coming. So I gave it to her.

I can't say I blame her. I walked the same path. The main difference was my delusion in thinking I could follow through, knowing it was coming by my own hand, and subsequent failure.

Will Lizzy ever forgive me for causing her mother's death?

Rubbing my forehead to push aside the pain for now doesn't work.

It felt slimy to sneak away in order to get more supplies to Martin. I'm sure his stock was running low, if not gone already. He ought to be kept happy and stationary for now. *Can't risk him on the loose trying to scavenge. If he's even still there.*

What the fuck kind of web have I woven?

Down another rabbit hole, I go. As far as I can tell, Martin's a guy who snapped and got the book thrown at him. Paying back too large a debt ever since.

Of the pool of inmates I researched, he held no prior record or history of problems. There were a few reasons it worked to use him as a scapegoat. No small part was me wanting to see for myself if this man deserved prison.

I mean, I know I do. At least I'm cleaning up some of the other problems in my own spiral. It gives me purpose, like I am making a difference.

Most people say they could never kill. I used to be one of them. Then I gave in once to help a friend, and it became a great deal easier after.

Going around in circles isn't helping. What's the plan?

Tomorrow, I'll go check on Martin.

And talk to Geoffrey.

Running into him was piss-poor luck. Between him trying to intimidate me last night and watching those soulless eyes look Lizzy up and down today left me ready to throw a punch right there in the store. He could get dangerous ideas if he thought he needed to hurt me through her.

Geoffrey started out as a tool to help me, someone else I gave a chance to. More quickly than I expected, he's outrun his use. In the beginning, he was the perfect extra set of hands—anger issues, no family in the picture, and friends in high places who are more than happy to encourage his bad behavior.

Now I'm unraveling what really happened to his wife and kids. Tracking them down under the radar has not been easy. Apparently, they had great reason to *abandon* him.

Some resolution achieved, sleep becomes possible. Situating onto my side, an arm reaches over Lizzy to pull her in closer. My heart beats faster at her willingness to press against me in sleep. I ask myself if it's because she knows it's me and feels safe, or if she's seeking any kind of comfort for another bad dream?

I hope it's the former.

***

An alarm goes off too soon. Waking with a start slams me back to the bittersweet reality of where I am.

Lizzy stirs beside me as I relinquish my place in the warm bed. I'm immediately shivering and wide awake from the chill. Sleep blurs my vision, requiring several attempts to blink clear. Once it does, I note it's her alarm blaring. *Might as well get moving.*

My plan is to let it trill so she can shut it off on her own. A muffled groan of, "Five more minutes," from under the covers changes my mind. Chuckling, I snooze it on my way to the bathroom.

Water on as hot as it will go scalds to combat the chill shaking me. Right about now, I remember my clothes are in the dresser, out there. I didn't bring in any to change into. *Damn.*

Guess I won't be so *good* if I walk out in a towel. *A towel is better than nothing.* I saw her lingering gaze last night. It gave me far too much confidence.

Residuals of said carefree confidence urges me to sing random bits of song, enjoying the acoustics until I think better of it. Lizzy might still be sleeping.

At the end, hot water runs down me in a baptism of the new day. Pink and radiating warmth, I shut it off and wrap a towel around my waist.

Lizzy is already awake and mostly dressed when I exit the bathroom. Down to putting on socks, she faces me from a seated position on the bed. *Whew, thought I was going to get double scolded.*

Taking in her expression while she stares at me, I am hyperaware of the fact I'm only attired in a towel. *Might get a lecture anyway.*

"Sorry, I figured you were asleep." I try to dig myself out. She doesn't speak or stop roving her eyes over my…arms? "You good? I hope I didn't wake you." The accompanying grin forms, despite my best judgment.

Her eyes flick to it before it vanishes, providing an opportunity for her to recover. "How could anyone sleep through the caterwauling you were doing in there?"

"Caterwauling seems a bit harsh." My arms cross as I lean against the doorframe.

Pushing herself up places her directly in front of me. "You're right." A mischievous gleam lights her features. "It was more like—"

She pauses.

I'm waiting on edge for whatever sassy comment is thrown my way.

"Oh, I can't be mean this early. You actually sounded pretty good. I'm just jealous I don't sound that good in the shower." Her face turns beet red.

I assume her flush is due to thinking about the both of us together in the shower. That's what came to mind for me. My bottom lip burns, biting back the remark I've got lined up.

We have to get ready, I tell myself. *We have to get going. Now is not the time.*

Instead of speaking, a pivot on my heel points me to the dresser. While I'm retrieving clothes, she makes her exit downstairs. *A wise decision.*

Alone in her room, I get lost in my head for too long. How unreal this weekend has been makes everything fuzzy, my movements slow to react to commands.

Finally ready, the bottom stair creaking under me draws her attention.

She calls from the kitchen, "Hungry?"

My words are drowned out by the oven's beep. "Sure. Smells good."

Did I take that long to get dressed?

Scrambled eggs are already divvied up onto two plates. Biscuits steam on a pan she pulls out of the oven. Quick movements shuffle a golden lava puck to each dish.

Pointed fork gesturing to one, she stands at the counter, digging into the other. "How'd you sleep?" she asks between bites, trying—and failing—to sound disinterested. Her gaze wanders everywhere except to me.

Making her wait for an answer as I take up my plate, I decide to push my luck. "Fine. It was nice to have a cuddle buddy for once." My eyes don't leave her as I pick at the food in front of me.

She chokes on the bite she's in the middle of chewing.

I deserve a medal for holding in my laugh.

Face scrunched together while coughing around the food she's currently inhaling, she doesn't agree. "I should've let you sleep in the recliner. Maybe you'd have some more manners."

I can't help but crack. Her narrowed glare shifts to me, igniting remorse. "Sorry, sorry. I appreciate you trusting me to be a gentleman. I can relocate to a different room if I need to. I don't want to overstep."

The expression shifts almost imperceptibly to suspicion.

I continue, "I'm here to make you more comfortable…among other selfish reasons. I'll try to do better."

Adding an eyebrow quirk perks her up. *She usually smiles when I do that.* I never really noticed how often I do it until I started talking to her. *Maybe it's her fault.*

Silence follows. Not an awkward quiet. There's no urge to fill the empty space rambling or engaging in random small talk. It's peaceful.

Only as we're preparing to walk out the front door does she break it. "Should we take my car today since you drove yesterday?"

"I've actually got more errands to run, so I planned to drive." Briefly, I wonder if she's worried we might be seen together or if she's lacking control and freedom. I tack on, "You could drive yourself if you want to. We can meet later if it makes you more comfortable?"

I don't want to leave her. However, if she needs to feel independent, I will not stand in her way.

She shakes her head. "No sense in both of us driving to and from the same place. If it doesn't bother you, I love having a chauffeur."

Thank goodness.

I head outside to start the car, leaving her to collect whatever else she requires.

Propped against the passenger side so I can open her door, a piercing scream cuts me deeper than any cold.

Legs move me on their own toward the porch. Every muscle goes rigid, tense and ready to defend.

The reason for outburst quickly becomes apparent. Satisfied she is whole and unharmed, my attention falls on "ur next" written on the front door. Rusty brown, I believe it either is, or is supposed to resemble, blood. Thick in some places and thin in others, the crude lettering appears as though it were finger painted.

Lizzy has a hand cupped to her face, no other noise emitting though her shoulders' tremble. She easily collapses into the hug I pull her into to shield her from the message. Holding onto her gives me a place to put my energy. I know she's okay, but everything remains taut, waiting for something else to happen.

My vision tunnels, scanning the immediate area for a sign, some symbol to indicate what might come next. Last night's cruiser, no longer sitting in the street, really makes me hope the bastard waited for the cop to leave before writing this.

Keeping her face tucked to my chest, I call non-emergency services. A sleepy voice answers, inquiring as to my situation. Anger makes it difficult to hold an even tone. Somehow, I manage. He confirms the deputy on watch last night did check in this morning, relieving one weight off my mind.

As I'm explaining, Lizzy removes herself to finish locking up. Her door slams as she yanks it closed. This early, the abrupt crack is almost mistakable for a gunshot.

The officer advises they'll send someone to take a look around and let us know if they find anything, then disconnects.

Tears brim bright and shiny under a furrowed brow when her gaze falls upon me.

Putting a hand to each side of her face, I ask, "Do you still want to stay here?"

Her face sets. "I don't want to be cowed out of my own house."

Whether she's justifying to me or herself, I support her.

At my nod, her muscles relax a tad, as if she were waiting for approval.

Our drive to campus is silent. She watches the fields go by without a word. Several times, it sounds as if she sniffles or cries. I begin to extend an arm in her direction, then drop it as quickly. *If she wants comfort, she knows where to find it.*

Somehow, we gave ourselves plenty of time to still arrive first. No one out and about to pay us any attention, I open her door and take her hand.

Halfway to the art building, I break her reverie. "I'm going to administration and officially dropping your class, first thing."

Out of my periphery, her head turns toward me.

Willing myself to remain focused on faded red bricks forming the majority of campus, I wait to look at her as unfiltered words spill. "I probably won't see you before the end of the day. It might be smart to stay in your classroom until I can pick you up. I'll send you lunch. You don't have to worry or do anything. The last thing I want is to control you… Just, please, wait for me?"

My resolve caves as I face her to beg.

A mask, thrown into place over her regular features, flattens those ever-present dimples and pales her blush ready cheeks. Knowing a war wages underneath the surface of her blank expression hurts more having experienced it myself and understanding there isn't anything I can do to make it better.

Minimal hesitation grants me some relief in her stony agreement. "I won't leave my classroom, unless it's an emergency. This is a crappy situation, and I do appreciate you taking it seriously without acting possessive and overprotective."

Outside the entrance, other students meandering onto campus bids me to rethink any type of affectionate parting. "Call me if anything comes up, and I'll be right here. Okay?"

She opens the door, a nod as her reply. Her grip loosens in mine.

At this flippancy, I push a little, tugging on her hand while I can. "I'm serious. Even if it might seem stupid, call me."

A crack appears in the mask, bared to me again. *Did I cause it?*

Smiling through her answer, "I will" falls flat between us. Light doesn't reach her eyes. She does squeeze my hand prior to disappearing inside.

Shit. Moments tick by. I contemplate going in after her.

Space. Give her space. It takes everything I have in me to walk away.

Sighs and groans of how I could've handled everything differently create foggy puffs of breath that precede me toward the admin building.

Only one lady operates its office today. I patiently wait for a calm moment to interject.

Her, "What can I help you with?" is frazzled when she addresses me.

Me too, lady. "Hi, I'd like to drop a class, please," I say, short and sweet, in hopes my smile doesn't look forced. I'm too aware of it plastered on my face, making it difficult to tell. *Too big a smile implies you want or are hiding something. Too small and it doesn't look sincere.*

She barely glances up from her computer. Clicks and clacks pause for her to verify my name, student ID, and the class I want to drop. In under five minutes, I'm on my way. *Easy peasy. Whew.*

Lizzy officially no longer my instructor lifts more of the weight bogging me. I mean, I wasn't bothered in the least. Knowing it unsettled her was enough.

Primary task out of the way, my trajectory returns me to the parking lot.

The next errand is to check on Martin. If he's not at his hideout, if he's the one who is targeting Lizzy, any sympathy I hold for him will evaporate, and he'll require expeditious handling.

Damn, I can't let myself get so fired up. Neck cracking side to side and rolling my shoulders releases some of the tension starting to build.

An attempt at calming thoughts whisks me across the miles to Dacoma.

There isn't room for awe at the tenacity it would've taken for Martin to run all the way from Alva during his escape, hide in Dacoma under constant fear of exposure, and then risk travel to Hopeton. All in the freezing Oklahoma cold. *Under different circumstances, maybe.*

I'm nearing the end of my patience, pulling up in front of the house.

Great care is still taken to be aware of my surroundings the few steps to round the domicile. Spare glances are easy to toss over each shoulder for reassurance.

A bag of groceries sits beside the door where I left them. *As if he was never here to bring them in. Or if he's lucky, something happened to him.*

My eyes flick to neighboring houses for any possible audience. Evergreens growing close to the foundation hide me from view of the street and most adjacent yards.

Satisfied no one is watching, as far as I can tell, I peek in the windows. Cupping my hands to shield against the glare doesn't help. Inside is too dark to see past the thin curtains. Martin would be trying to stay out of sight anyway.

For shits and giggles, I jiggle the knob. *Locked.*

The lockpicking kit appears out of my jacket, and I get to work. Within seconds, it's swinging open.

Slow footsteps carry me through each room. A garbage pile rots in the kitchen, and an extra funk lingers in the hallway. Other than the assaults on my nose, there's no sign of him.

He was here. Not anymore. *This isn't looking good.*

I pace back and forth down the hall, pondering my next move. While the stench is atrocious, it provides an area I can safely think in peace until an idea comes to mind.

Upon exiting the house, I leave the door ajar and grab the grocery bag, tossing it into my trunk.

Guilt at Lizzy's proximity to danger because of my actions threatens to surpass my previous capacity for self-hatred on the drive to Alva. Reining in my emotions, I maintain composure long enough to purchase a burner cellphone at the superstore.

An anonymous call in regard to a break-in at the Dacoma house should hopefully start the police on Martin's trail. Maybe they'll get to him before I do. *I don't know if that's better or worse.*

Another item as checked off my list as it can be, Geoffrey's big rig loitering at the back of the lot reminds me of the next unpleasant task. He said he was taking the week off. *I guess he meant it.*

Having a destination renews my purpose. Even if I have to confront Geoffrey when I'm not quite ready to do so.

Few blocks span the distance between his house and the superstore. Time doesn't allot for me to plan what to say or prepare for how this interaction will go. *Guess I'm winging it. Might as well be today's motto.*

There is no indication of life exuding from his residence. I don't know what I expected to see. It's a miracle he doesn't dwell in a cave or straight out of his truck. He's a barely functioning drunk, so any curb appeal went out the window some time ago, giving the place an abandoned quality.

Mustering up the courage for this unpleasant task, I approach his door with caution. One ring of the bell stirs no reaction or sound inside. No stumbles, grumbles, stomps, or gripes. Relieved and annoyed, I bang on the door. Still no answer.

Curiosity overrides the opportunity presented to say I tried and walk away.

I wouldn't be surprised if he's passed out in the backyard.

A privacy fence splits the yard. Easy to hop, it's as empty back here as up front. Among overgrown weeds, succeeding in their takeover, and patches of dirt where grass has given up, nothing appears out of the ordinary.

Being in his domain makes my skin crawl.

No trace of life here either. I'm ready to put a pin in this endeavor when freshly tilled dirt catches my eye. There's no reason I should care about a hole, yet here I am.

One more glance toward the house solidifies I'm the only person out here. Silence within this and the surrounding yards instills confidence I should hear any impending approach.

Stiff, untouched ground doesn't give as I kneel beside the soft spot. Only in this small area does the dirt shift easily. Hardly below the surface, my hands come in contact against something solid. I cringe, retrieving them until more soil falls away to reveal an old boot box. *What an odd thing to bury*, is my single thought as I open it.

Smell doesn't hit me right away. Confronted by a mess of fur, blood, and bone, my vision clouds. Then, as my other senses heighten, stench rolls out of this tomb so vile, I don't know how I missed it.

Holding my breath does little to quell rising bile.

Sunlight soaks into my dark clothes. Its warmth does not comfort. Bite from the cold breeze stings bone-deep as I stare at this horror I've stumbled across.

Hacked apart, pieces of this puzzle clearly used to comprise a dog. Long clotted and covered in parasites, the deed itself must've taken place some time ago while the box and grave appear fresh, nowhere near as degraded as their contents.

Hands rattling, no longer due to the cold, I return the creature to its resting place.

I attempt to put the ingrained image out of my mind as I hop the fence to escape this hell. My eyes skirt windows for any movement. Unsettled gurgles ravage my stomach the entire way to my car.

I knew Geoffrey was fucked up, too recently beginning to realize how in depth, but this is bad. I don't doubt for an instant he would do the same to his family if given the chance.

To put distance between me and this hellscape, I drive over a couple of blocks to park somewhere his house can't watch me.

Shaking my uneasiness takes a few moments. Clearer-headed, I use the burner phone to call a number I've spent a long time tracking down.

After several rings, a woman answers.

Taking the plunge, I ask, "Hi, is this Sarah?"

Silence hangs between us until a tart, "Yes," responds.

"Sarah, Geoffrey's stepsister?" I contemplate ending the question here. Something spurs me to continue. "Please, don't hang up. He doesn't know I've been looking into him. I doubt he even remembers you exist, and I assume that is by design. I'm worried his wife and kids are really buried in the backyard when he's telling everyone they left. I just want to know if they're okay and if maybe I could talk to her?"

Allowing a moment for it all to resonate leaves me in deafening silence.

Distrust coats her tone. "Not that I'm confirming or denying anything, why should I believe you?"

Can't say I blame her.

"There is no good reason I can give," I answer honestly. "Geoffrey is an incredibly evil man, and I want to know how deep it runs. All I have to go on is his word, and the word of those who enable him. Not exactly trustworthy sources. I understand how difficult this must be in trying to stay hidden, out from under his thumb, and I can't imagine what she and those kids must be going through, what they've already gone through. I don't want to jeopardize their safety."

There is no reply for so long, I think we disconnected.

"Hang on," comes from her end.

Hushed bickers fill the background. Snippets can be picked out here and there, nothing coherent or pronounced enough for me to grasp.

Eventually, another voice whispers, "You promise he won't find us?"

Compared to the first, this one is shaky and frail. My heart aches for the woman wielding it.

Fighting to keep emotion from cracking my own, I promise, "I do. You deserve for people to know if he was hurting you." *And I want him to be punished for it.*

She takes a moment to respond. When she does, her words hold more weight. "*If he was hurting us.* All the man can do is hurt. He never got physical while we were dating, didn't lay a finger on me. After we got married, a switch flipped, and it all changed.

"I never knew how bad it would get. It might only be a slap and nothing more. Other times, I thought he'd send me to the hospital with broken bones or internal bleeding, but he never actually got so careless. His reactions grew increasingly more frequent and harsh all the time. At first, everything was aimed at me. Then, as the kids grew older, he'd shift to them.

"Most of our money was spent before he would make it home. He claims he kept food on the table—hardly. The kids taking on odd jobs as soon as they could did the bulk of providing because he wouldn't let me work.

"His friends would check in on us to make sure we were obeying his rules. I never knew when someone might drop by, and if I didn't answer the door or let them come in, then I'd be accused of cheating or being lazy behind his back. Then it'd be worse the next time he got home."

Her voice hardens the more she speaks. I am amazed at the strength this woman found to get herself free of him.

"Decided we were all going to leave. The kids got out first. I told Geoffrey they were spending the night at a friend's. They were supposed to pick me up once he blacked out, but I wanted some payback. The man wouldn't buy a car, even after finding out I was pregnant. He said we didn't need a family vehicle, his trusty two-door, thirty-year-old pickup was plenty. Which, of course, I wasn't allowed to drive. Finally, when the kids were old enough to drive and hold jobs of their own, he saw the value in having a second vehicle. I wanted to take something from him, the same way he took everything from us. He never loved me or the kids. I don't think he has the capacity. I hate how long it took me to see…"

Hesitation creeps in to break her voice. "Please don't let him find us. He would kill me and the kids if he were given the opportunity."

I wish I could disagree. "I want nothing more than for him to pay for what he's done to you and your family. He has no idea where you are, and it's driving him crazy. I do want to ask you one thing. Did you leave a family pet behind?"

She sucks in a breath. "Oh, I felt so bad when I remembered the dog. By then it was too late to go back without endangering ourselves. I hoped it might be better for Geoffrey to have something there to care for…" Trailing off at the end, she doesn't sound like she believes it herself, as if she knows where this is going. "Why do you ask?"

What would it benefit for her to know?

"I just think you're right. He would potentially kill you if he were to ever find you. Stay hidden, move on, and find happiness. He's got to slip up, especially the way he drinks." Too shaken, I can't tell if I'm reassuring.

A single sniffle sounds. "I don't know about that. He has some powerful friends who enjoy encouraging him."

I hate to do this to her, although it is clarifying my next moves. *I wonder if she's ever received words of encouragement?* "Thank you so much, ma'am. For taking the time to talk to me and for trusting me. I can't tell you how deeply I admire you for leaving such a situation. That took a whole lot of courage. Hopefully, you can live a better life."

Muffled sobs come through the phone. "Thank you. I don't feel it yet, but we'll get there. Don't let him find out I've spoken to you."

"This conversation never happened. Good luck to you and your kids." Fighting tears of my own, I hang up and toss the phone into the glovebox.

More confident in what my next steps are, I pull away, leaving Geoffrey's house lighter in my soul. Still sick, but lighter.

Whether he was involved in the attack on Lizzy's neighbor or not, Geoffrey is no longer an asset to me.

Both him and Martin have worn out their usefulness.

18: Geoffrey

The taste of blood is thick in my mouth. *Did I try to bite through my tongue again?*

My bender from last night clings to me in a haze. *Was that last night? I guess I can't hang like I used to.*

Getting up there in years is starting to wear on me.

I will my eyes to open. Nothing happens. Telling my body to sit up invokes no physical response. Muscles are unreactive to the thoughts driving my hands toward a face I cannot feel in order to rub this sensation away. There is no response from them either.

Forcing myself to roll over results in nausea, no movement. *Whoa, must've tied one on pretty hard if I'm paralyzed.*

Concession granted for now, I fall back into the abyss lurking at the edge of my fading consciousness. She plays coy, staying right outside of grasp until deciding to overtake me all at once.

Then, I am gone once more.

19: Martin

Darkness everywhere.

I search for an escape, but it clings, weighing on my soul.

What is happening to me? *Can't answer that one.*

How did I get here? *Ah, there lies some answers.*

Images play across my vision. *I left my hideout.*

***

Crossing miles of fields, skirting houses and dirt roads under the cover of night, a pull drew me to my brother's house. *To where it all went wrong.*

After my brother's death, his wife couldn't stand living in their house anymore. She sold the place and moved away.

I knew they weren't there. Still, an urge to return pushed me on, wondering, *Who lives there now?*

Sloppy mud dragged me down, and frozen wasteland showed no quarter. Crops and tree rows planted in my path, as well as winding creeks with a will all their own, formed debilitating obstacles.

Daylight snuck up the horizon by the time Hopeton came into view. Sun rays illuminated the final stretches of a single field left to trample. Shadows no longer claiming the land, they'd also begun to recede inside my mind, making it easier to think. Claustrophobic darkness retreating from all allowed leeway for a few moments of sanity.

Part of me regrets that night. Never had I actually believed I was capable of violence. It lurked, hiding in the background. Presence of this ability wasn't foreign. Ignoring its whispers were easy. When giving into it hit me in the moment, my life changed.

Anger boiled away any lingering regret at the memory. Steps, closing the distance between me and my destination, were easier to take.

Reminiscing carried me the last mile, past the neighboring houses, and into the familiar backyard. At a slight noise, my head swiveled to check if I were alone. Of course, I was.

Focus dialed in for an access point, an upward heave not moving it, a rear window dashed any hope I had to make an inconspicuous entry. Surprisingly little force was needed to break the glass.

Unlocked, the window went up without any noise or issue, as if it was meant to be.

The layout of the house has remained ingrained into my essence. Muscle memory guided me through the house as if I were there only yesterday. Updated furniture and new photos lining the walls made no difference. It took me right back in time. My senses became hypervigilant.

Snores, echoing from the master bedroom, were the only discernable noise.

I crept down the hall, bedroom door opening under my steady hand.

Unsure what else to do, I continued forward. In the bed lay a small man, sporting an unfortunate choice of moustache.

Beyond his appearance, my mind knew it wasn't my brother asleep in the bed. This pitiful creature couldn't compare to the burly brute he had been. It made no difference. *He would do.*

A pillow discarded to the floor wound up in my grasp.

His raspy breathing grew louder as I got close. Cushion in place, the sound ceased. My body pinned his before he was conscious enough to put up a fight. Arms thrashed, and he bucked what little he could, too late. I easily maintained pressure to hold him.

Reliving the finger poking me in the chest, I remained in place well after he'd stopped moving.

Comforted in my successful kill, the pillow dropped away to peer at his face. Scrawny, taut, and possibly undernourished.

"Such a shame." I tsked aloud. "He would have been no match for me, even if he'd tried."

The nagging itch of darkness receded completely, temporarily satiated. *It always comes back.*

Mind and vision cleared, I felt more in control, less manic.

No need to rush departure, my return trek was slow and meandering. Dropping into the grass outside the window, I finally acknowledged the cold sting against my skin.

A moment to take in the morning beauty was ruined as sirens assaulted my ears. Steadily, they rose.

My head spun in search of a spectator. At the very last house, a figure loomed on their rooftop.

Without thought, my arm raised in accusation. The figure stiffened. They didn't think I could see them. *I know you're there.*

Spite renewing was the driving force to pry me from where I stood. It carried me the lengths of several yards to get out of sight.

Thinking about them surrounding the house propelled me to move faster than I had in a long time.

Soreness could and would be dealt with later. *As I'm experiencing now.*

Farther to the north, well distanced from my kill, I realized the field I was running beside held something beautiful: cotton.

No questions bombarded my mind of why it hadn't been harvested yet, how did I not see it previously, or would it be enough? Those came later.

Rows of overgrowth provided perfect cover. Hunching as far as my body would allow gained me access to the maze. White fluff whipped into my face. Stems sticking every which way clawed at my clothes and skin.

Only a short while could I carry on in such a state, reduced to crawling to continue. Dragging myself along the frozen, somehow still wet ground, put plenty of space between me and the town in the time it took my arms to give out.

One last shove flopped me onto my back. Cold seeped into the thin fabric adorning me. Everything had long gone numb.

By then, darkness started clouding the edges of my vision again. Consciousness beginning to slip away, I welcomed it.

Let the cold and darkness take me, whether I awaken or not.

Too bad. I woke up.

There I lay, in the field, contemplating so many choices made to land me in it. Dull throbs in my worn feet pulsated to the beat of my heart. Clouds fogging my mind vanished in the wake of clarity at how I physically got there.

It's still dark.

Open your eyes.

They are open.

Stars winked from their heavenly post. *Ah, night.*

Not a single nerve end worked throughout my body. An upright position took an inordinate amount of time to attain. Let alone the return trudge to Hopeton.

To the house on the end.

Faint light originated from its direction, providing a beacon to guide me. Fire rekindled in my gut warm enough for movement. Night reigning once more, there was no need for extra energy waste on sneaking.

Stiff and weak, my body successfully completed the journey. My guiding light extinguished prior to arrival at this destination.

Closer inspection of my target brought a police cruiser into view. *Damn watchdog.*

Stationed in front of the house, this interloper put a damper on any plan. Blind rage ebbed. Less fueling, it forced stronger conniving under greater odds against me.

In my inhibited condition, I would be no match for him. *Or anybody, really.* Recovery was a must.

Prickly evergreens clustered to one side of the house provided temporary shelter. Awake, I remained under them the rest of the night, shivering, waiting for darkness to sweep me into its arms. It never came to soothe. *Fickle bitch.*

The sun cresting on the horizon shed light onto a sight I was hoping not to see. My extremities were a concerning mixture of black and blue. Several fingers starting to ooze and bleed. *That couldn't be good.*

As if playing tag with daylight, the cruiser departed.

An urge to send a message twitched unfeeling digits resting at my side.

Creaks and groans from the upper structure implied movement inside the house. This did not stop me from mounting the steps of its front porch.

No pain hindered the fingertip I used to write "ur next" on the door. *Hopefully it will be the truth.*

A hasty retreat returned me to the trees, where I waited and listened for my audience to happen upon their note.

Wooden creaks and groans excited me as the door opened. Footsteps faded, and it opened again.

This time, a scream immediately followed. Music to my ears. The sound brought a smile to my weary face.

Amidst the small celebration I threw, a voice carried on the crisp morning air. *Shh,* I told myself. *I want to hear what they're saying.*

After a few moments of what sounded to be a one-sided conversation, it became apparent a man was on the phone with police. *Dirty narcs.*

Their car drove off once they were done tattling. My concern shifted to obtaining better accommodations for a chance to recuperate.

Around the house, a window at the back porch promised easy access. Few steps to climb drained any residual energy left within me. Vision spinning and suddenly top heavy, my body collapsed. Bouncing off what was most likely the very window I was going to use as my entry point, darkness enshrouded me.

20: Geoffrey

Though the haze persists, now less intense, it is finally relinquishing its hold.

Little movements, brought on by my body beginning to stir, send sharp twinges up my back. Lightheadedness grows stronger the more I rouse. The pounding of my heart roars as if it were inside my head. Each beat is a knock against my skull.

Glue holds my eyelids together, unable to pry open.

Arms reach up to rub them into submission. Gravity aides the limbs rather than slowing their progress. Effort is required to not hit myself in the face. *Weird.*

My legs pull in to start the process of shifting positions.

Stairs dig in wherever their edges push against me. Able to gaze upon my surroundings, this is more than simply a hangover. Nothing sits quite right in how I've landed at the bottom of the stairs. Head down, my legs have fallen to rest above my torso.

Ah, I remember now.

Running into Casey with some girl stirred up far too many impulses to ignore. By the time I made it home, shaking and shuddering took control.

Beers were no longer cutting it to take the edge off. Upgrading to mixed drinks hardly made a difference. I had to skip the mixer and go for straight whiskey, bourbon, anything available.

As the night progressed, my brain started playing tricks on me. That's the only logical explanation for the noises throughout the house. Bangs and stomps sounded from rooms I knew were empty. I swore someone or something was here with me.

After investigating to find myself alone, barks came from downstairs. They were plain as day, the same annoying yap as the one I'd permanently silenced.

In my haste to figure out what the fuck was going on in the basement, the stairs turned out to be more of an obstacle than I anticipated.

I fell down the fucking things.

Somehow, my head hangs off the bottom step while the rest of me sprawls above. Blood pooled in it for so long, it feels swollen, a pimple ready to burst.

Pain cripples as it swiftly overtakes every muscle and joint. Eventually, I slide off the steps to lie flat. Limbs fall into their normal placement.

I don't move until all sharp pain ceases. Dull ache replaces intense stabs. Prepared for it all to come sweeping in again, I push myself to a seated position against the wall.

Propped and stationary, the room continues to spin. Time loses meaning as I sit here for who knows how long.

Unable to do much else, scanning the room brings my phone into view. A couple feet away, it mocks me, just out of arm's reach.

Groaning helps to hold down the bile trying to vacate my stomach. An arm extends to reach for the device. Blood doesn't run in my veins. It can't exist alongside the liquid fire burning away everything. Shards spear up my side and down my spine.

Fingers curl to ensnare the object they've met. Sweat drips into my brow from the effort. *Don't be dead,* whispers through my mind.

All I could've hoped for was the fall to be enough to kill me. Disappointed, yet again.

The lock screen proclaims three percent battery life on this Monday afternoon. *Fuck. Good thing I already wanted to take off work.*

My body remains a lump of useless flesh. I give it as much time as I think it'll require, waiting to see how quickly recovery may take before growing impatient.

A deep breath precursors my half-assed plan to reach for the railing, push beyond the pain, don't let go, and heave until I am, begrudgingly, vertical.

Pain consumes all. Geoffrey is no more.

Legs buckle underneath me. Shakes rattle my frame from head to toe. I'm my own personal earthquake. Maintaining a grip on the banister becomes the most difficult task I've ever had to complete as the volcano inside me erupts, sending magma to every corner of my being. *And that's prior to ascending any of the stairs.*

White-knuckled grip and agonizingly slow movements are the only reason I end up at the top. Shuffling steps drag my feet across the carpet to a dining room chair. *If I fall into the couch, I'll never get out of it.*

Unfortunately, I might be messed up bad enough for a trip to the hospital.

The last thing I want to do is call Casey. At the moment, he's all I can think of as an option.

Answering after a couple rings, "What?" is all he says. *Curt little shit today.*

I don't like this any more than he does. "I fell down the stairs last night, and I'm pretty torn up. Can it not be a big deal for you to take me to the hospital?"

Silence from the other end. *What kind of game does he think this is?*

"Look, I didn't *want* to call you. I can't hardly walk.

There's pain all up and down my back—"

"I'll be right there." Then he hangs up.

Damn it. That kid needs an attitude adjustment.

The phone, no longer of use, falls to the floor. Merely sitting has started to send waves of ache through my body. Too long passes before there is a knock at the door.

"It's open!" I yell past the agony.

Casey enters slowly, as if expecting a trap.

My eyes roll, unable to stimy little impulses for nicety's sake. "I'm not fooling. Get over here and help me." A grimace replaces my frown.

Not moving any closer, he instead asks questions. "You were here Saturday night and all day yesterday besides our run-in at the grocery store? You didn't go out or pull any stunts?"

Whatever the expression on his face means, it reminds me how pissed I am. "Yeah. I was mad at you for not planning something Saturday night. I was here, throwing 'em back. Sunday, I needed some shit and went to the store, still pissed. Came home and threw a bunch more back, waking up just now at the bottom of the stairs. What of it?"

The rush of words expends my minimal energy supply. Suddenly, staying upright in the chair is impossible. Bobbing side to side a moment, I tumble onto the floor. An explosion lights up every vein and nerve as I hit the ground with a dull thud.

One hand instinctively reaches toward Casey. My conscious mind hates this show of weakness. *What else can I do?*

His face is stone cold, unreadable.

The edges of my vision go dark as Casey squats next to me. Making no move to help, all he does is stare. *Bastard.*

Then, my sweet mistress surrounds me, and nothing else matters.

21: Lizzy

Classes drag forever.

What makes it worse is I've found myself jumping at the slightest provocation. One student tapped my shoulder in the hall, another coughed during silent study, and an administrator came knocking in the middle of class. These normal, daily expectations sent my heart rate straight into the atmosphere.

Twice, I had to clamp my mouth shut on a scream because I was so startled. Breathing normally requires conscious effort, unwilling to comply as a basic body function necessary for survival. I swear, I constantly sound as if I've ascended multiple flights of stairs.

Casey did order lunch for me. The delivery person emphasized how she was tipped *very* well to hand the food off personally.

I'm going to punch him.

He's made this entire ordeal less overwhelming. Several times, bringing me back from the edge of a larger breakdown. It's crazy to know someone is trying to have my best interest in mind while proving to be reliable.

I didn't realize how badly I'd needed that.

He's making everything harder to process is what he's doing. Of course, I can't let myself enjoy anything. There has to be a catch; the other shoe has to drop.

Swallowing a sigh, the barrage continues. *How can I properly process this fiasco when he's throwing my life into its own uproar? I'm losing control one facet at a time. What's next?*

To detract from the oncoming spiral if I maintain this thought pattern, I force myself to address positives. One relief is knowing home won't be some dark and looming structure of solitude where my time will be spent alone, worrying myself into a tizzy.

There's always the option to temporarily relocate. Hotel, motel, or Casey's place. A glance around the room shows everyone focused on themselves. No one pays attention to my shiver or accompanying blush at the notion of staying at Casey's.

After how long the day has taken, this last class is the worst perpetrator. Eye flicks to the clock every couple of minutes can't be helped, causing time to virtually cease.

I'm running on fumes when Casey walks in. He kindly waits until the last student departs.

Standing no longer comes easily. This conclusion is brought about due to my legs turning to mush the moment I attempt it.

Casey catches me in time to avert my face making acquaintance with the ground. Concern thickens his voice. "Are you okay?"

"It's been a long day," I start, tucking some hair behind my ear. "I've been a little skittish. Getting in my head and psyching myself up." Using him to regain composure, I take advantage of the proximity to extract a hug that's teased my thoughts all day.

His arms encircle me, delivering much-needed pressure. All my broken pieces begin to meld together. A deep exhale breathes into his chest.

Too soon, it ends.

He pulls away only enough to look in my eyes. "Anything I can do?" His forehead wrinkles, crossing the line to paranoia with how fervently his dart between mine.

"I'm fine, just clumsy. Nothing I can't handle." A nervous smile pulls at the corners of my mouth before reverting to serious. "Did you drop the class?"

He has the audacity to laugh. "Yeah, dropped it first thing this morning." His upper eyelid twitches as if struggling to keep his own brow down.

The relief his words bring to my weary form is adequate distraction from his sass. "Good. Let's get out of here. I'm exhausted."

Taking my hand, he escorts me to the parking lot. I forgot how cold it was today. As I slide into the passenger seat, that cold is significantly reduced as the car is already warm.

Without thinking, I open my mouth. "Did you skip today?"

All color leaves his face. *Shit.*

Guilt colors my own. Quickly, I backtrack, "Sorry, it's none of my business and doesn't matter. I should be happy to be warm."

Whatever the cause, his face shifts into smug repose. "I said I had some errands to run. They ended up taking longer than I expected."

My smarmy remark is shut down when his phone rings.

Eyes lock on mine as he answers, "Hello." A few seconds go by. Incoherent words babble nonsense on the other end. Removing it from his ear, he puts the call on speakerphone. "What's the update, Officer?"

Lunch forms a rock in my stomach.

Gruff words continue. "When we searched the premises, we found the message you referred to. In addition, there was blood found at the home's rear entrance. Someone may have attempted to break in."

Any air privileged to remain in my lungs up to this instant expeditiously exits as a choked gasp. Struggling to smother a hacking cough, teetering at the back of my throat, takes top priority.

Shortly, the call ends as Casey thanks the officer. Wishing him a good evening, he sounds so calm, deadpan, and monotone. *Is he a psychopath or a superhero?*

Either way, his gaze firmly holds mine while I recover in some capacity.

Once he believes me capable of conversing, he hits me with, "Are you okay?"

No.

Then he follows it up. "You are going to *be* okay. Are you okay right now?"

Oh, I *am* breathing. *That's good.* "Not really."

He cups my cheek. "Do you want to stay at my place?"

Deep breaths are all I can manage at first. *Now air wants to flow.* An exhale melts into a sigh. "Would that not be giving up?"

His lips pull into a flat line.

My brain flies through a messy array of thoughts at breakneck speed, not accomplishing anything. "Do I have to decide right now?"

"No." Authority behind how he says it grounds me. "We can go to your house and talk, think, whatever you need."

Retrieving his hand, he pulls out of the parking lot.

The drive gives me time to bounce between dread and potentialities threatening to overthrow my sanity. Sorting what I can into questions forces me to address and identify. *What is it I am worried about?* Everything, all the time. *Not helpful.* A murderer is out to get me. *The police don't sound super concerned, so why should I be?* Despite this, do I not think I'll be safe in my own home? *I can hardly call it my home. Why would I be upset if there's another reason I'm uncomfortable there?*

It is an odd experience to live my life as normal when

I don't even know what normal is anymore. *How can I compare anything to a nonexistent baseline?*

Aside from my personal struggles, the community itself has been in an uproar lately. Instances one would expect to find in bigger cities, a setting where chaos is anticipated, have been on the rise here. *Maybe that's it.* It isn't right.

Hopeton's grain elevator grows larger on the horizon. A stout guardian over town, it implies a watchful presence, offering peace and safety, yet no way of supporting its claim.

This hollow promise sinks my heart lower.

During quiet periods today, to ease some of my nerves, I looked into recent headlines around the county. An endeavor to uncover hometown nostalgia, to restore my faith in small-town community, gave me quite the opposite.

Besides the upsetting news of an escaped convict, which is upheaval enough, it turns out the couple whose house caught fire were drug dealers.

Another resident has gone missing. Having not shown up for work or court appearances, a welfare check was done. They found his house empty and his car still in the garage. The crazy part is he was in the middle of fighting child predator charges.

I couldn't believe what I'd read. A tiny voice in my head speculates the insane, whispering doubt over my mother's death. *I've got plenty going on without adding conspiracy theories into the mix.*

I'm so tired of life happening to me. *What do I want? Right now?*

I blurt, "What if we get out of town for a few days?"

As if prepared for an outburst, Casey readily responds, "If that's what you want."

Second-guessing myself begins immediately. "Do you

think it would help? I'm beginning to regret moving into my mom's house, and I want a chance to think straight. Preferably before I do anything else drastic."

Explaining it out loud justifies the concept to myself. Simply discussing getting away lifts my shoulders.

He doesn't require convincing. "I think you know what you need. Where did you have in mind?"

"I know it's silly, but really, I want to go to Oklahoma City. Not too far, and it's more familiar. I might be able to breathe a little easier, blend into the crowds. If it ends up not being far enough, we'll keep going." Pressure tightening my chest lessens as I grow more excited at the idea of leaving. "I'll text my boss right now. With everything going on, she won't be able to tell me no."

My phone is in hand and a message half drafted before I think to ask, "Are you okay with that?"

A smile pushes up his cheeks. "It sounds awesome. I'm just glad to be included. I didn't want to assume I'd be allowed to tag along."

"Duh. You're practically my bodyguard now. I don't want to go alone." My enthusiasm falls away. "Plus, I might not be able to afford it by myself. Especially since I'm taking off work already." Shame heats my cheeks.

Unoffended, his smile not only stays in place, but it also grows radiant. "Perfect. I'll consider it brownie points in my favor." A wink teases at the end.

Details regarding work are settled as we pull into the driveway. Giddiness adds a bounce to my steps down the front walk until seeing the message again sucks all wind from my sails. *Gah, they couldn't get rid of that for me?*

My eyes train on the knob to unlock the door. Shivers infiltrate, nearly causing me to break and stare at the nasty writing. Gaze never lifting to take in the letters, anger still manages to replace the elation slipping from my grasp.

Shoving the door open, any comfort I'd begun to find

in these walls is gone.

Casey is right on my heels to close and lock it. The deadbolt clicks into place.

Hardly pausing to kick off my shoes and shed outer layers, I stomp up the stairs. Rubbing my temples is a vain attempt to stave off the headache building.

Creaks to follow from his ascent comfort my brain. Knowing he is right behind me, one of my hands leaves my temple to reach for his. In it, I receive a reassuring squeeze.

Merely a whisper, his voice is low. "Let's pack. We can leave tonight. Or first thing."

A war wages within me. Partly, I feel violated and have no desire to stay. On the other hand, I want to know I can last the night. Just because.

Mulling it over, I turn to Casey. "First thing. I have no capacity to travel or make decisions at the moment."

He takes on the gentlest tone I think I've ever heard from him. "I can handle everything if you would like. If that's the main reason you don't want to go now."

One hand reaches up to cup my cheek. His thumb rubs beneath my eye.

My heart pounds heavier. *I love when he does this.*

I sigh into his hand. "No. I want my own bed and familiarity. We can get an early start." Not posing it as a question leaves a weird taste in my mouth.

Without missing a beat, he's nodding in agreement. "Sounds good."

His genuine smile, the intensity of it, is reflected in his eyes. Everything in the way he looks at me sets my stomach aflutter. *It's as if I'm all that matters.*

Such scrutiny causes me to squirm. I tell myself to knuckle under, better get used to it. *This is him showing he cares, and I need to learn how to accept affection.*

He pulls me in for a hug, easing my face to his chest.

I think this is my new happy place. A chuckle escapes, muffled by his shirt.

His head tilts to stare at me in question. Probably to make sure I'm not having a breakdown.

Furrowed brows, seemingly as far as they will go, stare me in the face. I find myself biting my lip to hold in the urge to giggle. My struggle somehow deepens those creases lining his forehead.

The onslaught wins, and I devolve into laughter, apologizing once it subsides. "Sorry. I was trying to think myself out of a spiral, and the most random thought pulled me out of it."

Please don't ask what it was.

My explanation relaxes his frown a fraction. "Well, good." He doesn't sound relieved.

Exhaustion sweeps over me. "I am so ready to not exist. Let's pack so we can get some sleep,"

We spend the evening getting packed and squared away. I'm changed into pajamas and climbing under the covers as my energy gives out.

I can't find it in me to care what time it is. *Dark outside equals bedtime.*

Casey, warm and real beside me, allows for easy drifting.

22: Martin

My body cramps.

The twinges nearly send me into a fit before I fully awaken and remember where I am. *Inside the narcs' house.*

I couldn't describe how I entered this place. Everything leading up to how I arrived here is foggy and brings on the worst headache when I try to delve deeper to process it.

Hope, that the familiar position of stretching out on the floor would bring me some peace, dies as it becomes claustrophobic underneath this bed.

Flashes of panicked memory remind me of what I'd planned to do with myself once I was inside the house. A bare bedroom on the ground floor seemed like the perfect place to hole up and recover. Face to face with the bottom of a mattress, this is where I am now.

The bed skirt nearly reaching the floor completely hides me from view of the open door. Faint moonlight teases an outline of the curtain over a window.

Before I have further chance to gather my bearings and figure out the next step, creaks sound above.

I suck in a breath and hold it until the noise ceases overhead. Ready to let it out as a sigh, periodic groans pick up directly outside.

Someone is down here.

To reinforce this, a light switches on in another room to illuminate my surroundings.

My breath escapes in a silent groan.

Accompanying someone's weight shifting across the floor, cupboards open and close, and a faucet runs.

This is my chance.

For better or worse, I relinquish my hiding spot again. I remind myself why it is I'm here at all.

The fun continues.

23: Lizzy

In sleep, creaking tickles my ears. Rousing from the frays of a dream I can't recall, I believe it to be an alarm going off.

A falling sensation jolts me wide awake. Creaks persist outside the dream.

It takes a moment to sink in. *Someone is on the stairs.*

Heart in my throat, I roll over to find myself alone in the bed. Casey isn't next to me. Rationalization slows my breathing, and a hysterical laugh squeaks out. *He must've gone downstairs.*

The pillow catches me as I collapse. My eyes close, and I wait for him to return so I can tell him how he scared me.

Forcing them open to not fall asleep, blurry vision unveils a figure standing over me.

"What are you doing?" I ask the mass of shadow.

His hand weaving into my hair catches me off guard. Expecting a kiss, my half-conscious reaction is to face him and accept. Instead, I'm dragged from under the covers in a vise grip. A yelp sounds as I follow my hair to keep it from being yanked out.

Sleep and confusion hinders my fight or flight, halting any type of defense. Husky grunts accompany the effort it requires to subdue me.

Pulled tight against him, heavy breaths heat my ear. Damp clothing presses into my back. The stench of body odor and death descends upon me, overwhelming any other senses.

Before my brain catches up, telling me to scream, a hand clamps down on my mouth.

Instinctively, I try to face my attacker. Rough hands force my head straight. Using his body to propel me forward, he guides us out of the bedroom and downstairs.

Attempts to stymie our progress or break away elicit a harsher grip wherever his hands hold me.

My search for Casey grows more frantic as we make our way through the house. No sign of him causes me to wonder if he's even here, until we get to the too bright kitchen, where several blinks to acclimate reveal him sprawled across the floor.

Tears spring at the sight. I fight them, knowing I need to stay calm and think. *This must be my murderer.*

Ragged breaths continue in my ear. His weight shifts onto me. I can't tell if it's to wrangle me under control or because he's using me to stand.

His voice right beside me sends an abhorrent stink directly up my nose. "Don't you dare scream."

The removal of his hand cripples any restraint over my gag reflex.

Calmly, I somehow ask, "What do you want?" without throwing up.

Nasty chortles answer. Hairs on my neck stand. "I want you to know how much you fucked up. I just wanted to enjoy my second chance at freedom. You tried to get them to take me. You're gonna pay for that."

"Did you kill him?" The words fall flat. My head gestures to Casey's limp form.

"He should come to any minute, with a raging headache to match mine." The solace this provides is snatched away immediately. "Now, dear, I do need something from you."

A gulp does little to help stifle what my stomach is trying to reject. "What?" comes out more confident than I feel.

The man doesn't appreciate it. "Oh, don't you go putting on a brave face now. I want you to act scared and hysterical, for his sake. He has to see how I've got the upper hand. Can you play along for me?"

Stench assaults anew after every word. In need of a deep breath, I'm too nervous to take one. "If you don't let me have some fresh air, the only thing I'm going to be capable of is throwing up."

The sass isn't intentional. I'm extremely serious. An exaggerated exhale punctuates the statement.

He surprises me with another chuckle. "Fair. Ope, his foot twitched. Now why don't you be a good little meat shield and cry out for me."

Unwilling to partake in goading Casey, I weigh my options. *I have no options.* Getting this man off me may mean nothing, depending on the arsenal he has.

Instant relief from his hand releasing my hair is quickly replaced by a sharp pain at my side. I cry out as a reflex.

Casey jerks awake. Slowly, he pushes himself to sit on his knees where he wobbles as if he were prepared to throw up himself or pass out again. His hands splay for balance to remain upright.

Vacant eyes rove the kitchen. Once they catch mine, his blank expression recedes.

I mouth, "Trap," while he regains composure.

Stinky re-covers my mouth before I know if Casey understands.

I can't hurl if his hand is in the way.

"Ah, you shut your pretty lips, or I'll cut them off," he coos into my neck.

Squirming under his touch, vomit noises do nothing to affect him.

Casey stares at me. Trying to figure out what's going on?

All I can do is mirror his gaze.

"Don't keep us waiting all night, lad," the man tosses at him. He sounds stronger in addressing Casey.

Must have taken a lot of energy, considering how heavily he leans on me. Supporting both of us has my legs ready to give. *There's an idea.*

As Casey teeters to stand, they do just that. My legs fold.

Unfortunately, Stinky holds up the both of us. Hauling me onto my feet, his hand nearly dislocates my chin. Grunts rumble down my spine at his strain.

Our struggle allows Casey time to come around.

With the man's face far too close to mine, his gaze narrows at us. Venom coats every word as he spits, "Martin, is that you?"

We stumble a step backwards at the name.

Intrigue enters the voice in my ear. "Oh, do you know me because of my conviction? Or are you one of the mystery people who helped me escape?" After a pause, any joviality is gone as he proceeds. "Nevertheless, in regard to our current predicament, you tried to turn me in. Both of you. Now we have a debt to settle."

Casey looks between us. I assume he's calculating the risk of busting us apart versus playing along with whatever this Martin's game is.

It crosses my mind to try to get out from under him again. My side throbs to remind where he already succeeded in getting me to cry out. Since he won't let me move my head to inspect, it could've been a sharp pinch. *Or worse.*

Martin resumes inching us towards the living room.

Instinct screams for me to resist. Reluctantly, I pull against him to remain closer to Casey.

He hisses in dissatisfaction. "Move, you little bitch, or I'll remove you from this equation. I don't need you alive for this to be fun, so I can make that happen if you'd prefer." Spittle sprays as his lips brush my ear.

Not moving to follow, Casey stays rigid and silent. His reaction takes us both off guard.

"What do you think, son?" Martin glances at him and then to where we're walking. "You wouldn't leave your girl in my grimy fingers, would you? Let me walk right out with her?"

Casey doesn't move an inch.

I don't know what his plan is, and Martin is becoming unsettled, not having a compliant pawn.

Martin sucks in a breath. "You don't want us to spend any alone time together, do you?"

Almost to the front door, his head swivels, and I take advantage. Whether it gets me killed or not, fuck this guy.

Shaking loose enough to bite down on the hand covering my mouth, I put as much force into it as I can, simultaneously throwing a fist behind me in hopes to hit him in the groin. *I don't want to go anywhere near it, but desperate times, as they say.*

Despite these attempts, he doesn't let go. A low groan is his only reaction as he pulls me harder by the hair. It doesn't slow him down. There is no prying his hands off me.

At the bottom of the stairs, he switches course, ushering us up.

What is Casey doing?

One last time, I try to free myself from Martin's grip. Dead-weighting myself to fall down the steps does nothing except infuriate him further.

He rips my head back to face him. "I will pick a limb

to lighten your load if you don't get your ass moving."

A knife flashes inches in front of my eyes. Even though light from the kitchen is dimmer this far away, dark stains tint the blade.

We get to the top of the stairs without further issue.

Inside my room, he kicks the door shut. Throwing me onto the bed, there's no time to react before he's on top, pinning me face down.

Duct tape rips from a roll to tie my wrists behind me. Flailing and kicking doesn't hinder him.

Hands secure, he binds my ankles and flips me over, caring little for the amount of hair and skin it'll rip coming off. *That is not going to be a fun wax.*

Lizzy, you might not live to see the tape come off.

Less concerned about me once I'm immobile, he pushes the dresser in front of the door as far as it'll go. Partway successful, he gives up, still making it more difficult to get in.

Doubled over to catch his breath, Martin addresses me, "Where is your dumb-fuck boyfriend, girlie? He has to play, or he's going to make it worse for you."

There isn't really anything for me to say, so I remain quiet.

He flicks on the bedside lamp and inspects the duct tape holding me. A nasty hand pats my cheek. "Good. Don't cause any more trouble, and I promise to consider ending it quick for you."

My eyes widen to saucers. *What an enthralling promise.*

Pacing the small space, his knife still gleams in the low light as he mumbles to himself. Steps concluding to point the blade at me, glints of shiny red tighten my jaw. *That's my fucking blood.* Dull pulsing from my side confirms the thought.

"What's your fella's name?" comes his unexpected question.

I hesitate.

Wrong move.

A strong grip takes one of my bound arms. Holding it steady, he drags the knife along my bicep. Shock and pain cause me to cry out.

"What. Is. His. Name? I'll not ask again." Hot breath fans my face.

Fighting a losing battle to tears, I mumble, "Casey."

Fingers tighten around the wound. "Speak up, missy."

"Casey. His name is Casey," I blurt, hating my show of weakness.

"Oh, Casey, my boy," Martin calls over his shoulder toward the door.

No response from beyond. *Hopefully, he got out and went for help.*

"He isn't making this very fun for me." Disappointment furrows Martin's brow as his gaze returns to mine. The tip of the knife meets his lips as if he were lost in thought, leaving a bloodstain behind. "Well, if he's not going to play, I'll just have to get my fun out of you first."

His frown melts into a sneer. The ugly grin sends a shudder through my soul.

I swallow a scream as he shoves me back down and climbs to perch on top of me, taking a seat on my pelvis.

Not allowing time to examine my options, he pushes up my shirt to expose my stomach and ribs. Shivers rattle me. *From the cold, the knife, or his proximity—take your pick.*

At first, the knife traces over my skin, leaving tingling trails to torture me in expectation. Of course, it can't stay this way for long.

Martin starts to make actual cuts. Pain erupts wherever the knife pierces.

Biting my lip to refrain from making anymore sound works for a cut or two. Beyond that, I can't stop grunts or gasps made in vain to assuage the burning.

I yell Casey's name.

My eyes close for most of it so I can't watch Martin's face contort as he hurts me. The one thing I don't do is beg him to stop. *He won't get that satisfaction.*

At last, he lets up. *Probably to admire his work.*

Consciousness clings to me by a thread, or vice versa.

It takes a moment for me to realize Martin is talking. *Talking to me?*

"—self-defense, and they called it murder. Can you believe it?" he asks as if we were mid-conversation.

In my daze, fighting to stay awake, he receives no reply. Apparently, I'm not upholding my end properly.

A slap across my face is the next thing to register. Its sting is effective in rousing me. Darkness retreats for now.

"Pay attention," he scolds as if it were my choice. "He kept inciting me. Then everything was my fault when I finally snapped."

His voice fades in and out as I focus on staying awake.

"I stopped trying to be good and started acting on the intrusive thoughts. It was terrifying at first, then it became easier. My dear, do stay with me. We're not done yet, and you're not listening."

My eyelids flutter as unconsciousness looms closer. I want to give in so I don't have to bear the dizzying ache. Arms tied beneath me strain at my shoulders. Fingers and hands are long numb under our combined weight.

He delivers a lighter pat to my cheek. "People were afraid of me. I finally gave them something to respect."

I don't know what possesses me to speak. "Fear and respect aren't the same," tumbles out of my mouth, cracked and raspy.

His own drops open. "Have you not been listening? It doesn't matter."

Another slap follows, causing me to wince. The pain it evokes nearly sends me spiraling straight into a blackout.

Only one thing keeps me from giving in and letting the dark take me.

A faint creak on the stairs.

Whether it's in my head or Martin simply didn't hear it, I don't want to take any chances. To cover any more potential noises, I start to mutter and groan.

This is a mistake.

Disturbing my throat enough for one cough opens the floodgates, and my body convulses from continuous hacking.

Either it was enough to hide Casey's approach, or I've started to hallucinate. The next time I am able to open my eyes, he's joined us in the room, pointing a gun at Martin.

Casey's eyes are lifeless. Black voids, stark against the blank expression he currently wears, hide any sign of cheekiness or sarcasm he usually has on deck. Despite his taut muscles, ready to pull the trigger, he appears torn.

Once the coughs and convulsions stop to where I can suck in a ragged breath, I say, "Fucking do it."

So badly do I want to close my eyes and rest. *I'd rather see this fucker go down.*

Martin's sick smile falters ever so slightly as he begins to follow my gaze.

Whatever internal conflict Casey has resolves.

He pulls the trigger, sending a bullet straight into Martin's head.

His body slumps to one side, falling mostly off of me.

Another coughing fit takes over as Casey fumbles to cut me free.

"Are you okay, Liz?" His voice is steady as ever.

Focusing falls to the backburner. I can't answer.

Freeing me of the dead weight, his hands cup my face, forcing me to look at him.

"I don't know," I think I whisper. Darkness rears, threatening to drown me.

It succeeds until pain dredges me from its depths. Casey is carrying me down the stairs. Compressing my body irritates the fresh wounds.

"Damn son-of-a-bitch motherfucker," is the most I can articulate as jostling creates waves of searing agony.

"Sorry, Liz, I had to get you out of there." He is barely holding himself together as his façade cracks. More than mere concern dims the fire in his eyes.

Unless I'm still hallucinating.

"Casey, you're hurt too. Get an ambulance and police here. I don't want to go to a hospital or for you to drive."

My words cause him to stop at the bottom of the stairs.

"I beg your finest pardon?" he sputters. "You need a hospital. I probably do, too. I don't want you to stay a minute longer while that monster is here."

As his bravery wanes, pain of his own shows underneath.

It almost gets me to fold. Almost. "Please, don't drive. Get them here, check us out, glue me up, and let me shower."

Now, I'm okay with begging.

Tears trickling down my cheeks destroy the rest of his resolve. "I'm going to grab our stuff. If anything, we'll be going to my place for the rest of the night."

Placing me in a dining room chair, he disappears. I let it do most of the work to hold me upright. Consciousness fades in and out.

Before he returns, he's already on the phone. Nothing he says make an impression on my mind. His voice soothes, though the words are meaningless.

Dried blood streaks down the side of his head. Hair is clumped and matted in it near a small gash.

One minute, the house is silent. The next, everyone arrives, and it is far too crowded.

Police go through every room. Most of their time is spent upstairs. Paramedics check us over and stitch or patch up what they can. At the same time, several indistinguishable uniforms ask us never-ending questions. Disappointment shows clear in their faces at our refusal to go to the hospital. *Let them be disappointed. Most of it is surface level.*

Martin is loaded and carted away in an ambulance, pronounced dead on scene. Too numb to express emotion, I don't find joy or sadness in them wheeling out his corpse.

Total silence descends after everyone clears from the house. Without the din, a thick vacuum of quiet fills the space. *Better than all of those people.*

"Are you okay?" Casey's words echo as if he yelled them. They couldn't have been more than a whisper.

A laugh catches in my throat. Pain medicine severely reduces the effects of constricting my stomach. *"Okay" is not the word I would use.* Instead, I offer, "Okay enough. Are you sure you're good to drive, Mr. Head Injury?"

His worry lines disappear, transforming into false bravado at the mention of his own well-being. *Double-standard-having cheeky bastard.*

"I'm fit as a fiddle, ma'am." His pretense falters. "I'll be fine once I can lie down. Are you ready?"

In lieu of a response, my body heaves up from the chair. One groan escapes. More a testament to exhaustion than pain.

The entire drive, I am fighting for my life to stay awake. This makes the miles drag on for hours. If the pain meds weren't working so well, I'd poke my stomach to perk myself up. *Casey would probably scold me.*

My misery ends at an apartment complex, where he pulls straight into a handicap space.

His place is quaint. It's bare, as one would expect a bachelor's apartment to be. I don't know what else I expected.

Casey leads the way down a short hall into the bedroom. My steps, swallowed by the rough carpet, tread quietly behind.

He drops our bags onto the floor and immediately begins to undress.

Meandering to the kitchen in search of cling wrap, I try not to take too long in case he decides to follow.

Triumphant, I return for his help to wrap my bandages and undress myself.

Staring at him while we're both so exposed doesn't cross my mind.

Any embarrassment or shame I would normally experience under his gaze, in my current state of undress, is clouded.

Not a single blush exchanged, I motion for him to shower first. He starts the water and proceeds to push me in.

If he's going to be sassy… I adjust the water as hot as I can stand as he climbs in to stabilize me. The temperature doesn't faze him.

We take turns washing off blood, sweat, and filth left from our encounter, careful of our newly acquired wounds. My face is raw after scrubbing to rid myself of the lingering stench still haunting me.

When Martin's touch is gone, I stand motionless under the water, allowing it to wash over me as I breathe easier.

Casey chuckles.

"What's so funny?" I ask, finally comfortable.

"I do the same at the end of my showers. A baptism, freeing me from the sins of the day."

Ah, I'd already started to miss his cocky grin.

I sigh into the water. "It's the best part of my day."

My legs buckle by the time we dry off and change.

Casey takes a seat on the edge of his bed rather than climb in. Deep in thought, as I sit beside him, he hunches over. Elbows propped on his knees hold up his chin.

"Don't hurt yourself thinking too hard," is my attempt to jest.

One side of his mouth ticks up, though his eyes remain lost in the distance. He gives no verbal response.

For a long time, we sit in silence. As I begin to doze, swaying where I sit, my neck snaps up to him speaking.

"Did you ever get a last letter from your mother? Anything right around when you found out she died?"

What an odd question. "No, I hadn't heard from her in a long time. We really weren't close."

His pause leads me to believe I misheard the question until he continues. "Is there a chance you have mail at your old place? Maybe that didn't get forwarded?"

Between yawns, I offer, "It's possible. We can check once we're in Oklahoma City."

Not looking at me, his eyes close. "You still want to go together?"

What the fuck? Has my low self-esteem rubbed off on him? "Of course. You just saved my life, Casey." My hand moves to his leg.

Flinching at my touch, he sits ups and faces me. Tears glisten in the dim light, choking up his words. "Let's get some sleep. It's been a long night, and we're getting the hell out of here tomorrow."

He brings me in for a gentle hug, kissing the top of my head.

At last, under the covers, his warmth radiating beside

me, it doesn't take long to fall asleep after my head hits the pillow.

24: Casey

I can't believe I almost got us killed.

The first rays of sun seep in through closed blinds. Lizzy's light snoring almost lulls me to sleep. My thoughts race, again stalling such bliss.

I don't know how I'll bear knowing she was hurt and nearly killed because of me. Let alone how the monster even got the chance to put hands on her due to my cockiness. *He should've had a tighter leash from the start.*

How could I let my guard down for a second when I knew there was a potential threat? At least now I know there is no question—he deserved prison. Maybe not at the time he was first sentenced. The shell of a man I saw tonight had been consumed by the evil he permitted to rule.

There was definitely darkness whispering to him. Darkness he greatly lacked the capacity or will to ignore. He should've never been a candidate for our plan. *My plan. Fuck.*

Lizzy shifts beside me. In my bed. *Now there's a better line of thinking.*

Though I don't deserve it, I allow myself to smile and soak in this peace.

Only for a moment.

My head aches. Whatever blow I took from Martin, compressing my skull between my hands provides no relief. The pain is dizzying. *I better suffer the consequences of my actions.*

We should've come here after we packed. *Then she might have resented me for controlling or manipulating her.*

Relinquishing their pressure, my arms fall to the mattress.

It sucks this happened. She made the decision. I didn't encroach on her freedom. Maybe now she'll more comfortably delegate to me. The last thing I want is to possess or manipulate Lizzy. *I want her to trust me, to choose me.*

Shifting to reach an arm over her chest, careful of the bandages covering her abdomen, I pull her close.

Thank goodness that bastard didn't do worse. I worried I'd wasted too much time suppressing the noise of climbing those damn stairs. Retrieving my gun from the car was another hurdle itself. While it might have given him more time to hurt her, he might've grown desperate if he'd heard me coming.

I'm not doing a great job as a bodyguard.

There I go, ruining our time together, thinking. Stop. Enjoy the present.

We are together. We are whole, if not intact. We are cozy in my bed.

As if reading my mind, she settles against me. A flinch from leaning on her wounded arm makes me tense too.

I really hope she isn't having another nightmare. There isn't a thing I can do to help with those.

Relaxing, sinking into the bed, my brain begins to shut off. Eyelids shut out the growing light. Our alarms will wake us soon enough.

***

Cold emptiness replaces her presence.

Slow blinks, muddled by sleep fuzz, bring Lizzy into

focus. She's sitting on the edge of the mattress, similar to how I was earlier this morning.

Still for a beat, her shoulders begin to quake as whimpers break the silence.

Untangling myself from the covers proves difficult in order to wrap my arms around her as full-on sobs arise.

Her body convulsing has to hurt. Knowing it won't make a difference in her ache, I kiss the top of her head.

Choked gasps eventually subside into soft, shaky breaths.

I keep her embraced until she pulls away. Then my grip releases.

Red and puffy, she faces me.

Damn, I wish I could take away her pain. All I can do is offer myself. "Do you want to talk about it?"

Wet eyes flick between mine. "I had a nightmare that Martin killed my mom, killed you, and then came to kill me. I tried to calm down when I woke up and realized it was a dream. You were right there next to me, but it didn't matter. It felt so real."

My hand weaves into the hair behind her ear. She leans into my arm, reaching up to caress it.

If it weren't for her grief, I would want to stay this way forever. I can't believe I'm here with her, that she wants to be here with me. *At least, I think she does.*

Her question surprises me. "What were you thinking when you had the gun to Martin's head?"

I automatically tense.

She is unfazed. "You looked confused. I wasn't sure why."

Tingles race along my skull. "I didn't want him to collapse on you or his blood to touch you." Speaking the words is more difficult than thinking them. "It was hard enough to see him perched over you. Seeing you trapped beneath him." *Do I sound angry? I feel angry.* "I wasn't sure if you were still alive. There was a lot of blood, and your face was so pale." Forcing the last few words, my teeth clench on reignited rage.

A few deep breaths allow me to shake away the memory. Focus shifts to Lizzy. Easing her face to mine gives her time to object. When she doesn't resist, I bring her in for a kiss. Nothing too intense. Something to remind me she is here, she is real. Martin didn't take her from me.

As I'm about to release her, she renews it.

That's my girl. Take what you want.

Reciprocating as passionately as she gives me, we kiss for an eternity.

Our alarms ring us back to reality. Their noise fills the space between us as we drift apart.

In the time it takes us to shut them off, her expression rumples.

We should stop while we're ahead. "Are you ready to get up and get out of here?" I will not stand for her hating herself or me for anything we do.

Worry lines smooth. Relief dips her head in a nod.

Standing too quickly forces me to pause, waiting for the vertigo it creates to wear off. Recovering myself, I dig out some old clothes and toss them on the bed. "If you like or want anything, you can have it. And there's another bathroom down the hall if I'm taking too long."

The door closes on my wink.

My morning routine is far more satisfying, knowing she's here. This apartment has never been anything other than a place to live. Suddenly, her existence within these walls gives them meaning.

Put together as I can be, I open the door to find her dressed in my old stuff. An overwhelming peace calms my mind. A smile forms before I can stop it.

"What's so amusing?" she asks, catching me mid-stare.

"I just can't get enough of you." *Why not let her know?*

Squirming under my gaze, a blush highlights her cheeks. *Ah, some normalcy.*

We finish getting ready and vacate the handicap spot without anyone noticing.

It's a quiet drive. The radio plays low to be able to hold a conversation if we wanted to. Neither of us speak for a while. I figured she would ask me questions. Either she doesn't want to or isn't concerned. I'm not going to push her to talk. There's no way I'm ruining whatever peace we have going.

Frost reflects bright sunshine in crystals scattered throughout tree rows, fields, and yellowed pastures. *A Midwest winter wonderland.* Though I've hated being stuck here, there are worse places to be.

As we get closer to the city, I broach my questions. "Where did you used to work? We could go there first, or would you rather later? Where do you want to stay, and we can go drop our stuff at a hotel?"

Choices might be what she needs to provide focus. Or the indecision will drive her crazy.

She doesn't answer right away, continuing to stare out the window. "Let's get a hotel first. If we could get somewhere with a view of downtown, that would be nice." Her voice, hardly above a whisper, falls silent again.

Several miles further puts us in view of the OKC skyline.

A gasp followed by her head snapping toward me is startling. My heart rate skyrockets until her excited words destabilize the conclusion I'd jumped to.

"There's a cute little bookstore across from the mall. I love stopping there whenever I'm in town. Can we go at some point?" Her elation immediately lessens. As if she doesn't want to get her hopes up if I have no interest in going.

Well, good news for her, I am extremely interested in anything she finds enjoyment in. *Especially if it involves books.* "We can go to any or as many bookstores as you want. Is that where you want to start after the hotel?"

Her eyes light up again, though she pretends to act cool. The thought of anyone trying to tone down her excitement because it was too much for them breaks my heart.

She clears her throat to respond in a calm, controlled manner, "Yes, please."

Returning my attention to the road does nothing to hinder my view of her happy dance. A valiant attempt is made on my part to tamp down a chuckle. It doesn't work.

Her head whips back to me.

My eyes remain forward.

One of the older, downtown adjacent hotels is my destination. Riding the elevator up to a higher floor, Lizzy grows antsier each level it passes.

Plenty of morning light pours into our room. Filtered between buildings and partial cloud cover, gold and pink hues reflect off the many windows aimed at ours. We are just far enough away to perfectly overlook the skyline.

Another gasp sounds as she soaks in the view. Running to the window, she all but flings herself against the glass.

Despite her awe, she is able to articulate, "This is amazing, except it's way too expensive and nice. Have you stayed here before?"

How dare she doubt the way I want to treat her.

"It is beautiful, isn't it? I love this place." Placing our bags down, silent steps tread across the carpet, drawing me closer. Glare blurs our reflections together. "Don't you worry one bit. Not another negative word unless it's a legitimate complaint."

I come to a standstill behind her. Careful to keep off her midsection, my arms wrap to lay across her chest. My cheek rests against her hair.

At first, I expect her to jump or shrink away at the contact. To my surprise, she accepts the gesture and sighs. *Hopefully as content as I am.*

"Do you want to relax or head straight out?" I ask. It's so selfish to have her all to myself. Alone and apart from our daily lives, it's like cheating my way into her affections. *Don't ruin this.*

Facing me, she spins under my arms, wrapping her own around my waist. "Let's hit some bookstores and walk the mall. I want to move."

***

The first bookstore we visit is the one she was excited about. It appears smaller on the outside. Apparently, an amazing illusion dispelled once inside.

Floor-to-ceiling shelves wind through the store. They create the kind of labyrinth I would love to get lost in. At the same time, it has a remodeled newness while maintaining a secondhand, antique quality. Bright overhead lights shine down on thousands of books placed in every nook and cranny.

We meander rooms of shelves. I linger in classic literature and poetry. She eyes the romance and new fiction.

After some searching on my own, I join her, a potential purchase tucked under my arm. Asking to see what I picked, she scoffs at the fact it's an autobiography.

My eyes roll. "What, is a nonfiction book too boring for you?"

Her tone is serious. "Actually, yes, it is very difficult for a nonfiction book to keep my attention. I read to escape my own reality, not remember facts and statistics. I want to live in someone else's problems and catch a break from my own." The wheels in her head turn, pivoting her response. "Sometimes I'll give a nonfiction book a chance. Like an autobiography I read recently, written by a German Knight of the Holy Roman Empire." Her explanation quickens as she gets more excited. "His hand was blown off in battle by a canon and replaced with an iron prosthetic he used to write poetry. He's accredited with the first written use of the phrase, 'Lick my ass.' Now *there* is some nonfiction I can get behind!"

I make a mental note to add it to my reading list. "Sounds awesome. I can't wait to read it myself."

Ignoring my smile, she instead searches the immediate area. A hand covers her mouth as if she's admonishing herself for anyone she may have disturbed in her excitement. *We'll work on that together.* She shouldn't be so worried over what others think or taking up space. For now, I leave it alone.

"Come on," I prod. "What are you perusing so I can appropriately *ooh* and *ahh*."

Her attention falls on the book in her hand. "I haven't found one I really want yet. There are a couple I'd consider if I don't find anything else. Nothing screams for my attention, you know?" She returns the book to its place.

A choked gasp accompanies the snatching of a book off the shelf below it. Quickly scanning the front and back, she rounds on me. The flush of her cheeks battles her gaping mouth to prove the depth of enthusiasm I hope she's experiencing. "I've really wanted this one. I'd heard good things but hadn't happened across it." She winces, hugging the book to her chest. It doesn't make her let up.

"Perfect. Let's move on to the next store, or we can walk the mall if you want to go there first?" I chuckle, starting towards the checkout.

"I'm getting hungry. Can we grab a bite to eat and then walk around the mall?" Pulling the book from my hands, she places both of ours on the counter while making her request.

I somehow manage to holster an eyeroll. "Good plan." The question follows without approval. "What are you doing?" *I know what she's doing.*

"You've paid for everything and done so much for me. I will buy these books and make myself feel like slightly less of a loser."

Her response frazzles every nerve I possess.

We'll work on it, I remind myself, taking a deep breath and keeping my mouth shut for now.

Our day from there is a blur of food, walking the mall, checking out other stores, and admiring or making fun of each other's book selections.

It's hands down one of the best days of my life, if not *the* best.

We finally make our way to the hotel at the end of it and curl up on the bed, switching back and forth between TV shows.

Deciding on a movie to fall asleep to, the last thing I remember is her drifting off in my arms.

25: Geoffrey

I no longer process the pain ravaging my body.

It's been long hours of riding the line between unconsciousness and unfettered daydreaming, allowing another level of rage to move in and take control. The fog it brought on suppresses anything not deemed productive.

The walk to my truck is long, but it gives me time to either collect or lose myself further. A couple of people honk and holler, asking me if I want a ride. Answering or acknowledging them threatens to rip apart the spell. So I ignore it all.

Sunlight reflects off the metallic paint of my rig. Pointed directly at me, I stare down the rays until my eyes water rather than face away. I welcome the sting of any other sensation.

Moving slower than usual, it takes some time to get comfortable in my seat.

The ole girl starts right up as I chuckle. *Casey can't really think he got rid of me so easily.* It's almost insulting.

He can be dealt with at a later time. There's no rush.

My first priority, I believe, will be shifted to where it should've been this entire time.

Tracking down my property.

26: Lizzy

This is another dream. *Nightmare.*

Knowing doesn't change the fact there isn't a thing I can do except let it play out.

Casey holds the gun to my head this time. His finger is on the trigger while he stares off into oblivion. Blank eyes wander everywhere, except to me.

For whatever reason, my cheeks are as high as they will go, smiling ear to ear. *Do I want to die?*

My dream-self screams. The sound is sucked away as it leaves my lips. Lowering my jaw to release the nonexistent note has no effect on their grotesque formation.

His expression doesn't change. There is no acknowledgement of me at all or any sign of recognition.

Blood stains his shirt.

Turning my gargoyle expression onto myself, blood seeps from my own reopened wounds. Pressure radiates through my stomach. I want to scream, cry, or vomit if I could. *Maybe all three.*

As I look up, he's finally noticed me. His face remains deadpan beneath tear streaks and more blood. Familiarity softens the hard eyes until they begin to bug out of his head. Wider and larger they grow, as if trying to convey a voiceless message.

A message I can't understand. Dream me tells him so in disappearing words.

Maintaining eye contact, he sheds new tears. His grip tightens on the gun.

I inhale as he squeezes the trigger. The smile on my face never falters.

A real scream accompanies the gunshot, ripping me out of the nightmare.

My heart beats double time as I shoot straight up from the bed, slick with sweat. Rational thoughts attempt to console me that it was only a bad dream. Breaths drag in and out of my substandard lungs. The sensation of doom doesn't dissipate in the wake of conscious clarity.

Casey's face appears in mine, scrunched by my scream. He pulls me into him. His words are soft. "Shh, shh. It's okay, Liz. I've got you. You're safe." Repeating them, he gently rocks us.

The sound of his voice, intentional breaths to the rhythm of our sway, and forcing my mind to tune out everything except his comfort are eventually enough to settle my nerves. I relax against him.

When he notices the tension subside, he kisses my forehead, asking if I want to talk about it.

At first, I can't bring myself to say anything. *Should I tell him?* What would be the point? *What would be the point in not?* "You had a gun to my head. And the same soulless stare you gave Martin. Both of us were covered in blood, and I was…smiling. Like I was excited for you to kill me."

Immediately, I hate myself for saying it.

His arms tense around me.

I dive straight into an apology. "I'm sorry. I should've kept it to myself."

Hardly after I get the words out, the scolding begins. "Do not apologize to me. Not for something you can't control, and I asked if you wanted to talk about it. You are telling me. There is nothing to be sorry for. Please, continue if you're comfortable."

Hesitation stalls me for a second. "I cried for you to stop. You didn't or couldn't hear me. Then you pulled the trigger, and I still had this sadistic smile. That's when I woke up screaming."

Explaining my own terror, it dawns on me that I haven't checked in to see how Casey is handling all this. *Martin did attack both of us.* This man has gone out of his way to make sure I'm as alright as I can be, given the extremely extenuating circumstances. With how strong and unbreakable he acts, I've assumed he's fine. *Maybe he's better at hiding it.*

"Are you okay, Casey?" I ask into his chest.

His muscles relax a fraction.

Worried I'd upset him, I word vomit, "You've been through a lot too. I'm sorry I haven't asked how you're holding up. Just because you act strong doesn't mean you aren't hurting. I thought you were dead, sprawled out on the floor. Then hearing you describe what you saw Martin doing, it has to affect you."

As the flow of babble stops, I pull away to inspect his face for any hint at what might be showing.

An unfamiliar mask stares at me. The blank expression, devoid of any and all emotion, is the opposite of what I expected. If anything, I assumed there would be an internal struggle battling it out like I've seen before. This is…empty.

One thing is familiar: pain.

Pain deeply set behind his eyes. A kind that stems from holding onto something, enduring alone, for too long.

The dam collapses.

His voice matches the hardness stiffening his usually fluid features. No tone I've ever heard out of him. "You're right. There are some things I need to get off my chest."

I'd begun to retreat from this stranger now in front of me. My back hits the headboard. *Nowhere else to go.*

He proceeds in the same robotic monotone. "It's a lot. You might feel differently about me by the end. Once I start, I can't stop until it's done."

"What?" is all I can whisper.

Knees tucked up to my chest as a barrier between us, I listen as he explains. Everything. *Every. Thing.*

Not a single time does he break eye contact as he talks. I return the favor, unintentionally. It's a spell I worry may induce hysteria if broken too soon.

Only at the end does he remove the mask, allowing several silent minutes for his many words to sink in.

Blood pounds through my veins. Each pulse throbs, barreling beneath my skin. A ring develops in my ears. My stomach forms into a pit, swallowing me from the inside out. *I'm in shock.*

Casey doesn't laugh. He doesn't rip the rug out from under me. This isn't a silly story. Whatever he transformed into to tell me the horrid, despicable truth is proof for me to believe every bit of it. The man he embodied to look me dead in my soul I believe is a man capable of unspeakable horrors.

Part of me wishes he hadn't told me. Selfishly, I want to stay in the dreamlike trance I've lived in since our date.

Another part is relieved. Here is this guy, who on paper is an awful, murderous, detestable piece of crap. Yet he scolds me when I talk badly about myself. He shows care and devotion on a level previously incomprehensible to me. *Maybe it's unhealthy.* So are a ton of other relationships.

His *arguably larger* flaws do make my own shortcomings insignificant by comparison.

Am I processing this properly? *This is insanity, right?*

Then the dumb little voice at the back of my mind pipes up, *He killed Mom.* As if there weren't plenty for me to already be overwhelmed by. *My head hurts.*

Casey's normal tone breaks into my spiral. "Lizzy?"

Our eyes lock, though my mind continues running rampant.

The sound of my name from him stirs up the normal butterflies. I worry there might be loathing, hatred, or other normal reactions, but no. *Maybe it's the shock.*

Since I don't respond out loud, he grows more concerned. "Are you okay?" His arm lifts, wanting to reach out, hesitating to touch me. It falls to his side.

My vision blurs as the room spins. *Damn.* Lightheadedness mutes all other senses. Darkness envelopes me. Only for a second.

When I come to, Casey is supporting my head. *What a monster.*

Realization cuts through the gobbledygook slowing my synapses.

"Did I just fucking faint?" I ask, incredulous.

He frowns, stifling a nervous chuckle. "Appears so. Are you okay? I know that was a lot. Did you hear everything I said?"

Spoken like a man who doesn't want to repeat any of it.

Sarcasm is my default reflex. "Okay? No. A lot? Yeah. Hear it? I think so. Understand? Fuck if I know." Fingernails end up in my mouth to assist the thought process. They don't do much. "What the hell am I even supposed to say? *Good job? What the fuck? Thanks for taking out the trash? Thanks for unloading all this bullshit on me?*"

Watching him cringe at my flippancy almost makes me regret it.

I sigh, nowhere near big enough to match the weight behind it. "So, what do we do now?"

Confusion raises his motherfucking eyebrow. "What do you mean?" he has the audacity to ask.

"Well, as of right now, there is no proof to confirm or deny what you're telling me. I have to take you at your word. That's an insane amount of pressure to put on someone, by the way. I'm choosing to judge you based on the actions I've seen, not the stories you're telling." I tack on, "At least for now."

He cracks a smile. "That seems very unwise."

My lips pull into a tight line. *Tell me about it.*

Keeping his smile in place, he continues, slightly more confident, "Well, since I'm already dumping all this on you. Let's round it out with my favorite part. No more secrets, no more holding anything back. I promise."

What other worrisome thing could he possibly tell me?

"I love you, Lizzy."

Oh.

Still startled by the abruptness of this entire morning, my response is slow. "You know I want to say it." The inside of my cheek ends up between my teeth. "If you'd have said it before, I would've returned the words immediately." Tears threaten to overthrow my composure. "I do love you. But now I need to figure out if it's going to be enough."

Confidence shaken, his face falls, fighting tears of his own. "Do you want me to leave so you can have some time alone?"

The notion of him leaving me here nearly sends me down another spiral. I blurt, "No," way too fast. *I did not go through the bullshit of these last few days to wind up in Oklahoma City alone again.* "How about we go to my old place to check the mail?"

Possibly not ready to trust himself to speak, he merely nods.

Getting up and dressed in silence, it's another long, quiet car ride.

I'm permitted far too much time to be buried by my thoughts. *Am I crazy?* Well, that answer is the same as usual—*yes*. This time, maybe it's a touch more legitimate. *I'm literally in the car next to a serial killer.*

The worst part is, not to justify it, I can understand what he did and why. I've always had similar reflexes. Intrusive ideations I know better than to act on. *Maybe under the right circumstances, I could, and there's what is so terrifying.* Maybe I admire Casey for being able to use them for something *productive*.

What the fuck has my life become? This has to be insanity. I belong in an asylum. *Maybe a lobotomy would fix me up.*

Shaking myself off is supposed to be a metaphor. I choose this moment to do it literally. Although, it's more of a full-body twitch to reflect my atrocity of a mental state. My gaze shifts to take note of any reaction.

Casey is locked on the road. He either didn't see, or he's pretending not to. *What a gentleman.* Well, apparently not. *Ahhh, why did he have to do this to me?*

I'm ready to crack my head into the passenger window by the time we get there.

A sigh changes into a swear under my breath as I throw open my door. Heated steps carry me to the front of the building. My hand reaches for the heavy glass monstrosity of a door when it hits me I am alone. Glancing over my shoulder, Casey has remained in the car.

He waves to usher me on.

I manage to avoid all eye contact on the way to the building manager's office. Casually existing among other people is strange, knowing what I know. It puts me on edge. I'm hyperaware of my existence.

Several shaky knocks bring footsteps to the door.

"What do you want?" my old manager shouts, angry at the disruption. Until he realizes who it is bothering him. "Oh, Eliza. How are you? Come in."

He steps back to open the door wider. His cramped office is less than welcoming.

I see the crush he has on me hasn't lost any momentum. Don't make a face, idiot!

Stifling my grimace, I manage to form words. "Um, good. Thanks. But is there any mail here for me that hasn't been forwarded?" I should've had Casey come in with me, or even for me.

The manager's eyes widen. "Oh yeah, I've got—uh— there are a couple of things here for you. Let me grab them."

Previously inviting me in, he now shuts the door in my face. Desk drawers rattle as he rifles to retrieve whatever he's kept.

Finally, a little winded, he opens the door holding various envelopes. Rather than hand them over, he tries to make small talk. "Here they are. Hey, since you're in the area, would you want to go out for lunch or a coffee or something?"

His eyelids lower, and he leans against the doorframe. I assume in an attempt to be seductive.

Practically ripping the papers out of his hand, my throat clears to cover a laugh. "Sorry, I'm here with my boyfriend, and we have plans." All overthinking aside, it still causes me to shiver to be able to call him that.

My old manager's disappointment is obvious. It reminds me of the tantrum he threw the last time I turned him down. The night I'd accidentally locked myself out of my apartment, he said I could stay in his. He wouldn't unlock it until morning, during *business hours*. It was the middle of the night, and I was in my pajamas. No way was that happening. Opting instead to sleep in the hallway, he'd pouted and gotten really upset I'd rather sleep there than at his place.

It's crazy how subjective the term "creepy" is.

I say goodbye and spin on my heel, stopping in the lobby to peruse the small stack accumulated. Most of it is junk or bills not due yet. Mom's handwriting is on one of the last envelopes.

Her familiar scribble hitches my heart, and my legs start to wobble. Sinking down into one of the chairs, I tear open the letter and read as blood pumping in my ears tunes out all while I concentrate. Not everything is legible, but I get the gist.

Beginning with *Dear Eliza,* the version of my name I've always struggled to consider my own, it reiterates how Casey described her end. *Left here, alone in this house, surrounded by the memories of what I can no longer call mine, I find there is no fight left in me.* How she'd given up on life and was ready to be done. *I wouldn't approve of this if I hadn't already exhausted every option or opportunity I could think of to give life meaning again.* Even here, she tried to retain some semblance of high ground. *I've done all I can think of and nothing makes a difference.* She goes on to ramble about how we fell out of touch, and she didn't know how to bridge the gap between us.

At this point, I can't read anymore. *She's such a hypocrite.*

Exhaust every option or opportunity to give life meaning. Except to try and to make amends with your estranged child?

I would have preferred to think she could set our differences aside for one last attempt, at the possibility to live and maybe see us reunite. She was the mother, after all. Supposedly older and wiser.

Instead, she got her way out.

I felt so guilty for not trying harder. I thought I'd wasted the last chances presented to me for us to reconnect, squandered my potential presence in her last days, weeks, months because I couldn't put my own ego aside. I'd grieved the death of our relationship long ago, now re-experiencing it all in the wake of her true death. It's not that I don't care. My grief then and now is no less excruciatingly real. Knowing she went out on her own terms, knowing she let go of me as much as I had her, why go through it again?

She made her choice. And now I can make mine.

Any potential tears, ready to shed, dry up as a giant weight lifts from my shoulders. A smile appears. For a split second, I worry I'm on the verge of hysteria.

No. I'm just ready to get back to Casey.

Renewed strength floods me. I march out to him sitting patiently in the car.

In my seat, I lean over the center console and initiate a long, firm kiss. Tense at first, his lips relax against mine.

Releasing him, his face is full of questions.

I'm surprised he holds them in. I laugh as I tell him, "My old building manager has had a crush on me and tried to ask me out. I'll have to tell you some stories about him. He made it pretty hard to live here sometimes."

Fire ignites in Casey's eyes.

Am I selfish to want this dangerous man on my side? This man who wants to show me affection and have me see him as a better person. Who listens to the darkness I try to drown out and pretend doesn't exist. *It's exhilarating.*

Trying to focus, he asks, "Did your mom send you a letter?"

"She did, and it helped a lot." I leave it at that for now. Except to mention I'm starving.

His face furrows in concern, but he doesn't press for more. Throwing the car into gear, he makes far more noise than is necessary as we pull away.

I laugh, lighter than I've felt in months, maybe years.

27: Casey

There's no way I'm this lucky.

Lizzy is choosing to disregard my flaws and accept me for the monster I am, knowing good resides underneath.

I thought she would look at me differently. The light behind her eyes might dim, rather than brighten. Our brief silence after I told her everything was my only penance to pay. Such a short time with the rift between us, even this stint was just a small reminder of how easily the darkness could move in and take control.

Whatever Debbie wrote in her letter, I am thankful it helped Lizzy. I worried I'd broken her, pushed her away and shut the door myself by my deceit and actions.

Instead, we spend another few days exploring Oklahoma City. Nothing we do is necessarily extraordinary, besides it consisting of me, her, and time together.

Towards dinner one evening, when the sun begins to disappear behind the downtown structures, Lizzy asks to go dancing.

"I'm sorry, you want to what?" I make her repeat, thinking I must've misheard.

"Dance. I want to go somewhere and dance. I used to go with a couple of the girls from college, back in the day, but that's been some time ago. And I never had a boyfriend to dance with." Her eyelashes flutter.

As if I weren't prepared to give her anything and

everything she could ask for. "How could you think you'd have to talk me into that? I get to hold you, manhandle you in front of jealous onlookers? That sounds like a great time."

Her eyes roll. Yet the little happy shimmy commences anyway.

"Do you know where you want to go?" *I have no idea what the options are.*

"There are a couple of country dance halls I really like." She's already got them pulled up on her phone. "Their vibe is more chill, especially if you get there when they open and leave by nine or ten, when the younger crowd shows up."

Destination decided, we change.

She throws on a pair of tight, black pants. The way they cling to her makes my knees wobble. I'm ready to fall to the floor, reduced to a puddle before her. Somehow, I keep my composure.

As if those weren't enough, she picks a shirt that practically screams *come hither*. Here, I do. Wrapping her into a hug from behind, I kiss down her neck. A playful smack between giggles is my reward.

Her face turns to mine, expecting a kiss there, too. Happy to oblige, we do. Passion electrifies the air. Tingles race along my skin, everywhere we touch. *A kiss to rock our socks.*

Sparks fly as I leave her to continue getting ready in peace, donning my own pair of dark jeans and a long sleeve, maroon pearl snap.

Her eyes linger as I roll up my sleeves, prolonging my progress. I revel under her stare.

Our gazes meet in the mirror. A flush colors her cheeks.

Hopefully, we aren't out late.

When both of us are ready, we head for the club she

chose. Unable to contain her excitement, she fidgets the entire way. The part she says she's most excited for is a dedicated dance partner.

I can't wait.

Upon arrival, bouncers advise all guys to pay a cover. I pretend to shoot her a pointed look. Already swaying to the beat pounding through the walls, she's so pumped, it goes right over her head.

Sparse groups mingle around the bar-height edges of a large dancefloor. Colored spotlights flash periodically while main overheads remain on and low. Less than a handful of couples are dancing.

We take up a place to people-watch for a song or two, until I pull her out onto the floor. Stumbling some at first, she finds her groove. Then we move faster.

She laughs into my chest after every spin. Her body presses against mine to navigate the growing flow of dancers. Our hands are quick to find purchase wherever they can along each other, as we shift from swing dancing to two-step. Slower sways allow us to catch our breath and give my throbbing calves a break.

What songs play don't matter to me. I'm happy to continue as long as she is willing.

All at once, the sensation of being watched tenses my movements. Despite the ever-increasing crowd, the presence of eyes specifically trained on us unsettles me. I try to scan faces as we make another pass. Smoke and flashing lights drown out any details amid the array of bodies.

Lizzy notices my attention shift, my distracted lead causing her steps to falter.

In her ear, I whisper as low as I can, above the noise, "Stay close to me. I feel like someone's watching us."

Her hold on me tightens.

I hate to make her nervous without cause. *I did promise*

not to hold anything back. "I'm sorry. I'd say maybe one more song, and then we need to skedaddle."

Whatever this is, there's malice to it. And I will not dismiss my gut reaction again.

She nods in agreement. Clearly disturbed, her face still drops, not ready to leave.

It's wrong to rip her away from the fun. "We can try another place if you don't want to go straight to the hotel, but let's talk about it outside."

The smile this induces is almost sufficient to push away the dark cloud looming over me.

We dance to one last song. Then, I angle us towards the door.

"I have to go to the bathroom first," she pipes up.

I nod and walk her to them. Posting up outside the door, arms crossed, my eyes are alert for anything out of place.

A couple of minutes pass as groups of girls go in and come out in waves. One, about to fall flat on her ass, grabs hold of me to keep steady. Her face has a faraway expression, present and not at the same time. *The lights are on, but nobody's home.*

She shakes herself off, at least enough to hit on me. "Wow. You're really strong. Are you here with someone?"

Practically shouting in my face makes it easier to smell the vodka cranberry on her breath.

Getting her to stand on her own two feet is a feat. "I'm here with my girlfriend. Waiting for her." My thumb gestures to the restroom.

"What a gentleman," she mumbles as her eyes blink separately of each other. "Unless you're overbearing and possessive?" Cocking her brow in an attempt to reevaluate me appears to take every ounce of concentration she can manage.

"Just protective. Please be careful." Her steps are shaky as I hold the door open.

Lizzy walks out around her, and I breathe a sigh of relief.

"Did you make a friend?" she taunts.

I narrow my eyes and whisper in her ear, "Get me out of here before I throw you over my shoulder and haul you back to the hotel room."

Pulling away, I catch her eyes widen and the gulp she suppresses.

My laugh is lost to the music and chatter.

Outside, open air and the sting from the cold reduces the sensation of prying eyes. *That doesn't mean I let my guard down.* Walls and crowds no longer closing us in provide freedom of movement as well as exposure.

Once Lizzy is in the car, my nerves start to settle. Only when we are both inside and the doors are locked do I truly relax.

The urge to apologize floods me. "I'm sorry to cut our fun short. I don't know why I'm so on edge all of a sudden."

"Don't apologize. The younger crowd is showing up now, so the music is about to change over anyway." Losing herself in thought, it takes her a moment to continue. "There's another not too far, and it's closer to the hotel."

"Of course. Anything for my girl." I reach across to kiss her cheek.

Turning the key, my car sputters and clicks. It does not start. Trying again, to no avail, something definitely isn't right.

"Stay here, please." My voice is calm. Meanwhile, every hair on my body bristles.

Thankfully, she doesn't respond with a snarky remark or get out alongside me.

I relock the doors and pop the hood. Nothing immediately appears to be out of place.

Leaning in for a closer look, footsteps grate on the asphalt behind me.

Too late, sharp pain accompanies Lizzy screaming my name.

28: Geoffrey

Man, that felt good.

The bat falls to my side, similar to how Casey's body slumps to the ground in front of his stupid sports car. His moan is music to my ears.

That scream was unnecessary, though. Stepping from behind the hood, I can see into the passenger seat. There sits the girl he had with him at the grocery store. Eliza Dern. What a fun surprise.

A phone is already dialed in her hand. *Tsk, tsk.* My head shakes as the bat lifts to point at her.

Her face pales. She might scream again. Gulping it down instead, she lowers the phone from her ear.

Damn, my head hurts like a son of a bitch.

Slow movements bring me to her door. I try to open it. The handle does nothing. Rather than look at me, her eyes are glued to the spot where Casey was standing.

I tap my finger on the glass to gain her attention. Once her eyes lock on mine, I point to the handle, gesturing for her to open it.

She doesn't move.

I am not in the mood for that. Bringing the bat up, I swing at the window. It busts before another thought runs through her head.

To her credit, she only shouts once.

Door open, I drag her out by the arm. Her moans and groans about being injured flow in one ear and out the other. *Like I give a damn.*

She tries to rip herself out of my grip.

I tighten my hold and give her a shake. "Let's not make this harder than it has to be. It's not my fault you got caught up with the wrong guy."

Biting down on another cry, she goes silent.

Good.

We sidestep Casey's crumpled form. He groans, so I know he's alive. *Oh, how the tables have turned, eh, Casey boy?* Last time he saw me, I was the one groaning on the ground.

Eliza keeps glancing back. Each time she pulls at me, pissing me off more.

"Focus," I spit, tugging her forward. "Don't give me reason to want to hurt you."

Whether she believes the threat or not, her stride picks up. We make our way to my rig at the edge of the lot. Streetlight reflections gleam off its metallic paint.

The passenger door flings wide as I shove her into the steps. "Get in the back. No shenanigans."

She stares dumbly at the truck, then at me.

"I didn't ask a question." At each repeated word, I lean in closer. "Get. In. The back."

Her recoil isn't much of a reaction, but it's enough to satisfy. For a second, those eyes narrow like she might try something. *Hopefully she isn't that stupid.* Luckily, she climbs into the cab without further issue.

Several people exit the club and pause to watch us. *They don't matter.*

They're probably going to alert club security. *They also don't matter. We're fixin' to be gone.*

Slamming the door once her ass is finally clear, I stalk to mine. Clicks sound as she attempts to open it from inside. Her brave stupidity brings a smile to my face, knowing how pointless it is. She gives up as soon she realizes it too and climbs into the sleeper.

The driver seat bounces while I situate. My vantage point offers an unobstructed view of Casey pushing up off the ground. I get to witness his moment of clarity as I wave and pull away. Staggering steps he takes toward us shift into a useless, outright run.

We're merged into traffic and gone long before he has a chance to close the gap. *It won't take him much to get his car working.* All I needed was a little head start.

I didn't plan any of this.

There was no way I could've known I'd run into Casey so soon.

The reason I'm even in Oklahoma City was to try to start tracking down my family. My wife used to go to the country dance bars all the time, before I found her and made her quit going to those meat markets.

She always wanted to dance and never shut up about trying again someday. I figured checking them out was a decent place to start.

Then, whose car did I find in the parking lot but Casey's?

Since there wasn't time for a plan, I winged it. Disabling his car was all I could come up with on the spot. After that, I went inside to search for him. Too many bodies in the way made it nearly impossible to pick him out.

Eventually, there he was, swinging around the dance floor. I watched for a while, allowing my rage to simmer. He looked happy, the fucker.

He had to know something was off because he started frowning at the crowd. Like he knew my eyes were on him. As they were getting ready to leave, I came out and grabbed the bat from my truck to wait. I wanted it to be up close and personal. *That part was awesome.*

Except now, I still don't have a plan. So we're

continuing to wing it. Aimlessly, I navigate the city, highway hopping to change from one direction to another. No specific route or destination in mind, only knowing I want to lose myself among the twists and turns.

Little miss is behaving for now. That's good. I was hoping she wouldn't put up too much of a fight. *I want the struggle. My body isn't quite up to snuff for it yet.*

At the thought, I reach under the seat for my emergency fluid. There isn't a lot left. Upending it, the rest goes down the hatch.

Eliza sucks in a breath that I ignore.

"Where are we going?" she mumbles, barely loud enough for me to hear.

I ignore that too.

When she doesn't get a response, she asks another question. "What do you want?"

My foot slams the brake pedal. Unprepared, she tumbles forward to land beside me between the seats. She narrowly catches herself to avoid bouncing her pretty little head off the center dash.

Her glare focuses on me.

Ooo, if looks could kill.

It's a struggle not to bust out laughing. Though it is a nice change from the cowing that made up my wife's typical response. This fuels the fires of my rage rather than pacify.

My hand tangles in her hair. Gripping tightly, I put my foot in the accelerator. "We are going to make Casey fret and worry and be as helpless as he left me when he thought he'd killed me."

With each word, I bring her closer to my face, throwing her back into the sleeper once I've finished.

Maybe this will be fun.

The thin fragment of joy I'd begun to grasp is

interrupted by my low fuel light. *At last, something to give me direction.*

Choosing a truck stop is easy. I know where they all are.

She quietly picks herself up and climbs into the sleeper. We continue in silence until reaching one of the twenty-four-hour places.

Parked in a truck stall, my eyes find hers in the mirror. "Don't do anything stupid. I'll be right outside."

Standing in the cold, coughs become more difficult to suppress as the rig fuels. I walk to the front of the hood and inspect the lot. Not many other drivers are here to post up for this time of night.

A neon sign in the window catches my eye. Cutting off the pump once there's plenty to get us by for a while, I'm drawn toward the liquor section for another restock.

Little miss shouldn't cause too much trouble locked in the cab for a few minutes.

My smile returns as I walk inside.

29: Lizzy

"Did you get all that?" I whisper into my phone.

Really, I'm amazed he never double-checked to verify my call disconnected or took the device himself.

I want to be relieved as he walks away, though it doesn't instill the level of confidence I wish it would. Bright lights inside the store allow me to watch him wander the aisles.

This has to be the Geoffrey Casey told me about.

Lowering myself onto the floor, I squeeze between the pedals and his seat to try the driver's handle. *Locked.* There is no manual locking tab to be seen on the door itself. *What kind of deathtrap is this?*

Cringes twitch my body at every dingy surface I touch.

Everything I know passed on, the 911 operator assures me they have people close who are on the way.

I hope so. He shouldn't be gone long.

Poor Casey has been blowing up my phone ever since he regained consciousness. Perched on the edge of this grungy mattress, content that police are enroute, I call him, hopeful that doing so doesn't disconnect me from the 911 operator.

He answers by the end of the first ring, on the edge of panic. "Liz? Are you okay? Where are you? Did he hurt you?"

"I don't have time to talk. I've been on the phone with police. They know where we are."

His voice is tight, breaking my heart as he asks again, "Did he hurt you?"

He's about to have a conniption.

"I'm fine—shit, here he comes," I cut off, stuffing the phone back into my waistband.

Arms loaded, Geoffrey directs an ugly sneer at me, holding up his purchases as trophies. This truck already reeks. I'm in desperate need of a deep breath. *A more difficult task while I'm actively trying not to gag.* Chancing it, all I get is dizzy from fumes.

Sirens sound nearby. *Not close enough.*

Geoffrey flinches and begins to walk faster. The door opens as I'm attempting to choke down a dry heave.

"Let's hit the road, Jack," he says to himself, settling into the driver seat.

We're on the road and gone by the time any flashing lights come into view.

A sigh arises. Immediately, I squash the impulse. *No need to draw attention.*

Unable to do anything besides take in my surroundings, I try not to examine anything too closely and focus on where he's driving. From the smell to the thought of what he does in here, I shudder and gag again.

Meeting my disgust in the mirror, all he does is smile. *Gross.*

Miles later, his question makes me jump. "Where are the two of you staying?"

Internal debates wage over withholding versus lying. Flustered stutters to clear my throat buy myself a second to decide. *What would I gain by deceiving him?*

He remains quiet as I tell him the name of our hotel.

More silence while he drives puts me on edge. Not enough to make up for the adrenaline wearing off. My eyelids droop. Gears shift. Air periodically purges only to build back up. The truck sways from lane to lane, weaving through intermittent traffic. At one point, I start to fall asleep and slump to one side, jolting upright once I realize what's happening. This is about the time we slow to a stop.

Searching surrounding details to focus on, the sign for our hotel flashes outside the windshield. My heart sinks.

"Why are we at our hotel?" The question spills out before I can filter it.

"Haven't you learned your lesson, asking me shit? Be quiet and do as I say." Opening the door, Geoffrey faces me. "Get up. We're going in so I can think. You better act cool. Don't try anything. I have my gun on me." He climbs out the driver door and waits in the street for me to step down next to him.

To an unsuspecting onlooker, it might appear as though he's a gentleman, holding the door for me. *We probably more closely resemble a trucker and his lot lizard, if I'm being totally honest.*

I dressed to go dancing. I didn't plan on getting abducted.

Gripping my shoulder, he pushes me in front of him, steering me towards the entrance. Inside, he leans on me and starts mumbling as if he were drunk. Something heavy presses into my side. It takes immense effort not to scream and shove him away. The sensation takes me straight back to my night in Martin's grasp.

A security guard barely notices us.

Putting on a tight smile, I nod and give a small wave when the front desk person glances up as we hit the elevator. It's a small miracle no one is on it. Geoffrey rests against the wall instead of allowing all his weight to stay on me, though the hold he maintains on my arm is strong.

As soon as we come to a stop on our floor, he's already pushing. The doors hardly get a chance to retract, and I'm squeezing out into the hallway.

Outside our room, he extends a hand to me for the door key. Pressure digging into my side disappears. I didn't think his grip on my arm could grow any tighter, but it does even more as he takes the card.

His forceful shove inside, releasing my arm at last sends me tripping over Casey's suitcase, where I land on the floor. Geoffrey faces the room too quickly for me to reach a hand in and rummage for the gun. His back presses to the door.

I push myself up and try to get him talking. "What now, Geoffrey? What's the plan? You hurt Casey. You've got me. What's next?"

He doesn't take the bait. "Shut up. I need to think."

White-knuckled, his hand pulls a gun from somewhere. Mumbling to himself, all I can make out is something about a wife.

"What's her name?" I try, sitting down on the bed.

His eyes burn holes in me. "None of your damn business. Shut. Up. So I can think." He stalks to the window and stares out at the lighted streets below. Glare from a table lamp reflects the room back to me.

Silence descends as we sit uncomfortably for a while. The time gives me plenty of chance to scold myself for not thinking more quickly on my feet. For letting this happen to myself.

"I have to go to the bathroom," comes out as a whisper. May as well have been a shout for how loud it sounds.

He answers without turning around, "Nothing funny. Leave the door open." Watching my reflection in the glass.

There is little consolation in the fact he can't see directly in. This moment, I check to make sure my call is still active. Unable to talk, it's reassuring to know Casey is there.

Phone safely returned to my waistband, I leave the bathroom.

Geoffrey hasn't moved an inch when I walk out. Seeing my reflection, he spins to face me and the room. His eyes rove over the small area as he sinks down into a chair beside the window.

I reclaim my seat, perched on the edge of the bed.

After soaking up seemingly every inch of the room, his gaze falls on me, picking me apart piece by piece.

I can't help but squirm under his scrutiny. Eyes making their way from my face and hair down to my waist and legs. They flick again to my waist where they pause, his brows furrowing.

"Empty your pockets," he barks.

Patting at the pockets with nothing in them, worried he'll take over without something to show, I present my wallet and chapstick.

"What happened to your phone." Phrased as one, his tone leaves no room for question.

"I dropped it when you bashed in my window." In the attempt to drown any snarkiness out of my response, my voice hitches. I change tactics and lean into it. Tears that have somehow remained reined in begin to fall.

Before dropping my face into my hands, I catch him shifting uncomfortably in his seat.

"What do you want from me?" I draw out a little dramatically. Perhaps too much.

Blurred, his face hardens. The chair bangs against the wall as he shoves out of it.

Uh-oh.

Shrinking into the bed doesn't keep enough distance between us.

His hands firmly plant on my knees, locking me in place while depositing his face directly in mine.

Not wanting my fear on full display goes out the window as my body begins to tremble. Tears blur my vision. I force my eyes to the wall behind him.

One hand withdraws from my leg, reaching up to grab my chin. Unlike Casey, he aggressively yanks my head to look him squarely in the face. A face worn and withered from the life he's lived. Eyes dim and lifeless.

"I want Casey to hurt as bad as I do."

Whiskey breath blows directly up my nose. It adds to the cotton mouth I've developed as well as the frog in my throat.

Sliding the hand down my chin, he brings the other up to meet it around my throat.

Instant, overwhelming pressure incapacitates me. Weight descends upon my entire body, immediately restricting movement. Not seizing my last chance to inhale, all oxygen disappears in a single gasp. Instinct raises my hands to claw at his, to no avail.

As darkness clouds my vision, I contemplate letting go and falling into blissful oblivion.

30: Geoffrey

My grip doesn't let up until her body goes limp, relaxing beneath me after minimal struggle.

Damn, I love this feeling.

Easing up slightly at first, when she doesn't move, I release her completely.

Now I can have some real peace and quiet.

She stays flat on the bed, unable to watch me or ask questions.

I switch the bedside lamp off before returning to stare out the window. *The light was ruining my view.*

Hours, it feels like, I stand there watching the night melt away. Artificial lights give in to the sun's rays growing on the horizon.

Eventually, it becomes easier to think, allowing me to focus on Eliza's breathing. It was nothing to tune out at first, though it's far more pronounced now. *Maybe she's about to wake up.*

As I go to turn, my head bumps against something heavy. Ragged breaths sound right behind me. *Ah, she is awake.*

Continuing to spin, she smacks the back of my head again with whatever it is she's holding. "Keep your fucking eyes out that window," rasps from her. "Now I have a gun, too."

A chuckle escapes me at the notion she thinks she has any power in this situation. Not afraid of her threats, I take my chances in facing her.

Holy shit, she does have a gun.

Dark, shiny metal gleams inches in front of my nose.

There's fire in her eyes. Fight. Will. It's invigorating.

I find myself stepping forward, pushing her and her gun back. She orders me to stop.

I want to see what she thinks she's going to do.

Another step forward forces her to retreat another. Removing the gun from my face, she shoots me in the leg.

I guffaw. She actually shot me.

Pain doesn't register right away, so I take another step.

Another shot hits me.

This time I don't see or feel it. I only know the embrace of my mistress as she takes me, for hopefully the last time.

31: Lizzy

Holy shit, I shot the bastard.

I stand there with the gun pointed at him for a while. Eventually it begins to quake in my hands. No idea how long I'm frozen this way, part of me waits for him to get up and come at me again.

Dried tears sting my cheeks.

Time is meaningless, until I remember Casey on the other end of the line.

Digging the phone out of my pants, I fumble under the weight of the gun before laying it down on the bed. Our call is still going. Never mind my battery is nearly dead. I put it to my ear. "Casey? Are you there?"

No response.

"Casey?" I yell, hoarse.

Breaths, more ragged than mine, pant back, "Liz, you okay?"

Relief is nowhere to be found. "Casey, where are you?"

Silence.

"Casey?" I shout. My ears ring from the gunshots.

"His truck. Can't get down. Sorry."

"Hang on. I'm coming to get you," grinds painfully out of my throat.

Walking on shaky legs, a rail in the elevator is the only thing allowing me to remain upright. Silence spans between the ding at every floor provide opportunity for the shock to take effect. My limbs tremble with nothing to focus on. The whir of the downward thrust upsets what little balance I have left.

By some luck, the doors open to the security guard still stationed in the lobby. I thought I'd have to persuade him to help me. Before I make it to the desk, something about my appearance drives him to stand and follow without a word uttered.

It registers somewhere in my brain that he does ask me questions—*What happened? Are you alright, miss?*—while we walk. I can't find it in me to produce answers.

The cold slows my hastened pace. Exhaustion sweeps over me in waves as we head toward the truck parked along the sidewalk. Seeing it again reignites some of the lingering adrenaline as my heart rate spikes.

Red and blue lights flash a little farther up the road. They don't induce the same relief seeing Casey does when he all but falls out as the door swings open.

Satisfied in knowing Casey is at least alive for now, I find the words to explain the short version of whatever just happened to us to the security guard. The man helps us inside so we can sit together on one of the lobby couches and wait. Hearing the words come out of my mouth doesn't help me to believe that they are mine.

Eventually, police officers arrive. Their radios beep and crackle with one update after another.

All the noise isn't enough to dispel my thoughts. Rather than be lost in spiraling questions and distractions, my mind quiets. I can focus.

Initially they want to question us separately. I tell them there's no way in hell we're separating, so they question us together.

32: Casey

Fuck, I feel like hot garbage.

I remember trying to chase Geoffrey's truck on foot. Barely able to stand, I didn't want to lose them. Dark and with no noticeable identifying decals, his rig could easily blend in alongside many other trucks on the road. *He could've kept driving and I might've never seen either of them again.*

Several people called for help while I fell in and out of consciousness. Getting through on Liz's phone was my last glimmer of hope. I remember begging her not to hang up on me once I could finally talk to her.

One of the club security guys let me borrow his car to follow them as soon as Lizzy could tell me where to go. It was stupid of me to come alone, but I didn't want to put anybody else in danger. Somewhere in my head, I told myself I had to be the one to save her. *I am the one who got her into this.*

Following Geoffrey, based only on what information Lizzy could pass along, was awful.

I was running on fumes by the time I made it to the truck. When I saw it, I thought they might still be in there. Hauling myself into the cab to check it was where my strength ran out. It was too late for me to be useful. I wasted precious time and effort for nothing.

If I'd tried to climb down, I would have face planted in the street. *Still should've.*

Unable to contribute much to the officer's questions

now, I rest, fluttering in and out of it as Lizzy does most of the talking. It's better this way. Cops still give me the creeps, even though they are precisely what she needs. *These first responders are who can help her. Not me.*

Her voice soothes a fraction of the chaos unleashing inside me. Every now and then it does hitch because of what that monster did to her. *Am I really any better than him?*

Paramedics check us over. Aside from a raging headache, concussion, and I'm sure they said something else too, there isn't anything that sounds bad enough for a trip to the hospital. We promise to keep an eye on ourselves and go straight in if anything gets worse.

Well, she promises. I not-so-politely agree.

Thousands of questions later, we're able to be moved into a different room.

Lizzy is amazing for handling herself and the situation so well. *She deserves all the praise.* Guilt eats away at me for so many things. Especially for not being there to protect her.

As we lie on the bed, completely exhausted, I use any energy left to apologize. For everything. "I am so sorry I let you down, Liz. I set myself up for destruction, and then here I am, dragging you down with me. This is all my fault."

My head falls to one side as tears flow. If she were smart, she'd duck out while she can.

She doesn't.

Rather, she takes my chin and gently tilts it up, forcing me to look her in the eyes. "Shut up. You need to do some healing. And you shouldn't talk to yourself like that." Her voice is strong and confident.

I may not understand it, but I think we're going to be okay.

Cupping her cheek in my hand, I rub under her eye. "That's my girl."

Final Note

There is no *good* or *bad* guy to this story.

Lizzy wrote her mother off when she found out she could have had a last-ditch effort for a relationship and was denied it because her mother chose suicide, then wrote off her murderous boyfriend's past as she came into her own self confidence.

Casey is a murderer under the guise of a vigilante. Still, he has some good internal messages, however corrupt he may be.

Geoffrey is an abusive alcoholic with sociopathic-psychopathic tendencies, also a murderer with blatant disregard for the lives of anyone or anything around him. Is he simply a product of his own addiction and enablers?

Martin might have had a justifiable moment of weakness under the cover of self-defense, but he let the intrusive thoughts win and then continued to allow them reign over him.

Debbie had suicidal ideation, and even though she tried to make life have meaning, she didn't reach out to her daughter to give her the chance to repair their broken relationship and ultimately decided what she thought was best for her, regardless of anyone else.

Everyone has their own demons and battles to fight. We all have to ignore the dark whispers, however loud or quiet in our minds. It's not always easy to see the reason for being here. Sometimes we have to make our own, and that is so much easier said than done.

Our actions impact others, whether we want them to or not.

Thank you for coming along on this journey.

Please make sure you are taking care of yourself. If you
need help, don't be afraid to ask for it.

988 Suicide and Crisis Lifeline
National Domestic Violence Hotline 800-799-7233
National Human Trafficking Hotline 888-373-7888

ACKNOWLEDGMENTS

My in-laws are the reason I ever got to see Waynoka and the dunes in the first place. Dad would tell us stories about when he used to go, but he never got the chance to take us. From a wedding on the sand, to yearly rides that we don't always make it to, Woods County, Oklahoma has dug itself a special place in my heart.

The first time I drove by Hopeton, a bump in the road, I saw a scene from this story unfold in my head. No context or know-how on how I would do it, over ten years later, we have a story.

The escaping inmates sign is real. This road sign, coupled with one of my favorite dad jokes about a truck driver picking up a hitchhiker -

Hitchhiker: "Thanks for the lift, but aren't you worried about giving rides to sketchy people?"

Truck driver: "Eh, what are the odds the both of us would be serial killers?"

- became the basis for this story. I want this book to pay homage to the real communities where it takes place. It may not have turned out how I initially expected, (there was never supposed to be any romance) but I am so happy it finally exists.

Alva, Dacoma, Hopeton, and Waynoka all have their own history that my work of fiction does not tap into. I didn't want to chance botching anything related to the true lore of the towns themselves. This story just so happens to take place among them, a fictional version of them, I should say.

Their real history, you'd have to research and experience for yourself.

Of course, there's no way I could have accomplished this without a team to help me stay motivated through the roller coaster of emotions from day to day, really hour to hour.

Early readers:

Adrien, Bri, Jacy, Kami, Katie, Laura, Morgan, and Tory

You all are so much more than alpha and beta readers. You helped me keep going when I thought I would give up on this, for sure.

Thank you for helping hold me accountable.

Thank you for giving me someone to be excited with while this was all happening in the background.

My biggest supporters, my family. I love you all so damn much!

Cover art by: Julian Bauer
https://julianbauer.com/
mail@julianbauer.com

I found Julian and his work on Reedsy. Hopeton Horror was the second cover I asked him to make. Seeing what he could do with my limited vision on our first commission helped me decide what I wanted for this book. I cannot express enough gratitude for him and his work.

Thank you, Julian.

Edited by: Clara Abigail
https://clarabigail.ca/

I found Clara's TikTok when I was still in the early stages of self-editing. I cannot thank her enough for her patience and helping me to see my story in a way I could not have otherwise.

Thank you, Clara.

This book is sponsored by my dad. Thank You, Dad.

Came across these on my first trip to the dunes, October 2014

"Bears"

Photo Credit: Shelby Doll

Socials:

TikTok: @tpmw_author

Instagram: tpmw_author

Facebook: TPMW Author

Email: tpmwauthor@yahoo.com

www.ingramcontent.com/pod-product-compliance
Lightning Source LLC
Chambersburg PA
CBHW031141160726
47991CB00004B/1521